Praise for
A DASH OF DRAGON

★ "Fast-paced, funny, and chock-full of action."
—*Shelf Awareness*, starred review

"This novel is a recipe for success—perfect for
Top Chef fans with a penchant for the fantastical."
—*Kirkus Reviews*

"A wildly inventive fantasy with wide appeal."
—*Booklist*

"A zingy, buoyant adventure where the happy ending is
certain but the path to it is enjoyably twisty."
—*Bulletin of the Center for Children's Books*

Praise for
A HINT OF HYDRA

"[Lang and Bartkowski's] gripping tale is
chock-full of adventure and action."
—*School Library Journal*

"Solving the magical whodunit and battling against
steampunk-inspired automatons easily reinforce Lailu's
heroism and allow for an engaging, self-contained adventure."
—*Bulletin of the Center for Children's Books*

"Lang and Bartkowski continue Lailu's adventures in a
world that cooks up magic, fantastical beasts, steampunk
science, and a dash of murder mystery in a story that will
attract readers who enjoy not only fantasy adventure but
cooking TV shows, such as *MasterChef Junior*."
—*Booklist*

Something's always cooking!
A Dash of Dragon
A Hint of Hydra
A Pinch of Phoenix

A Hint of Hydra

Heidi Lang & Kati Bartkowski

ALADDIN

New York   London   Toronto   Sydney   New Delhi

This book is a work of fiction. Any references to historical events, real people, or real places are used fictitiously. Other names, characters, places, and events are products of the author's imagination, and any resemblance to actual events or places or persons, living or dead, is entirely coincidental.

ALADDIN
An imprint of Simon & Schuster Children's Publishing Division
1230 Avenue of the Americas, New York, New York 10020
First Aladdin paperback edition July 2019
Text copyright © 2018 by Heidi Lang and Kati Bartkowski
Cover illustration copyright © 2018 by Angela Li
Also available in an Aladdin hardcover edition.
All rights reserved, including the right of reproduction in whole or in part in any form.
ALADDIN and related logo are registered trademarks of Simon & Schuster, Inc.
For information about special discounts for bulk purchases, please contact Simon & Schuster Special Sales at 1-866-506-1949 or business@simonandschuster.com.
The Simon & Schuster Speakers Bureau can bring authors to your live event. For more information or to book an event contact the Simon & Schuster Speakers Bureau at 1-866-248-3049 or visit our website at www.simonspeakers.com.
Designed by Nina Simoneaux
The text of this book was set in Adobe Caslon Pro.
Manufactured in the United States of America 0619 OFF
2 4 6 8 10 9 7 5 3 1
The Library of Congress has cataloged the hardcover edition as follows:
Names: Lang, Heidi, author. | Bartkowski, Kati, author.
Title: A hint of hydra / by Heidi Lang and Kati Bartkowski.
Description: First Aladdin hardcover edition. | New York : Aladdin, 2018. |
Summary: "Thirteen-year-old chef Lailu must uncover the truth behind a murder before the elves and the scientists of Twin Rivers declare war on each other"—Provided by publisher.
Identifiers: LCCN 2017040024 (print) | LCCN 2017053143 (eBook) |
ISBN 9781481477970 (eBook) | ISBN 9781481477956 (hc)
Subjects: | CYAC: Cooking—Fiction. | Animals, Mythical—Fiction. |
Robots—Fiction. | Elves—Fiction. | Fantasy. | BISAC: JUVENILE FICTION / Humorous Stories. | JUVENILE FICTION / Animals / Mythical. | JUVENILE FICTION / Fantasy & Magic.
Classification: LCC PZ7.1.L3436 (eBook) | LCC PZ7.1.L3436 Him 2018 (print) |
DDC [Fic]—dc23
LC record available at https://lccn.loc.gov/2017040024
ISBN 9781481477963 (pbk)

For our sister Rosi Reed:

a judo black belt and physicist with an alliterative name,

who claims she's not a superhero . . . or villain.

Don't worry, your secret is safe with us.

1

GRIFFIN HUNT

Lailu stepped onto a stony outcropping, trying not to think about the thousand-foot drop beneath her. The autumn winds slammed into her back, threatening to throw her to her untimely death. And even though she had a harness securing her, something about that thin leather and rope just did not invite trust.

"Okay there, Pigtails?" asked her mentor and business partner, Master Slipshod, his graying hair blowing around his head.

"Of—of course." Lailu glanced down, then inched backward, feeling the weight of all that space between her and the thin ribbon of river below.

Master Slipshod smiled reassuringly as the man beside him fiddled with his harness. "Trust me, Caramel here—"

"Carbon. The name is Carbon. As I repeatedly tell you."

Carbon's bald head gleamed as he finished adjusting the straps around Slipshod's waist and chest. He usually wore a large black bowler hat, but the wind had taken it almost immediately. Between the long climb up, the lost hat, and Slipshod's repeated insistence on calling him "Caramel," it was clear Carbon's patience was unraveling faster than a plate full of vibber pasta. Lailu got the distinct impression that he didn't like either of them and wouldn't be bothered one bit by their deaths. Not the most comforting feeling when his invention was all that stood between her and a long fall.

"Carbon knows what he's doing," Slipshod continued cheerfully. "Isn't that right, my good man? And so kind of you to set us up with these."

Carbon grumbled something under his breath. Lailu caught the words "Starling" and "favor."

Oh yes, that was the other reason Lailu didn't trust the harnesses. They had been a "gift" from Starling Volan, the leader of the local up-and-coming scientists. Even though the scientists seemed quite capable of overcoming the impossible with their inventions involving steam and clockwork engines, Lailu felt they were up to no good. Nothing had been proven against them, but she knew they were the ones responsible for kidnapping elves and experimenting on their blood a few months ago. And she wasn't sure why they were suddenly so keen on outfitting her and Slipshod with new gadgets. It almost felt like a bribe, and it gave Lailu a bad taste in her mouth.

Carbon flicked a switch on the metal gadget attached to the front of Slipshod's harness. It began vibrating ominously.

"Um, is it supposed to make that sound?" Lailu asked.

"Yes, yes, of course, of course," Carbon snapped. "You should be all set, Sullivan. If you'd care to try it?" Carbon adjusted the spectacles on his pinched face and stepped back.

"Watch this, Pigtails." With a whoop of pure glee, Slipshod leaped backward off the cliff. For a few panicked moments, Lailu saw him plummeting to his death.

But the harness held, and his plummeting turned into a gentle downward drift.

"Your turn, your turn." Carbon waved his hands impatiently until Lailu inched toward him. He double-checked the straps that looped around her thighs and made sure the belt they were attached to was secure. "Keep that tight, or if you flip upside down, you'll fall right out," he advised.

"Wait, *what*?" Lailu pulled the belt of the harness tighter until it dug into her waist.

"Better, better." Carbon flicked the switch on her harness, the vibrations rattling Lailu's teeth. "Here is where you control it," Carbon said, tapping the small box that attached to the front of the belt.

Lailu looked down at the levers and clockwork gears dubiously, following the rope that led from them over to the large square contraption Carbon had bolted to the top of the cliff. He called it the auto-belayer, and it was supposed to lower her down and bring her back up easily, all without any effort on her part beyond the flip of a switch. Steam puffed out of it in small, irregular circles as it clicked and whirred. It did not look stable.

"You're set," Carbon said.

"Are you sure? I mean, you spent a lot more time checking Slipshod's harness."

Carbon's face flushed, his whole head glowing a soft pink. "I am very sure. Very sure. I don't know what you've heard, but I don't make mistakes. *My* inventions are sound. Very sound." He added something else, something about "lies" and "misrepresentations," the wind snatching his words and tossing them over the cliff, where Lailu could imagine them falling in long, angry streaks to puddle at the bottom.

It was only too easy to imagine herself falling with those words. . . .

Lailu gulped, but if she didn't start trusting Carbon's device, Slipshod would be facing the griffins alone, and griffins were not creatures you take lightly. Sure, they tasted great with a good dry rub and seasoning, but they really were monsters on the cliff who held nothing back, attacking with talons and claws and flying in all directions. Lailu only hoped she and Slipshod could get to one without attracting the attention of the rest of the flock.

Slowly, Lailu turned and leaned back in the harness, cringing at every little creak the leather gave. "Please hold, please hold," she whispered. "O God of Cookery, please let it hold."

"It will hold. Trust me," Carbon said.

"Not really," Lailu muttered, but there was nothing left to do but jump.

Lailu took a deep breath, then let it out. She was the youngest master chef in the land. She'd faced dragons and loan sharks and manipulative elves. She could handle a little jump. Without letting herself dwell on what would happen if the harness snapped, she pushed off from the cliff, leaping backward and out over the open air.

For one heart-stopping moment, she fell through the sky, the wind buffeting her from all directions, the side of the cliff racing by in a blur. Then the harness made a soft *click-click* noise and caught, gently slowing her descent until she hung next to Master Slipshod.

Lailu realized she'd been screaming and slapped both hands to her mouth, embarrassed. Such an amateur reaction. She glanced sideways at Master Slipshod to see his response, but if he noticed her slip-up, he gave no sign. She frowned. That wasn't like him. When it came to hunting and cooking, he had all his spices lined up in a row, but lately he seemed . . . off. She'd noticed the bags under his eyes and the way his apron hung limply on his frame, not to mention how often he'd been distracted while they were preparing meals. Something was up.

She just hoped that whatever troubled Slipshod wouldn't come back to bite her in the butt like last time.

"There's a nice older male in the cave below us," Master Slipshod said, shouting over the howling wind. "He's preening his feathers. See?"

Lailu leaned back in her harness to study the cave below their feet, her heart doing somersaults at the thought of the fall beneath. A griffin crouched near the edge, cleaning his golden feathers with his beak, his tail swishing back and forth.

"So what's the plan?" Lailu asked.

"I'll go zooming down past his cave. When he sees me, he'll come flying out. At that point, you drop onto his back and try to take out a wing."

"So wait. . . . You want me to take out his wing while I'm *sitting* on his *back*?" Maybe she should have asked him about the plan before they strapped on their harnesses.

Slipshod nodded. "It will be the ride of your life."

Lailu looked down at the glint of the river far below and swallowed.

"Don't worry, you'll be in your harness. Perfectly safe."

"Yeah, right."

"Oh, and don't injure the wing too badly until he loses altitude." Slipshod flicked the lever at the front of his harness, and before Lailu could argue, he was gone, zipping past the griffin, so close he could have reached out and touched the beast.

The griffin raised his massive head, feathers ruffling, tail standing straight out. Then he opened his beak and roared before leaping after Master Slipshod.

Before she could talk herself out of it, Lailu twisted the switch on her harness. She dropped immediately, so fast her eyes stung and her breath caught in her throat. And there he was—her griffin.

Lailu blinked her watery eyes, sure she hadn't seen correctly. The griffin blurred and became two, then three, then a dozen griffins, all bursting out of their own cave openings and soaring down toward Master Slipshod's unprotected head.

"O God of Cookery," Lailu whispered, mentally taking stock of her weapons. She had a large chef's knife at her hip and a pair of weighted steak knives tucked into each boot, but that was it. Since they would be hunting through the air, she'd purposely gone light. Would she be able to do enough to save her mentor? Or would the griffins just tear both of them to pieces?

Master Slipshod flicked the switch on his harness again and jerked to a sudden stop. The griffins and Lailu all hurtled past, leaving him safely above them. There was a brief pause while the griffins adjusted to this new development, changing direction and flying upward, and Lailu spotted her opportunity. She leaped, pushing off the cliff wall and hitting the button on her harness to give her slack. Her legs clamped around a griffin's waist just under his wings, and her fingers tangled in the feathers at the back of his neck.

The griffin squawked, plummeting beneath the added weight, his wings pumping furiously. He bucked and twisted but couldn't reach Lailu with his cruel beak. Slowly he managed to rise until the rest of his flock was just above, circling Master Slipshod.

"Ride of your life, yeah?" Master Slipshod shouted, looking way too cheerful for a man about to be ripped apart by the descending horde of beasts. Then he pressed a button on his harness.

Nothing happened.

Master Slipshod frowned, then pressed the button again.

Still nothing.

"Blasted contraption—" was all Lailu had time to hear before her own griffin lost altitude and began falling, tired wings unable to keep them up any longer. Lailu clung to his feathers, dodging the halfhearted stabs of the creature's beak. As the ground came into view below them, Lailu let go with one hand and pulled her chef's knife out of her sheath, waiting. Almost time. She looked at the soft, unprotected niche where the wing met the body of the griffin. It would be easy to slice there. She laid the edge of the blade against it and felt the griffin tense, then buck, then twist again in the air, but he was too tired. As they fell farther, close enough now that Lailu could leap free and roll safely, the griffin managed to turn his huge head around, one beady eye on her.

Lailu stared into that eye and saw herself reflected, her black hair tangled around her head, face flushed, knife poised. She wavered, her knife barely resting against his wing. He made a sad little sound, and Lailu bit her lip, steeling her resolve. She was a master chef. This was what she did for a living. She had bested this beast fairly, and his life was hers.

She raised her knife, about to strike, then sighed and shoved it angrily into her sheath. She couldn't do it. She just couldn't. All those years, and this was the first time she'd ever lost her resolve when it came time to make the kill.

The griffin's sad squawking turned into a roar of triumph, and with a sudden burst of energy, he flipped completely upside down. Distracted by her failure, Lailu slid immediately off the griffin and tumbled backward.

"You lousy, sneaky, feathered—"

Whump!

Lailu hit the ground hard, all the air knocked out of her lungs. As she lay there, she swore she heard the griffin laughing at her. *I hate birds*, she thought furiously, watching the beast fly away. What would she tell Master Slipshod?

Master Slipshod . . . Lailu had forgotten about him. What if the rest of the griffins had already torn him to pieces? "Might serve him right." She pushed herself up. Her whole body groaned in protest, but she managed to stagger back toward the cliff.

She pressed the button on her harness to pull her back up the cliff. It buzzed angrily and then went quiet, the harness barely twitching. Frowning, Lailu tried again. Nothing. "Yeah, he sure knew what he was doing," she muttered. She found handholds in the rock and began to climb. She wasn't sure she'd make it up there in time to be any help, but she knew she couldn't just sit down there doing nothing while her mentor was fighting for his life. Even if his plan was stupid. Even if he'd brought this on himself.

Before she'd gone more than a few feet, there was a loud splash from the river behind her, and Lailu lost her grip and fell. Again.

Master Slipshod burst out from the river, coughing and spluttering. "Pigtails!" he choked.

She scrambled to the bank and caught the rope he tossed her, hauling him closer until he reached a calm little outlet where the water flowed sluggishly, barely rippling, and he could climb out on his own. He waded through it, disrupting the glassy surface, and collapsed on the stony shore.

Groaning, he raised his head. "That plan," he said slowly, "was terrible."

"I know."

"You knew? Why didn't you speak up sooner, then? You really need to take a bigger leadership role here. I'm not going to be around forever, and then who's going to look out for Mystic Cooking?"

Lailu found this to be completely unfair. "You didn't tell me the plan until we were in the middle of it! It's not *my* fault. And I'd look out for our restaurant just fine on my own."

"Oh yeah?" Master Slipshod's eyes narrowed in his bruised face. He considered her, tilting his head to the side. "Perhaps," he muttered. "Perhaps." Then he climbed to his feet, pulled his chef's hat out of a back pocket, and wrung it out. "Well, at least you got the one griffin. I'd hate to think this had been a complete waste of time."

Lailu looked down at her feet and didn't say anything.

"You did get the one griffin, right?"

Lailu coughed, her toe drawing patterns in the dirt.

"Pigtails?"

Finally, reluctantly, she looked up at him. "It ... sort of got away from me."

Master Slipshod sighed, carefully placing his chef's hat over his tangled hair. "Well, I guess there's nothing for it." He looked past Lailu, back at the cliff they'd been on. "Time for try number two."

"W-what? We're going after those things again?"

"Of course. A good chef never gives up a tasty meal. Plus I promised we'd thin out the flock for the city. There are too many of these things here and not enough food to sustain them all, so they've been harassing the nearby village." Master Slipshod stretched, his back cracking audibly. "If we don't take out a couple of them, they'll send in one of those bloody heroes, and you know how *they* are. Stupid honor-seeking fools would probably wipe out the whole lot of these beasts, and then what would we do for future ingredients?"

"They're not *all* stupid honor-seeking fools," Lailu said, but softly, thinking of a certain blond-haired, blue-eyed boy. Vahn had been her childhood crush, and even though she was over him now, mostly, she still thought he made a great hero. She sighed and looked back at the cliff. "So what's our next plan?"

Master Slipshod grinned. It wasn't a very nice grin. Then he told her the plan. It wasn't a very nice plan.

"It's too bad the griffins didn't get you" was all Lailu could think to say. And then she reluctantly turned and started to climb the cliff. Apparently, it was her turn to be bait.

Ryon's Request

Lailu dragged the corner of her apron across her sweat-soaked brow. The whole kitchen blazed hotter than a raging phoenix as her Starling Volan stove worked overtime, all the burners turned on full blast. Tomorrow was the first day of the Week of Masks, the largest holiday in all of Savoria. People slept through the day and reveled through the night, chasing away the year's demons with parties and feasts, costumes and masks. Lailu and Slipshod had promised to cater a meal for Lord Elister's grand opening party celebrating the start of the festivities.

Lailu tried hard not to think about the party, about the extravagant guests and, most terrifying of all, Lord Elister himself. He was the royal executioner, and the man who essentially ruled the country right now until the young king came of age. Instead, she focused on the only thing she could control: making the best griffin feast any of those swanky aristocrats had ever tasted.

Hannah, Lailu's best friend and roommate, swept into the room. "Whew, it's warm in here." She flopped onto the kitchen's only chair, her teal skirts spreading around her like a wave. "That family of four just left," she added, adjusting the ugly comb in her long black hair. "Finally."

Lailu nodded, barely looking up from her cutting board.

"I flipped the sign to 'closed,'" Hannah went on, "and I picked up a letter for you."

"A letter?" Lailu wiped her hands on the front of her apron. "Who sent it?"

"A secret admirer." Hannah pulled a small folded paper out from her bodice. "And by *secret admirer*, I mean Greg. Naturally."

Lailu's face burned. "He's not my secret admirer."

"True. It's no secret."

"You're being silly."

"Is that so? Then why did he send you a love letter, hmm?" Hannah's dark eyes twinkled.

"He did not!" Lailu snatched the paper, her face now so hot she was pretty sure she could cook over it. She opened the letter and read quickly.

Lailu–

Remember that time I helped you take down a dragon? And then helped you cook it? And even helped you serve it up to almost the entire gang of elves? Oh yeah, and stuck around to clean up afterward? Because I sure do!

I also remember a little, tiny promise you made. I think the words "Lailu owes" and "favor" were used together.

Guess what? I'm calling it in. Sunrise hunt on the Third Day of Masks. I'll pick you up.

—Greg

P.S. Don't make any plans for the street festival, either—I'm going to need a cooking assistant.

"Oh . . . no . . ." Lailu groaned and crumpled the paper.

"So I take it, not a love note?" Hannah asked innocently.

"Like you didn't read it."

Hannah grinned. "What do you think you'll be hunting?"

Lailu shrugged. "It just better not be fyrian chickens. Favor or not, I'm not going after those beasts again." Still, she really did owe him—both a hunt *and* a cooking session, since he'd done both of those things for her.

Greg had been her rival all through the Chef Academy and was still her rival in the restaurant business. But he had also become . . . sort of . . . almost . . . her friend. Definitely *not* an admirer, secret or otherwise, but their relationship had certainly become more complicated after the events several months ago, when he'd helped Lailu save herself and Hannah from a gruesome fate involving a vicious gang of elves.

She shivered, a mixture of nerves and excitement running through her as she tried to guess what kind of beast they'd be after. It had to be something challenging, or why else would Greg be calling her in as backup?

Knock-knock.

Lailu frowned at the back door. Almost no one came through that way, except the elves, but her next payment to them wasn't due for another week.

She opened the door a crack, just wide enough to see a boy standing out there in dark clothing he'd done his best to make casual, the neck of his shirt loose and his vest undone beneath his thick wool coat.

"Ryon?" Her heart leaped. He hadn't been by Mystic Cooking since the night they helped rescue the kidnapped elves.

"The one and only."

"Where the spatula did you go? It's been months!" She would never admit it, but she was relieved to see him. More than relieved. Happy, even.

"I've been making myself scarce. Can I come in?"

"If you must."

"What a delightful invitation. I have never felt more welcomed." He made a show of stepping through her door, stopping when he caught sight of Hannah. "Resident thief Hannah," he said, inclining his head.

"Former loan shark lackey Ryon," Hannah retorted, rising from her chair.

Ryon's eyes widened, and he threw back his head and laughed. "Good to see your wits are as quick as your fingers. But I really prefer the term *henchman*."

"So I've heard. And I prefer the term . . ." Hannah hesitated.

"Hmm, I take back the quick wits comment."

"Hey!" Lailu said. "Be nice."

"Oh, it's okay, Lailu." Hannah looked Ryon up and down. "I might not know what term I'd prefer, but I'll take *thief* over *henchman* or *lackey* any day." Her smile was as sharp as steak knives as she added, "At least I've never been someone else's lapdog."

"I suppose I deserve that," Ryon said.

"If you're done insulting my friend, want to tell us why you're here?" Lailu said.

"Maybe I just wanted to visit my favorite chef."

"You've been gone months. Months, without a single word. And you expect me to believe you're just now dropping in for a visit?" She crossed her arms. "I don't buy it. What are you up to?"

"I'm wounded. I really did miss you." He smiled.

Lailu found herself smiling too.

"And . . . I might need a tiny favor," he added, pinching his thumb and forefinger together.

Lailu's smile fell faster than a one-winged griffin. "Absolutely not."

"I'll tell you where I've been these past few months."

Lailu debated, but in the end her curiosity got the better of her. "How about you tell me where you've been, and what you need, and then I'll consider it?" she said carefully.

Ryon laughed. "You're learning. I'm so proud. Okay, first I had some things I had to take care of after Mr. Boss's sudden death, and it was important to keep a low profile. And then I've been living with the elves the past few weeks."

Hannah gasped, then narrowed her eyes, giving Ryon the same kind of scrutiny she usually reserved for Slipshod.

"Why?" Lailu asked.

"I thought I should keep an eye on them, see how they were handling . . . everything," Ryon said. By "everything," Lailu knew he meant the discovery that their people were being kidnapped and drained of blood. There had been no casualties, but Lailu knew the elves did not tolerate insult or injury from anyone.

"Do they . . . do they know who was behind the kidnappings?" Lailu asked warily.

"You mean, do they know it was Starling?" Ryon snorted. "Obviously. They're not stupid."

"Then why haven't they done anything to the scientists?" Hannah spoke up. "I mean, they were ready to cut off my limbs over a hair comb."

"They don't have any proof yet, and Fahr is trying to go through official channels. He's worked hard to preserve peace with Elister. I don't think he's willing to throw that all away just yet."

Lailu thought of Fahr, the beautiful black-haired leader of the gang of elves. She'd only met him a few times and didn't know anything about him. But Eirad, his icy-eyed second . . . he didn't seem like the patient type. "What does Eirad think of this delay?" she asked.

Ryon grinned. "You're so clever. That's exactly the favor I was going to ask you about."

"I'm . . . what? Really?" Lailu blinked.

"Oh yes. Clever and very perceptive."

"Don't try to compliment her into helping you. That's so sneaky." Hannah frowned.

"It is, isn't it?" Ryon's grin widened.

"Sneaky *and* manipulative," Hannah added.

"Both wonderful attributes I happen to be blessed with." He winked.

Hannah's frown deepened. "I see what you mean about the winking, Lailu. It *is* annoying. And *you*," she pointed at Ryon, practically jabbing him in the chest. "You know Lailu doesn't have any defenses against that kind of thing."

"I do so," Lailu protested.

"No, honey, you really don't."

"Let's stay on topic," Ryon said quickly. "What's important is Eirad. I know he's loyal to Fahr, but I don't trust him, and I want you to help me keep an eye on him. I think he's up to something."

"What kind of something?" Lailu asked.

Ryon looked at her, his gray eyes serious. "Revenge."

Crack!

Lailu spun around. One of her favorite pots had split, pieces of griffin and hot oil tumbling out to sizzle on the stove. "Oh, no no *no*," Lailu moaned, rummaging around for an oven mitt and trying to rescue her doomed meal. "Hannah, pass me a clean pot. Ryon, grab me some towels. Hurry! This is a disaster!"

"It's not that bad," Ryon began.

"You don't understand! This . . . this . . ." Lailu waved a hand in distress at her broken pot.

"It's a terrible sign," Hannah said quietly. "When something breaks the day before the Week of Masks, it means your life is about to be broken too."

"That's ridiculous. You just had the heat up too high," Ryon said.

"This is a cast-iron pot," Lailu said. "It shouldn't break like that. This was no accident." She bit her lip. "I never replaced Chushi's shrine." Her shrine to the God of Cookery had been smashed to pieces on her opening day by Mr. Boss after she refused to give him and his cronies free food. Of course, she and Slipshod *had* owed him a bunch of money. . . .

Maybe now her patron god was angry with her? Whatever the cause, Lailu's stomach filled with a sick, squirmy feeling, as if her intestines had turned into snakes and were devouring her from the inside out. Nothing good would come of this; she was sure of it.

"Cheer up, Lailu. I need to go now, but I'll see you at the feast tomorrow," Ryon said.

"You're going to the party?" Lailu asked.

"Naturally. I need somewhere to practice my dance steps."

"Ooh." Hannah clapped her hands. "Can you get Lailu to dance too?"

Ryon winked at her and then put a hand on Lailu's shoulder. "Think about my words, okay?" Then he slipped outside, closing the door softly behind him.

"I'm not dancing," Lailu said into the silence, but her heart wasn't in it. She went back to cleaning up the mess on her stove and salvaging the rest of her feast, her thoughts on Eirad. Her pot had cracked at talk of his revenge. Maybe it wasn't a bad sign at all, but a warning.

3

RIVALS AT THE DANCE

"Lailu!" Wren waved from across the crowded ballroom, her bright red hair standing out against the purple of her gown. Even with the silver cat mask over her eyes, there was no mistaking Starling Volan's daughter.

Lailu waved back. It felt good to see a familiar face in the sea of people around her. She had been feeling lost amid all the bright colors and extravagant masks, even with Slipshod beside her. True, everyone had been eating their feast with enthusiasm, but she still didn't feel like she belonged among these people. She could hardly wait to escape Elister's fancy ballroom and fancy guests and get back to Mystic Cooking.

Wren slipped under elbows and around skirts until she reached Lailu. "I heard you tried Carbon's newest invention," she said breathlessly. "How was it? Was it amazing?"

Lailu grimaced. "It was . . . *something*, all right."

"Fool things broke on us," Slipshod said. "The lever stuck, right in the middle of a fight. I think Lailu and I will stick to more conventional chef's tools from here on out."

Lailu breathed a sigh of relief, then felt guilty at Wren's crestfallen expression. "Er, no offense, Wren," she added.

Wren shrugged. "Wasn't *my* invention. Mama will not be pleased, though. She hates mistakes."

"Oh. Well, she doesn't have to know," Lailu began.

"No, I'll have to tell her. It's sort of my job. Someone has to keep those scientists in line."

"Is that what your mom has you doing these days, then?"

"Oh, that and other things." Wren leaned in closer. "I've started working on my own inventions," she confided.

"Really? I thought you wanted to be an actress."

Wren tossed her head. "Kids' stuff. I've given it up. Besides, inventing things is a lot more fun."

"That's great, Wren." Lailu hoped Wren was happy with this choice, and that it wasn't something she was doing just to please her mom.

"Unfortunately, my inventions do have a tendency to kind of burst into flames. But I'm working on it," Wren added hastily. "I think I've found a way for Mama to keep an eye on—"

"Ladies and gentlemen!" Elister's voice boomed from every direction, and all other noise in the room cut off, as if Elister himself had sliced the sounds with his infamous crescent-shaped knives.

"I'll see you around, Lailu," Wren whispered before scurrying off.

Lord Elister strode out into the middle of the ballroom, draped in a suit of the deepest crimson and wearing a black velvet version of the old executioner-style masks. Clearly he had taken the original purpose of the Week of Masks to heart—a week to ward off evil spirits. As someone who had earned the nickname "Elister the Bloody," Lailu figured he'd want to take this week seriously. There were probably a number of angry ghosts trailing him.

For a moment Lailu felt his icy green eyes settle on her before sweeping the rest of the crowd. She tried to shrink back behind Slipshod. Elister had saved her life a few months ago, and he seemed to respect her cooking, but she knew he'd never forget how she'd tried to spy on him. And she would never forget how easily he'd killed two men in front of her.

Lailu's breath caught as a tiny woman in a gown the color of pure gold moved to stand beside Elister, her snow-blond hair piled in coils and held up by her gleaming crown. Although Queen Alina rarely made public appearances, she was instantly recognizable. Only people from her home country of Mystalon had hair so blond-white or skin so pale.

After the old king died, Queen Alina had inherited the throne until her son was old enough to rule. But Lord Elister seemed to wield as much power as she did. Rumor had it they'd formed an alliance back when the old king first began to grow ill. Elister ruthlessly killed all rivals to the throne so Queen Alina's young son would be the only option, and in exchange, she had given him power equal to her own.

Next to Elister, the queen looked almost like a child as she raised a hand and beamed at the ballroom full of people.

"I thank you all for joining me on this, the first day of the Week of Masks," Elister said. "Later tonight you will all be graced with an unveiling of Starling Volan's newest invention, but before that . . . dancing!" On cue, the musicians in the corner struck up a tune. The first day of the Week of Masks was all about chasing away fear and dancing with your demons, and the dance floor quickly filled with people ready to do both.

"All right, Pigtails, time for you to get out there."

Lailu froze. "M-me? Dance? Out there?" She gazed out at the beautiful women in low-cut gowns of all colors and men in top hats and brightly decorated coats and cravats, their masks smiling and snarling at the world. Lailu looked down at her own outfit, a gold-and-black silk shirt belted over formfitting black pants—the finest things she'd ever owned, courtesy of Hannah. Still, she would stick out horribly in this swirling soup of colors and finery. She could *not* go out there. What was Slipshod even thinking? Stalling for time, she tried the first excuse that came to mind. "I don't have a mask."

"Don't you?" Slipshod opened a sack and pulled out a pair of glittery golden masks. He passed her one. It was beautifully made, with long, sweeping griffin feathers that would frame the wearer's face and little glass beads lining the eyeholes. Lailu recognized Hannah's work immediately.

"But . . . but I don't belong out there." She couldn't explain how she felt as out of place here as an appetizer in the dessert course.

Slipshod puffed out his chest. "Of course you belong. Lord Elister himself invited us."

"Yes, but just to cook."

"It's never *just* to cook. Remember, I used to do this sort of thing all the time, back—well, back in the day," he mumbled.

Slipshod never talked about his glory days, but Lailu knew he used to cook for the old king himself. He'd been the greatest chef in all of Savoria, coming up with new and unique recipes and literally writing the book on dragon cuisine. She still wasn't sure what happened; the few times she'd gotten up the courage to ask, Slipshod had changed the subject and then been moody and silent for days afterward.

"Look, after the feast is when the cooks get to mingle. You know, brush elbows with the upper crust." Slipshod ran a hand through his strangely glossy hair, then put on his own griffin mask. "Well, go on," he said, giving her a gentle push in the direction of the dance floor.

Lailu stumbled a few steps forward, then halted. People danced and laughed all around her, the music swirling until her head swam with it and she thought she might be sick. She spun around, trying to find an exit, but she was surrounded by thrashing, twining limbs. There was no escape.

"Where's your mask?" a boy asked.

Lailu turned. "Greg?" she asked. His curly hair had been tamed and stuffed under a shiny black top hat, but she still recognized her one-time rival turned sort-of friend, even under the fiery phoenix half-mask: Gregorian LaSilvian. Her heart beat faster. Which was ridiculous.

He tapped his mask, and Lailu hurriedly pulled her griffin mask down over her face.

"Definitely an improvement," Greg said.

"And there's my favorite chef." A slender boy in a fox mask strode between a pair of exuberant dancers and bowed to Lailu, his dark hair pulled back into a low ponytail that brushed the shoulders of his sleek green shirt. As he straightened, he winked.

"Um, excuse me, we were talk—" Greg began.

"You don't mind if I borrow her, do you?" Ryon cut in.

"Ryon? What are you do—*oof!* Hey!" Before she could do more than utter these words, Ryon had a hold of her hand and was dragging her farther onto the dance floor.

"I made a solemn promise to your friend that I would get you to dance." Ryon's other hand rested lightly on Lailu's hip, and she squirmed.

"You didn't promise her anything. You just winked."

"Ah, but I take my winking very seriously." He whirled her around in a circle. "Besides, if you must know, I ran into her again earlier this morning."

"You did?" Lailu wasn't sure how she felt about that.

"Oh yes, and we had a very illuminating conversation."

Lailu felt even more unsure about *that*. "About what?" she asked nervously.

"Oh, family, friends, your excellent dancing abilities."

"But I can't dance!"

"Nonsense—you're dancing right now." He spun her around like a top and then dipped her backward and up again.

As much as she hated to admit it, it was fun. He twirled her around again, her feet flying like she was sprinting after a beast.

"And look! You're smiling now too!" he said.

"I'm imagining I'm out hunting."

"Whatever works." He spun her so fast, the world became a blur.

She laughed in spite of herself, finally relaxing. *One dance*, she told herself. *It can't hurt, right?*

And then she saw him.

Greg's eyes met hers across the dance floor just as the song ended, his vibrant phoenix mask shadowing his expression. For some reason, Lailu couldn't look away, until Ryon released her waist, then bent over her hand and kissed it.

Lailu gasped, surprised, Greg forgotten.

"Thank you for the dance, Lailu." Ryon let go of her hand.

"N-no wink this time?" Lailu felt like she was strapped into Carbon's harness again, her balance all off.

"No wink. I am in all seriousness. You're . . . not a good dancer."

"Hey!"

"But you're a fun dancer, and that's much more important." With a final bow, Ryon weaved his way through the crowd just as the next song started up.

Lailu was frozen there a moment longer until an enthusiastic couple trod on her foot, and she realized the middle of the dance floor was not a safe place to stand still, especially when you were only five feet tall. Shaking her head, she pushed her way through, almost running right into Greg.

"Oh! Er, h-hey, Greg." Lailu hated how her voice was all shaky. It was the dancing. It made her dizzy and confused and not at all herself.

Greg didn't say anything, his face still beneath his mask.

"LaSilvian!" a lanky boy called out. He knocked into Lailu, bumping her backward, and clapped Greg on the shoulder.

"Um, excuse me?" Lailu said, staggering back.

The boy glanced over, his mask—a painted and bejeweled dog face—laughing at her. "Who are you?" he asked coldly, just as another boy in a dog mask trotted over. It was like facing down a pack.

"I'm Lail—"

"She's just the chef," Greg interrupted. "So maybe she should get back to cooking, yeah?" Greg's brown eyes were dark as he looked at her, the eyes of a stranger.

Lailu took a step back, then another, and Greg turned, laughing at something one of the boys in dog masks whispered in his ear. Lailu's vision blurred, and she stumbled away.

She reached the doors at the far end of the room, grateful for her mask. It hid the tears spilling out of her eyes. Not that she was crying—it was just the heat. It was just really hot in here. She didn't care if Greg was a jerk. She *knew* he was a jerk. She'd always known.

She tried to open one of the doors, but a man staggered in front of her, blocking her in. Lailu's hand reached for her chef's knife before she recognized Carbon's bowl of a hat.

"You have to tell Starling that my invention worked perfectly," Carbon slurred. His breath stank of fermented grapes, his eyes bloodshot and watery beneath a crooked white mask.

"But . . . it didn't work perfectly." Lailu inched away from him.

"No, no, no. That's not true, not true. You must not have been using it right. I can help, I can—"

A man seized Carbon roughly by the shoulder. "Go away, *pawn*."

Carbon looked up into cold blue eyes, half-hidden behind a black domino mask, and blanched, his face turning the color of his own mask. "Y-you. You wouldn't d-dare do—"

"Wouldn't I?"

Carbon threw one last frightened look at Lailu before scurrying away.

"Eirad?" She couldn't believe it. Eirad, the elves' second-in-command, here at Lord Elister's party? Even though his long, pointed ears were disguised beneath a black top hat, there was no mistaking those impossibly sharp cheekbones, the elvish point of his chin. But from far away, Lailu could see how he would fit right in here, his whole outfit designed to blend, from the simple but elegant cut of his peacock-blue coat to the subtle gray cravat.

"That one is weak," Eirad sneered. "Even Lord Elister's pet scientist thinks so. I'd be doing her a favor getting rid of him."

"What are you doing here?" Lailu asked carefully, remembering Ryon's words.

"Working."

Working? Coming from someone like Eirad, that sounded quite ominous.

"Ladies and gentlemen, a moment of your attention, if you please." Elister's voice boomed all around the room, and Lailu was forced to put the puzzle of Eirad away for now. Starling Volan's presentation was about to begin.

4

STARLING'S DEMONSTRATION

Starling Volan swept into the middle of the rapidly clearing floor. She gazed out at the crowd, her head thrown back, her red hair tumbling from a low ponytail. Beneath her dainty bird mask, her smile was wide and triumphant.

"Good evening, lords and ladies. Your Majesty." Starling inclined her head toward the queen. "Tonight you all bear witness to something . . . game-changing." She glanced at Elister. Even from this side of the room, Lailu could see the eager way he stood. "Tonight, you have the privilege of seeing our newest invention!" She spread her arms wide, the sleeves of her blue silk gown trailing around her like wings.

Carbon stumbled over, placing something small and boxlike into one of her outstretched hands. Starling fiddled with a knob on top, and a long, thin piece of metal extended out two feet. She hit a button, shifted a lever on the side, and with a flourish, held out the object for all to see.

An excited murmur broke out among the waiting guests. Lailu peeked at Eirad, who leaned casually against the wall next to her, a predatory look on his face. She noticed he was staring at Carbon, and not Starling and her invention.

"And now," Starling announced, jabbing dramatically at a large red button on the front of the contraption in her hand.

A moment passed. Then another. Nothing happened, and the crowd grew louder and more restless. On the other side of the ballroom, Elister whispered something to the queen as she nervously picked at the lace around her throat.

Starling frowned down at the box in her hand and pushed another button, jiggling the lever again. Still nothing. Her frown deepened, and she glared at the slouched, bald figure of Carbon. He shriveled under her stare like burnt vegetables on a frying pan.

Reaching into her wide belt, Starling pulled out a tool resembling a small chisel. She used it to pop the back off the box, then fiddled with the wires inside. A moment later, she put the box back together and looked up at the waiting crowd. "My apologies, honored guests. I wished to build up more suspense." She smiled, and a few people laughed nervously. "But without further ado . . ." Starling pushed the red button again, and in the hush, Lailu heard it.

Click-click-click, whirrrrrrrr.

The doors next to Lailu burst open.

Lailu jumped back, her hand falling to her chef knife as something roughly her height stepped slowly inside the now silent room. It looked almost like an overgrown child, but a nightmare child that had been twisted and dipped in metal, with long, spindly arms and legs. Its torso was lined with glass, giving a clear view of the many gears and spokes inside, each clicking and rotating constantly, and glowing blue lights lit up its faceplate where eyes should be. It just looked ... *wrong*.

It turned its brass head toward Lailu, fixing those glowing orbs on her, almost as if it could read her thoughts.

Lailu took a small step back.

The creature tilted its head to the side, then moved through the room with a long, gliding stride toward Starling. At the last moment, it turned and stood next to Carbon instead, who went white as milk.

Starling's expression was a frozen promise, an avalanche one breath from falling.

"It's not ... I didn't program it to ... I ...," Carbon said, flailing.

"My associate here will be assisting in this demonstration," Starling said, her voice sugary sweet. "Carbon, if you'd be so kind?"

Carbon lurched forward and took the gadget from her. His movements were jerky, abrupt, a strange contrast to the graceful motions of the machine moving beside him as it finally slid over to Starling's side.

Click-click-click, whirrrrrrrrr.

Starling rested her hand on top of its head like a proud parent. "Ladies and gentlemen of Twin Rivers, I present to you all—the automaton." She waited a beat, the silence thickening faster than griffin stew. "And what exactly is an automaton, you may ask?" Another beat. "Why, whatever we want it to be. This is our first prototype, but we have many more in progress. They are still learning, but eventually they will be able to mimic and then even surpass humans at all but the most complex of tasks."

The words "many more" and "still learning" filled Lailu with dread. It was like taking a mouthful of striped vibber stew and then noticing that some of the creatures were still slithering. Why wasn't anyone else worried? As she glanced around the crowd, all she saw were rapt and wondering faces. Except for Eirad, who had no expression at all.

"For instance," Starling said, nudging Carbon, "if you need a server, just call your local automaton."

Carbon fiddled with the remote, and the automaton stepped into the crowd, which immediately opened to let it pass. It picked up a tray and some empty glasses from a nearby table and carried them effortlessly back to the middle of the room.

"Entertainment? They can do that."

The automaton tossed the tray and glasses up into the air, then began juggling, its arms a blur.

"Or perhaps dancing?"

Smoothly, the automaton snatched the tray out of the air and used it to catch the glasses, while simultaneously dancing a jig. Lailu's mouth fell open. This was unbelievable!

All around her, people chattered excitedly. One man even stepped forward and danced in front of the metal creature while his friends laughed and cheered him on.

"Or maybe you need protection," Carbon said suddenly. He jabbed at a button on the remote, and the automaton slid from a dancing pose to a fighting stance.

Zing!

Knives extended from its fingers. It cocked its head at the dancing man, who stumbled back. A woman nearby screamed. The automaton spun toward her, and with a speed that even Lailu would have trouble matching, its arms sliced through the air, the knives glinting in the light as it moved. It ended with a backflip, then crouched, putting one knee to the ground and elbow to knee in a posture of respect and servitude in front of Carbon.

Carbon nodded once, and the knives slid back into its fingers. It stood, a motionless doll once more.

Starling was silent for a long moment as she studied Carbon, and then she turned back to the crowd. No one spoke. No one moved. "I think this performance has been very . . . informative. For everyone," she said into the stillness.

Informative indeed. Lailu could picture that thing moving relentlessly, cutting people down without a thought. It was a glorified tool. A dangerous tool. And Starling was the last person Lailu would trust with something like that. She shivered.

Elister stepped forward, bringing his hands together in sharp, ringing claps. "That is marvelous," he declared, still clapping. A couple of people picked it up, and then the room erupted in sound.

Lailu couldn't bring herself to join in.

"Maybe Fahr is correct, and times are changing," Eirad said, narrowing his eyes at the automaton and the clapping, cheering people around it. "We'll need to change with them." He was silent a moment before he turned to Lailu. "I'll be seeing you again soon, little chef." Then he slipped out the doors and was gone.

Lailu found Slipshod packing up their stuff.

"Enjoy the show, Pigtails?" He put the last of the leftovers into their Cooling and Containment cart, then closed and locked it.

"I'm not sure," Lailu admitted.

Slipshod grinned. "I understand what you mean. Times are changing."

His words were such a close echo of Eirad's that Lailu felt a momentary pang. "I think they're changing too fast," she said. She watched the crowd. The musicians had started another lively tune, and people were already drifting back out onto the dance floor. In the corner, Elister was examining the automaton as Starling gestured emphatically at it. There was no sign of the queen, or Wren, or Ryon, but Greg was still there, standing with one of the dog-masked boys a few feet away. Lailu caught him looking at her and deliberately turned her back on him.

"Should we get going?" Lailu asked Slipshod. No answer. "Master Slipshod?" she tried again.

He was smiling at a woman in the crowd wrapped in magenta velvet, the top of her face obscured by a peacock mask. And the weirdest thing about her was that she was smiling back. Right at Slipshod.

Lailu cleared her throat.

"Eh?" Slipshod jerked his gaze back to Lailu. "What? Go?"

"We're all packed up. They don't need us here anymore."

Slipshod adjusted his mask. "A good chef is always needed. Remember that, Pigtails. I'll see you back at home."

"You'll—what?"

"Opportunities abound here," Slipshod called over his shoulder as he stepped out into the swirling mass of people. They closed around him, leaving Lailu alone with the food.

5

Eirad Is Surprised

Lailu was grateful to Lord Elister for sending her home in a carriage. With all the parties and decorations for the Week of Masks, Twin Rivers had morphed into a creepy place to walk around at night. Emboldened by their masks and costumes, once the sun set, people were allowing their inner demons to run free as they tore through the streets, cackling and fighting and destroying things. Houses and apartments had candles lit in every window and carved pumpkins beside every door to chase away the darkness, but outside on the streets, anything went.

Lailu wasn't scared of monsters, but people were often scarier.

She thought of the automaton, the way it moved in graceful, short bursts, those glowing blue eyes . . . She wasn't scared of *most* monsters, she amended. But man-made monsters? They were a whole different story.

The carriage pulled to a stop in front of Mystic Cooking, and Lailu climbed out, lugging her Cooling and Containment cart after her.

"Don't forget to wear your mask," the carriage driver said.

Lailu instinctively pulled her griffin mask down over her face. It was considered bad luck to be out on the streets at night during the Week of Masks without one.

"That's quite unique. Did you get it from Melvin's Marvelous Masks?" the driver asked, studying her.

"From where?" Lailu asked.

"That little shop that just opened in the market. You haven't seen it?" The carriage driver tapped his own mask, an elaborate affair with a horse's muzzle, complete with a silky mane. "I picked this up there. Never thought I'd be able to afford something so nice, but the chap who runs the place is very reasonable, practically giving them away."

"Oh. That's . . . that's great," Lailu said. She closed the carriage door and stepped back.

"You be safe now, little miss." The driver clucked at the horses and headed back down the road. There was something comforting about the way his horses moved in step with the carriage. How soon before that ended and everyone drove those strange steam-powered contraptions instead?

Times are changing.

Lailu shivered.

A couple of men in bowler hats and their own cheap masks laughed boisterously as they walked down the cobblestones. They gave Lailu a halfhearted wave before disappearing into the brick complex across from her. Mystic Cooking had been open long enough that all the neighbors now seemed to recognize Lailu. Hannah had insisted on giving a "neighborhood" discount—appetizers on the house!—to anyone who lived on their street, which definitely increased Lailu's popularity in the area. Supposedly it was a strategic business move meant to generate positive word of mouth and harbor good feelings with the locals. Lailu had to admit, she just wasn't very good at anything that wasn't hunting or cooking, so she was forced to take Hannah's word for it.

Still, with Hannah and Slipshod's help, Lailu had managed to get Mystic Cooking up and running. She patted the front of her two-story establishment. It wasn't big, and it wasn't in the center of town, but she loved every inch of it. Feeling better, she unlocked the front door and pushed it open.

". . . not ready yet." Hannah's soft voice carried from the kitchen.

Lailu opened her mouth to call to her friend when she heard Vahn's voice. "Hannah, my beautiful Hannah, what can I do to change your mind? I feel like I've been waiting for you forever."

Lailu froze, her body going icy all over, even as her ears burned. Should she leave? She should. She shouldn't be listening to this. But somehow her feet stayed where they were, her eyes fixed on the blue curtain pulled shut across her kitchen doorway, hiding Hannah and Vahn from view.

"You've been waiting, huh?" Hannah said. "Is that what you call stolen kisses with Millie the Baker and Sandra SalConte?"

"Millie was *months* ago, and Sandra is just spreading jealous lies. You know you are the only one for me."

"What about Lailu?"

Lailu's heart stopped for one impossibly long moment. It was like coming face-to-face with a mountain dragon.

Vahn groaned. "Would you leave her out of this? She's just a silly kid with a silly crush."

Lailu's hand clenched on the door handle. After everything she'd done for him, how dare he? Silly kid? Without this *silly kid*, he'd never have solved his first quest. Lailu was the one who had figured out where the kidnapped elves were being held, and Lailu was the one who had helped him rescue them. Otherwise he would have failed, and the rest of the elves would probably be using him for spare parts right now, a thought that suddenly gave her a great deal of comfort. How had she ever liked that guy?

"That's harsh," Hannah said after a long minute, her voice as cold as Lailu's breaking heart. "She's my best friend, and if you can't even be nice to her, then how can I possibly date you?"

"But I *am* nice to her."

"You beg free food off her and then think it's a reward when you give her a smile. Where I come from, that doesn't qualify as nice."

"To be fair, I have an amazing smile."

"I'm serious, Vahn."

"So am I." He sighed. "All right, all right. So if I can play nice with your little friend, you'll go out with me?"

Lailu didn't bother to listen to the rest. First Greg at the party, and now Vahn? She was sick of boys and sick of feeling like something dropped off a plate.

Lailu put her Cooling and Containment cart just inside the

dining room, then left, closing the door silently behind her. As anger carried her down the long dirt road, she welcomed the way the chill of the night slipped beneath her shirt and froze her skin. All around her came the shouts and cries of people celebrating the Week of Masks, and as she left her restaurant farther and farther behind, Lailu found herself mingling with a growing crowd of costumed people. She brushed shoulders with leaping lizards, roaring tigers, a whole blessing of unicorns, a dragon or two, and even one memorable gaggle of batyrdactyls. Why anyone would dress like those bloodsuckers, she had no idea, but the trio of teenage girls seemed to be enjoying flapping around and giggling together.

Lailu adjusted her mask, suddenly feeling very alone, a solitary griffin surrounded by people out with their friends. She hunched her shoulders, no longer enjoying the cold.

"You look like you could use a warm beverage," a woman said, her voice as deep and rich as the hot cocoa she held out.

Lailu thanked the woman and took the drink gratefully, wrapping her hands around it as she continued down the street. All around her, other merchants and vendors passed out food and drink to anyone who wanted. During the Week of Masks, nobody went hungry or thirsty.

She noticed the new mask shop: Melvin's Marvelous Masks. The owner sat slumped in his booth, a stack of fantastical masks beside him, a giant hooded cobra mask covering his whole head. It looked a little too realistic for Lailu's comfort, and she stopped a few feet away.

Cautiously Lailu took a sip of her cocoa, then found herself drinking her entire mug in one long gulp. It tasted as rich and creamy as it smelled, with just a hint of something spicy. She closed her eyes, and it was like she was back home in her village, sitting in front of a fire on a cold evening, wrapped in her warmest quilt with her favorite book of recipes on her lap.

Lailu opened her eyes slowly, dreamily, then blinked.

A pair of familiar blue eyes regarded her from behind a plain black mask.

"Eirad?" she gasped. She flushed, feeling like he'd just caught her stealing ingredients from a feast.

"Obviously."

Lailu struggled for a less obvious question to ask him. "You're here?" She could have kicked herself. "I mean, of course you're here. Why were you staring at me?"

"I could see the emotions flitting over your face. Nostalgia, sentimentality, dreams of home." Eirad tapped his chin. "Very intriguing. And all because of a simple cup of cocoa." He plucked the empty mug from her fingers, then tossed it into the air. It turned into an owl and soared across the sky, screeching.

Lailu's blood ran cold. "I thought you couldn't do magic in the city," she whispered.

"My poor little chef, there are loopholes. There are *always* loopholes." He bared his teeth in a vicious smile. "Enjoy the rest of your night. I know I intend to." He nodded at Melvin, who immediately sat straight up, and then Eirad sauntered off.

Lailu thought of Ryon's words about Eirad: *I think he's up to something*. She hesitated as the elf moved farther away, and then she made up her mind. It was the First Night of Masks, after all. A night to celebrate monsters. She might as well spend some time with one of hers. "Wait, Eirad!"

He turned, raising his eyebrows in a silent challenge.

"Where are you going?" Lailu panted as she caught up.

"Why do you ask, little chef? Did you want to accompany me?" He looked her up and down, his lips curling in amusement.

"Actually . . ." Lailu took a deep breath. "Yes."

Eirad's eyes widened. It was the first time Lailu had ever seen him surprised. No matter what happened next, she thought it all might be worth it for that alone.

Eirad regarded her for a long moment, then inclined his head. "Very well. I did offer, after all." He extended a hand toward her, and Lailu hesitantly took it, Eirad's long fingers folding around hers.

He grinned wickedly. "This should be very entertaining."

6

THE WESTERN TRAVEL DISTRICT

Eirad oozed through the crowd of revelers, sliding past them like a sea serpent and wending his way farther into the city. Lailu managed to get stepped on, elbowed, and tripped, Eirad's hand the only thing keeping her on her feet. He dragged her along like a log caught in a river current. By the time he slowed, she felt completely disoriented, her hair coming loose from its pigtails, her mask askew.

"Where are we—" Lailu froze. "Going," she finished in a whisper, but she knew.

The Western Travel District.

It was impossible to miss. The grandiose domed buildings that had once been a source of pride for the city were now nothing more than crumbled remains, the white stone and gold of the buildings forming their own graves. The streets ahead shifted from cobblestones to obsidian, the dark stones even darker in abandon-ment. Without any candles, it felt like a long, empty tunnel.

Lailu stopped short in front of a toppled statue. Its head had rolled off and vanished long ago, and parts of its torso were missing. At its feet, engraved in the base, Lailu read:

ENTER HE WHO IS WORTHY. ALL OTHERS SHALL PERISH AT . . .

The rest of the words had faded to nothing. It lay on the border of the district, the road stretching past it.

Eirad stopped next to her. "Problem, little chef?"

"Most people who enter here don't come back out again," she whispered.

"That is a misconception. They all come out . . . eventually. They just might not be recognizable anymore." Eirad's smile looked even more feral than usual.

Was he joking? Lailu wasn't sure, but since elves couldn't tell lies . . .

"Perhaps you'll be one of the lucky ones. Unless you'd care to turn back?"

Lailu shook her head.

"Very well." Eirad deliberately stepped on the broken statue, crumbling more of it into dust beneath his boots as he strolled into the Western Travel District.

Lailu shuddered but followed him. She didn't know what drove her. Curiosity, maybe, about this abandoned slice of city.

Years ago, goblins had populated most of this district. Master craftsmen, they created wondrous tools and fantastical pieces of art, but they almost never shared any of these things with their human neighbors. They were only willing to trade on those rare occasions when they needed something their alchemy could not make. But unlike the elves, goblins could lie easily and often, and Lailu heard their "deals" were never very beneficial to those they did business with.

Everything had been fine until they started trading with the elves. No one knew exactly what happened, but it eventually led to a vicious feud. One that had only one winner.

Thanks to the deadly magic the elves wielded, this part of the city had never been fixable. Even now, Lailu thought she could feel the aftereffects of their magic brushing against her skin like oil spattering from a pan.

Lailu followed Eirad down the street and around the corner into the heart of the district. She gasped, freezing midstep. Just up ahead, the largest building loomed against the night sky, its rotting, twisted frame completely covered in shimmering, multi-colored lights.

"Wow," Lailu breathed. "Just . . . wow."

"Don't be too impressed. You haven't seen anything yet," Eirad said ominously.

As Lailu got closer, she saw that the lights were coming from small glass jars that had been strung together in long, colorful lines and then hung from the roof. Each jar was filled with . . .

"Pixies?" Lailu touched a jar, and the pixie inside put both tiny hands on the other side opposite Lailu's palm. She was only the size of Lailu's ring finger, her body covered in a thick mat of bright orange fur, her wings a complementary translucent orange. They beat rapidly, so fast they were a blur, and when she bared her teeth at Lailu, they were sharp and pointed.

"Does this . . . does it hurt them?"

"Funny question, coming from a girl who hunts down dragons and other beasties," Eirad said.

"That's different."

"Is it?"

"I'm not keeping them in jars or anything. And they're not . . . not human."

"Human." Eirad's lip curled. "Yes, well, neither is *that*." He flicked the jar, sending the pixie spinning. "These creatures have more in common with insects."

The pixie hissed, her hands on her hips.

"She doesn't look like an insect to me." Lailu didn't know very much about pixies; she heard they fed on elven magic, and they hid from humans, only clustering in the deepest parts of forests. She could hardly believe there were hundreds of them held captive here in this spot.

"Don't worry, little chef, we'll let them all go after the final night of the Week of Masks." He turned his back on the jars. "Come along now. There are wonders much greater than this waiting inside."

Lailu spared one last glance at the pixie in the jar, then followed Eirad to the front doors. They looked surprisingly new against the cracked stone of the rest of the building and gleamed with a faint reddish hue. Cherrywood? Or something . . . darker? It was hard to tell in the shifting light from the pixie jars. Lailu reached toward them.

"I wouldn't if I were you," Eirad said.

"What?"

"Only someone with elven blood can open these doors. Anyone else who touches them, well . . ." He tossed his mass of braids back behind his shoulders. "Let's just say it is not pleasant. Unless you don't mind losing your skin."

"My *skin*?" Lailu took a step back, tucking her hands under her armpits as if they might reach out on their own. "Is this another one of those magic loopholes?"

Eirad cocked his head to the side. "Tell me, what do you know of the treaty Fahr made with Elister?"

"Just that it's *supposed* to be illegal for elves to do magic in the city. And since you can't lie . . . *supposedly* . . . it should be binding."

He laughed, a surprisingly light, musical sound that reminded Lailu of wind chimes. "Oh, I am glad I brought you, little chef. Yes, we cannot lie, and so our promises are binding. This is true. But much like one of your meals, there are different flavors of truth."

"That makes no sense," Lailu said flatly.

"No? I thought the cooking metaphor would help."

"It doesn't."

"I'll be more forthright. Fahr promised Elister that as long as we remained denizens of Twin Rivers, we would not kill anyone under his protection. This was a requirement after that unfortunate misunderstanding with the goblins twenty years ago."

Unfortunate misunderstanding? Lailu glanced at the broken shards of buildings all around her and shook her head. Clearly this was a flavor of truth she couldn't taste.

"Elister also demanded we not do any magic within Twin Rivers' official city limits."

"Which you agreed to." What was Eirad getting at?

"Fahr did. He likes to play nice with you humans." Eirad's mouth twisted. "But here is the fun part: at that time, the city's official limits extended only to just past Gilded Island. Your foolish kings were not always so good at updating their maps."

Lailu gaped at him. "But . . . the city goes way past that point."

Eirad studied his fingernails, his lips curving in amusement. "It doesn't matter how far the city extends. What matters is the wording, which was not nearly exact enough. It also said nothing about us doing magic elsewhere, and then bringing that magic inside the city. As I said, little chef, there are always so many loopholes."

"Why are you telling me this?" Lailu asked.

"Because there is nothing you can do about it, except worry." He swept his long braids back. "I find that quite entertaining."

Lailu scowled.

"Just as I find *you* quite entertaining," Eirad laughed.

"I could report this to Elister."

"You *could* . . . but we both know you won't."

Lailu's scowl deepened. He was right, too. The last thing she wanted was to get involved in another feud.

"Come now, we wouldn't want to be late for the main event of the party. For tonight is our night to dance on the graves of our enemies."

And at that, he put both palms against the doors, which rippled beneath his touch like water and then melted away.

DANCING WITH MONSTERS

The mouth of the building gaped like some giant beast, and Lailu caught snatches of song, laughter, and the smells of something expertly spiced and exotic. She stepped inside, the air falling around her thick and heavy as gravy.

It wasn't what she'd expected. Instead of a sitting room, she stood in a long, narrow hall, the walls glowing a gentle green, like sunlight filtered through a forest. The air now smelled like mold and peeling paint, and there were no pictures on the walls, no carpet beneath their feet—just plain wood.

Eirad led her down the hall about a hundred paces, and then he stopped in front of a stretch of wall that looked exactly like the rest. He tapped it twice, and it slid away, revealing a giant room full of hazy colors. Through the haze, elves swayed and twisted, their movements illuminated by hundreds upon hundreds of pixies, some in glass jars, others flittering around near the ceiling in their own complicated dance.

Immediately Lailu was caught in the wave of sound: elves laughing, music twining, the roar of too many people in a small space all having a good time. And the smells! There was that exotic scent—maybe mandrake root with a hint of paprika? And underneath it all, an earthy, woodsy smell that Lailu recognized.

"Is that inside the Tree Fort?" Lailu asked.

"Obviously," Eirad said.

"But . . . we're in the Western Travel District."

"I know. Clever, isn't it? It was my idea to link them. Now put this on," he instructed, a mask appearing in his outstretched hand.

"Did you just magic this into existence?"

"Even I can't just magic something into being. Silly human. I had it made specially for you."

"Why? You didn't even know I would be here tonight."

"Didn't I?" Eirad smirked.

Lailu's stomach clenched. She'd thought coming here was her own idea. It was, right? Why did everything with the elves always have to be so complicated?

"Well, I already have a mask," Lailu said, tapping her griffin feathers.

"This one's better." He pushed it into her hands.

It was an elaborate mask covered in shiny bluish-gray scales and a snout that protruded a good four inches, and after a few seconds, Lailu realized it was a mountain dragon. He really had made it for her. Tentatively she pulled her griffin mask off and slipped the new mask over her head. The material inside was warm and pliant, practically molding over her skin as if it were part of her face.

Lailu had the sudden urge to rip it off and throw it far away from her, but Eirad was already pulling her into the room. She was immediately surrounded by tall, elegant figures, all masked and costumed. Music seemed to come from nowhere and everywhere. It wasn't like any music she had heard before, the high notes too pure as they danced above a throbbing beat that made Lailu's feet move instinctively to the rhythm. Something in it called to her, and she could feel it thrumming through her veins like the cry of the hunt.

Vahn's words slid from her like grease off a plate, Greg's scorn dripped away, and she was just herself. Just Lailu. She closed her eyes, sensing her body. Shorter than she'd like, but that no longer bothered her, not in this moment. Instead, she felt strong. Powerful. She let herself melt into her mask, let herself relax into this bizarre night and just go with it, twirling along with the mass of dancing elves.

"It's intoxicating, isn't it?" Eirad asked.

Lailu opened her eyes. Eirad danced next to her, his eyes wide with pure glee, feet moving in time with Lailu's.

"What is it?" Lailu asked, tipping her head back.

"It's what we feel all the time, what it means to be an elf. It's the releasing of your humanity."

"It's *what*?" Her feet slowed.

"Don't stop dancing, little chef. Inside everyone is a wild creature, untamed and untamable. Tonight, you get to let that beast out, get to *become* that beast. Every human should experience this." He grinned wickedly. "This is true freedom. And my gift to you."

He spun her around suddenly, tossing her in the air like a piece of dough, then flipping her away. She crashed into another elf, this one unfamiliar. Like all elves, he was tall and thin, his ears poking above the feathers in his mask, his hair the color of burnt wood as it flowed in beautiful spirals down his back.

"Ah, little human girl." The elf's sneer was full of malice. "And what are you doing here, so far from home?"

"I'm, uh . . ." Lailu's heart hammered, as trapped as she was, her hands held firmly in the elf's tight grip as he pulled her around in a mockery of a dance. This was supposed to be *freedom*? Suddenly the walls felt too close, and she was very aware of the elves pressing in on all sides of her. What had she been thinking, following Eirad to a place like this? What could she possibly learn here?

"I brought her." Eirad appeared suddenly beside them. "She's here as my guest." Then he was gone again, spinning away with another elf.

Lailu's partner stopped smirking immediately and let her go.

Lailu took a few steps away from him, bumping into another elf, a female with long silvery hair.

"And what have we here?" the female elf purred.

"This is Eirad's guest," the first elf said.

"Really?" She studied Lailu in surprise, her pale eyes half-hidden in the shadows beneath her snakeskin mask. "He invoked the Rite of Guest for a human? *Eirad?*"

Lailu could feel her face flushing beneath her own elaborate mask.

"Well, he *has* been in a dreadful mood lately. Perhaps all he needed was a new pet." She patted Lailu on the top of her head.

"I'm *not* a pet." Lailu twisted away from the elf, but she caught Lailu's wrist and spun her around. "And what's the Rite of Guest?" Lailu asked.

"Only elves are allowed to dance here on this night of all nights. Unless an elf claims Rite of Guest, in which case that elf claims responsibility for the creature brought among us."

"Creature?"

"A creature such as yourself." She lunged in and out, the fangs on her mask extending, until she seemed to become a snake herself.

Lailu jerked back in surprise.

No, she was just an elf in a costume.

Lailu's breath caught in her throat. She had to get out of here. She tried weaving her way through the throng of dancing bodies, occasionally getting caught, twirled, sent stumbling back into the middle of the room, while all around her the whisper of *Eirad's guest* spread like wildfire until the room vibrated with this knowledge. A room that suddenly felt too stuffy, too full of elves, all glittering and dangerous. Lailu rubbed her eyes. Sometimes they were elves, and sometimes they were . . .

Dragons. Griffins. Snakes. Unicorns. Even a pack of three elves, dancing so close together that their limbs twined as one, somehow turned into a hydra.

"You should have stayed in your safe little kitchen," a female elf said, her features hidden beneath the beak and feathers of a roc, one of the giant birds that live on the tallest of mountaintops.

"Do I know you?" Lailu asked desperately. The elf's voice was strangely familiar, and she clung to the thought of anyone who could help ground her in this shifting, moving world.

"Yes," the elf said, her arms moving, the feathers glued to her sleeves rustling in a sudden breeze. "I was at your dragon cuisine negotiation."

Lailu stiffened. She remembered that night all too well. In order to save Hannah from the elves, Lailu had promised to hunt and cook dragon cuisine for them. If she'd failed to cook the best cuisine they'd ever tasted, they would have kept her as a slave—forever. Luckily, she had managed to pull it off.

"You remember me now, I see," the elf said. Her sleeves blurred, the feathers thickening, spreading, until they became a pair of wings.

"Wha—" Lailu began as the elf charged forward, her mouth ending in a sharp, cruel beak, open and ready to snap. At this close range, Lailu would never be able to escape in time.

Someone caught her from behind and whirled her out of the way.

"Gwendyl!" Lailu's rescuer said disapprovingly.

"What?" Gwendyl complained, her wings and beak vanishing so completely that Lailu was left to wonder if they'd been there at all. "I'm just having a bit of fun."

The elf let go of Lailu, and she immediately recognized Fahr, the leader of the elves, with his silky crow-black hair and laughing gray eyes. He wore a simple black domino mask that did nothing to disguise his features.

"I'm glad you chose to come here tonight," Fahr said, his tone surprisingly gentle. "But perhaps you've had enough excitement? This next part of the dance is not really suitable for you. Unless you'd care to stay?"

"No, I—I would like to leave," Lailu said, relieved.

Fahr beckoned to someone. Someone with dark hair and a familiar fox mask.

Lailu's jaw dropped. "Ryon?" How did he seem to be everywhere?

"That's me." He winked, then took her arm. "You look a little lost."

"I feel completely lost." She followed him to the outskirts of the room, and this time the elves seemed to part, allowing them to pass.

"Are you here as someone's guest too?" she asked.

Ryon blinked in surprise. "No, I'm here on my own."

"I thought only elves could be here. Unless that Rite of Guest thing was invoked."

Ryon coughed into his hand. "I suppose you could say I'm here as Fahr's guest, then. In a way."

"What do you mean?"

"He's the reason my place here is secured." Ryon pushed his fox mask up. His gray eyes, normally full of mirth, were serious as he studied her face. "You really haven't figured it out, have you?"

Lailu pushed her own mask up. "Figured what out?"

Ryon jerked his chin back in the direction they'd come. Lailu frowned and looked at the mass of elves, not sure what she was looking for. . . .

She spotted Eirad again, dancing in a frenzy, braids moving so fast they were a golden blur. Fahr had joined him, both of them moving to the same beat. Their dance reminded Lailu of a fight, all grace and elegance and, beneath it all, a sense of danger, like a sheathed blade.

Lailu's eyes widened. She stared at Fahr, at his blue-gray eyes and dark hair, and then turned back to Ryon. Same dark hair, similar eyes, similar cheekbones . . . She'd noticed it before but hadn't believed it. Hadn't *wanted* to believe it. Instead, she'd let the thought slip away like water through a colander. "You're . . . you're an elf."

Ryon winked.

Lailu recoiled. "H-how? How are you—"

"Oh, relax, Lailu. I haven't changed. I'm still the same Ryon. And besides, I'm only half elf. I had a human mother."

"Is that even possible?"

"Not usually. Half-elves ordinarily are put to death when they're born. But Fahr is my half brother, and in my case he intervened. I have some very strict limitations put on me, but otherwise . . ." He shrugged.

"Limitations? What kind of limitations?"

"Oh, this and that. Anyhow, your friend knew what I was almost immediately. I just assumed you'd told her."

"My friend. You mean Hannah?" Lailu could hardly believe it. "She *knew*?" And when did Ryon talk to Hannah about this? Suddenly Lailu remembered Ryon's "illuminating conversation" with Hannah. "Wait a second. Is *this* what you were talking about this morning?"

Ryon chuckled. "Don't worry, we also talked about you."

"M-me?"

"Oh yes. Hannah bet me a meal on the house I couldn't get you to dance."

"She did *what*?"

"Full appetizers and everything."

"She can't do that!" Lailu thought about it. Hannah gave away free meals all the time. "Okay, I guess she can," she muttered. "And don't change the subject. How did *she* know after just meeting you?"

"I guess she's more perceptive than you are," Ryon suggested.

"I never said I was perceptive. You were the one who said that."

"And I take it all back."

"Hey!"

Ryon grinned. "Well, maybe not *all* of it."

"I can't believe she didn't tell me," Lailu grumbled.

"She's good at keeping secrets."

"Not from me."

Ryon raised his eyebrows.

Lailu remembered a few months back when Hannah hadn't told her about getting kicked out of school, or about her sticky-fingered problem when it came to other people's hair combs. *Was* Hannah keeping secrets?

"Why would she keep secrets from me?" Lailu asked, hurt.

"Perhaps because you're an open book, my friend. All your secrets are visible right across that cute little face of yours."

Lailu suddenly felt very warm. She pulled her mask down to cover her blush.

"And speaking of Hannah, I'd better get you on home to her," Ryon continued. "Things are about to get strange in here." He jerked his chin at the dance floor.

Lailu's jaw dropped as the elves tangling in front of her shifted, their limbs stretching, faces twisting beneath masks that flowed like water, transforming them into their costumes, turning them into beasts. Now she knew it wasn't just her eyes playing tricks on her.

Her face tingled, her blood roaring. Lailu could taste sulfur in the back of her throat, and suddenly she was all teeth and fire and *hunger*. Her body felt strange, too small and pitiful, but not for long. Already she was growing, her talons sharpening, tail lengthening. She could smell prey nearby and knew it would be no match for her.

Pain lanced through Lailu, and she cried out. All her strength was ripped from her, her power taken. *No! No! I am a dragon! I am . . .*

"I am . . . ," Lailu mumbled, blinking. She was Lailu. She was a girl, just a girl, without talons or tail or dragon's fire. She was on her knees on the ground, her body weak and shaky, her throat raw.

In front of her, her mask twisted on the ground, the snout opening wide.

Ryon stomped on it, and it shattered with a little cry. "Elf-made?" he asked.

She nodded, heart hammering. "Did you pull it off me?"

"Yes." Ryon ground his boot into the pieces of mask, turning them into a pile of glittering dust.

"Thank you."

"Maybe stick to masks made by people you trust, hmm?" he suggested.

Lailu nodded. She could still feel an echo of the dragon's hunger thrumming through her. "You know, I think I'm ready to go," she decided, her voice small.

Ryon laughed. "Yeah, me too." He pulled her to her feet and led her out of the room and back into the hallway full of paint and mold. Lailu picked up her discarded griffin mask, then followed Ryon outside and into the fresh air, where people were still people and animals were still animals, and the elves—those caught in between—could be forgotten.

8

MASTER SLIPSHOD IS
UP TO SOMETHING

*L*ailu pushed open the door of Mystic Cooking, her body heavier than any mountain dragon, her eyes gritty with sleep. The sun was just peeking over the horizon as she shut the door behind her and Ryon.

"Thanks for walking me home," she told him. She hated to admit it, but that whole experience with the elves and their creepy masks had really shaken her up.

"For you? Anything," he said.

Lailu's chest filled with warmth, like the comforting heat of her favorite stove.

"Besides, I had some business to attend to near here, anyhow."

Some of that warmth dissipated. "Oh." It would have been nice if Ryon didn't have another motive for spending time with her for once, but Lailu knew she should be used to it by now.

"Lailu? Is that you?" Hannah called from the kitchen.

"Yes." Lailu trudged across the dining room and pulled the curtain back to reveal Hannah wrapped in a large fluffy robe. She looked quite cozy sipping her tea and reading a newspaper by candlelight.

Hannah's eyes widened on Ryon. "What're you doing here so soon?"

"So . . . soon?" Lailu frowned.

Ryon coughed. "I'm actually on my way out. I'll see you around, Miss Lightning Fingers. Lailu." He winked.

"Miss Lightning Fingers?" Lailu asked as Ryon vanished, the front door chiming behind him. "What was *that* all about?"

"Oh, you know, just reminding me I'm a thief. *Former* thief," Hannah amended quickly. "Er, how was the party?"

"It was . . . an experience." Lailu sagged against the counter. "What are *you* doing up so early?"

Hannah looked down at her paper and made a show of turning a page. "Meeting someone."

Lailu scowled. Of course, she was probably meeting Vahn. Again.

Hannah glanced up. "You look grouchy. Did you dance?"

"Yes, yes," Lailu muttered.

"Really?" Hannah put the newspaper down. "You really danced? Did you dance with Greg?"

"Greg? Why would I dance with *him*?" Lailu snapped.

Hannah blinked. "Whoa. Okay, there's definitely a story in there." She leaned forward, her eyes sparkling. "Spill."

Lailu shook her head.

"Come on, you know you want to tell me all about it," Hannah coaxed. "I mean, unless you picked a fight with Greg, and he was totally innocent."

"Innocent? He's not innocent at all! It was all his fault." And Lailu found herself telling the whole story. "And now I'm stuck hunting with him tomorrow morning," she finished, her hands curled into fists.

"Hmm," Hannah said.

"*Hmm?* What do you mean, *hmm?*" Lailu demanded. "He was definitely being a jerk."

"Oh, undeniably. But, Lailu, honey, don't you think he was just jealous?"

"J-jealous?" Lailu sputtered. "That's ridiculous."

"Is it?" Hannah asked. "Well, no matter his motives, there's no excuse for him ignoring you like that. Would you like me to go and talk to him for you?"

"No!" The last time Hannah tried to fix things between her and Greg, it turned out as bad as garlic chocolate. Besides, there was nothing to fix. They were rivals—that was it. The sooner she finished this hunt with him, the sooner she could go back to having nothing to do with him, and that was definitely the way she preferred things.

Hannah wrinkled her nose.

"What? I don't have to be friends with him," Lailu began defensively.

"No, no, it's not that. It's just . . . is it true Starling wore her hair in a ponytail for Lord Elister's party? I mean, really? A *ponytail?*"

Hannah shook the paper at Lailu, almost as if the whole thing had personally offended her, and Lailu noticed the picture on the front page. Starling Volan stood proudly in the middle of the ballroom, one hand casually resting on her metal creation's smooth head. Underneath that picture was the caption: STARLING TRIUMPHANTLY PRESENTS THE AUTOMATON.

"Really? She created a creepy metal person, and it's her *hair* you're talking about?" Lailu said. Hannah was too much sometimes.

"Well, a person's appearance is very important," Hannah sniffed. "I'd think someone as powerful as Starling would have hired the very best hairdressers to help her present the very best image. Especially on such a big night."

"Maybe she fired her hairdresser."

Hannah tilted her head to the side. "Hmm," she said.

"And how did you get today's newspaper so early?"

"Lord Elister had it delivered." Hannah flipped it over to study the photo again. "Along with your payment, and a note explaining that there's a whole article in here dedicated to your scrumptious dinner."

Lailu lunged across the table, snatching the paper from Hannah's fingertips. Hannah laughed as Lailu flipped through to find the article.

Slipshod Savors the Day

First Day of the Week of Masks, Gilded Island—Master Chef Sullivan Slipshod wowed guests at Lord Elister's exclusive party last night with his full-course griffin feast.

He was assisted by young up-and-comer Lailu Loganberry. When asked about his assistant, he praised her hard work ethic and willingness to learn. "As you know, I used to cook for the old king himself, and under my expert tutelage, Lailu is well on her way to becoming a master chef to rival even my reputation."

Thanks to the success of Slipshod's restaurant, Mystic Cooking, that "reputation" of his is once again a good one. Many have speculated that . . .

(story continued on page 3)

As Lailu began flipping to page three, the bell chimed, and Master Slipshod waltzed in as if summoned.

"There you are." Lailu dropped the paper. "Where have you been?"

"Ah, Pigtails. I've been making connections. Building the old bridges up, that sort of thing."

"What 'old bridges'?" Hannah asked suspiciously. "Are you gambling again?"

Slipshod drew himself up to his full height. "I thought we agreed," he said stiffly, "not to bring that up anymore. After all, *I* don't ask you how you've gotten your latest hair combs, do I?"

Lailu winced. She should have known that Slipshod and Hannah's recent peace couldn't last forever. After all, there were only two things they agreed on: their affection for Lailu, and their belief that the other was a bad influence on her.

"I can't believe you." Hannah stood and crossed her arms. "I know you're up to something shady. And I also know you're probably going to pull Lailu right into it. Again."

"Me, shady? *Me*, shady? Thanks to your poor decisions, Lailu was forced to negotiate with the elves—"

"That was your fault too!" Hannah snapped.

"It's okay. It all turned out fine—" Lailu tried desperately, but no one was listening *to* her; they were too busy arguing *about* her.

"*I* was trying to teach *my* apprentice the dangers of running a business!" Slipshod roared.

"Well, *I* was trying to protect *my* best friend from your carelessness and cowardice!"

"Cowardice? Me? I have faced down dangers that would haunt your very dreams. Once you've come face-to-snout with a dragon, we can talk about cowardice."

"Then I guess now's a good time to talk, because I *have* done that." Hannah put her hands on her hips. "Or have you conveniently forgotten about the time you abandoned Lailu and I helped her hunt a mountain dragon?"

Slipshod's mouth moved silently for a few seconds. "Blast, I did forget," he muttered.

"Look, let's not fight," Lailu said quickly. "I think we can all agree, you both got me into a lot of trouble." Hannah and Slipshod turned their glares on her, and Lailu quailed. "I mean, uh, you also both got me *out* of trouble. . . ." She adjusted the neck of her tunic. It felt tight all of a sudden.

"I'm going for a walk," Hannah declared. She paused and looked down at her robe. "After I change." She stalked up the stairs.

Lailu shifted awkwardly in the silence. "So," she began slowly, trying to think of something, anything, to change the subject. "I'm hunting with Greg tomorrow at sunrise."

"Oh yes, LaSilvian told me all about it. You thought hunting griffins was exciting? Just you wait." Master Slipshod rubbed his hands together.

"What are we hunting? Greg told you?"

Master Slipshod smiled. "I promised not to ruin the surprise." He paused. "Be careful out there. A dead apprentice is no use to me."

"You're not coming with me?" Lailu's heart sank.

"Sunrise, I'm, er . . . no, I can't. Sorry, Pigtails."

"Why not?"

"It has nothing to do with cowardice," Slipshod said quickly, his scowl back in place. "But I have things to do, places to visit. Besides, you need to start hunting more without me."

Lailu frowned. "The last time I hunted something dangerous without you, you called me reckless."

"Yes, well, that was then. Now, what are we cooking for this evening's festivities, hmm?"

"We don't have a lot of griffin, but we still have some of that leftover goldhorn we hunted last week," Lailu said. She tried focusing on possible recipes, but she couldn't help but wonder if Hannah was right: Was her mentor gambling again? She didn't think so, but then she hadn't wanted to believe it last time either. And one thing was for sure: Master Slipshod was definitely up to something.

9

GREG'S FAVOR

After the last diners left at midnight, Lailu managed to snag a few hours of sleep before it was time to get ready for her hunt with Greg. The sun wouldn't be up for another few hours, but enough moonlight poured into the room for Lailu to weave around Hannah's stuff and get to her own. She tiptoed around, gathering all she would need for the hunt ahead. It was difficult, since Greg hadn't bothered telling her *what* they were hunting, but she did her best. A grappling hook, her two largest chef's knives, a couple of weighted steak knives for throwing, and her best, most supple pair of dragon-skinned boots.

Lailu adjusted her pigtails and pulled a hat low over her ears, then slung her pack of hunting gear over her shoulder before quietly making her way down the stairs. She didn't have to wait long before the heavy *clomp-clomp-clomp* of Greg's carriage announced his arrival.

Lailu wrote a quick note to Slipshod letting him know she would be back that afternoon in time to prep for the evening's crowd, and then she slipped out into the night. The damp cold wrapped around her like a soggy coat, the rest of the city quiet as people finally made their way to their beds after the night's festivities.

Lailu frowned at Greg's carriage. It was more of a cart—not his usual sleek affair at all. "This?" she demanded, gesturing to the large flatbed, the bales of old hay, and the completely open top. "This is what we're riding in to . . . wherever it is?"

"What's the matter?" Greg twitched the reins. "Not fancy enough for you?"

Lailu scowled and climbed up. She was *not* looking forward to the cold ride trapped with Greg.

"So, did you miss me?" Greg asked as she took a seat.

"Like an ulcer." Lailu pointedly turned away from him. If he could ignore her at a big event like Lord Elister's, then she could ignore him now.

They rode in tense silence for a few minutes. Lailu could feel Greg watching her, but she refused to look at him or say anything at all. There was nothing he could say that would make her talk to him. Nothing.

"So, we're hunting hydra, by the way."

"We're *what*?" Lailu spun around so fast her neck creaked.

Hydra were big, nasty creatures that bred like bunny rabbits, and their magic created swampy marshes wherever they nested.

Because they were so dangerous to people—not to mention destructive to the landscape—master chefs didn't often get a chance to go after these beasts; heroes were usually sent out immediately at the first sign of a swarm. To take one of them down would be glorious. To cook one would be absolutely delectable. Already a half-dozen different recipes sprang to mind. But as Greg's grin widened, Lailu remembered she was still mad at him. It didn't matter what they were hunting.

"Don't try to hide it. I know you're impressed," he said.

"Whatever." She stared at the passing scenery as their cart pulled out of the city, leaving the tall gates behind. The road they were on skirted the Velvet Forest, winding its way down onto a narrow wooden bridge and over the West Dancing River. The sky was just starting to get lighter on the horizon, a thin line of softness brushing the dark like a hint of butter on a well prepared pastry. Lailu could practically feel the city falling away from her as they crossed the river, heading deeper into the rolling hills and farmland of the outlying villages.

Greg cleared his throat.

Lailu kept her back to him.

"Lailu," he tried again.

She ignored him harder.

"Look, if we're going to be hunting together, don't you think we should at least be on speaking terms?"

She turned, but just so she could glare at him. "You weren't so big on speaking terms the other night."

"The other night? What do you . . . Oh. You mean at Lord

Elister's party? Is that what this is about?" Greg ran a hand through his hair. "I was busy with my friends. Just like you were busy with yours. I don't see how it's a big deal."

Lailu's eyes widened. Did he really not realize what a jerk he'd been? Unbelievable. "You *ignored* me." How could she explain how hurtful that had been? It was like being transported back to her early days when she was nothing but the scholarship student, the girl with the secondhand uniform and shabby books. The one no one wanted to be seen with.

"Well, you ignored me first," Greg said.

"When did I ignore you?"

Greg muttered something under his breath. Lailu just caught the words "dance" and "shifty guy."

"Excuse me?" she demanded. "What's it to you if I danced with Ryon?"

"Oh, so you admit he's shifty."

"Of course he's shifty. So?"

Greg's eyes were angry slits. "So maybe I was trying to ask you to dance, but you were too busy ignoring *me* and went dancing with him instead."

Lailu's jaw dropped. "When did you ask me to dance?"

He looked away.

"When?" she demanded.

"I never actually asked you," he mumbled. "But I was thinking about it."

Lailu opened her mouth, then shut it. *Greg* had wanted to ask her to dance? Her . . . and Greg? Dancing? For some reason, the cart seemed awfully stuffy all of a sudden, despite its open top. "Well, I'm not a mind reader," she managed.

Greg's shoulders slumped. "I know." A moment passed, then another, each as uncomfortable as eating cold soup. "I'm sorry," he said finally. "I shouldn't have been . . ."

"Such a jerk?" Lailu suggested.

"That's probably accurate."

She snorted.

"Okay, that's definitely accurate." He glanced sideways at her. "Does that mean you forgive me?"

She thought about it. "I'm still half hoping a hydra eats you," she decided.

"But only *half* hoping. Sounds like progress to me." He smiled. "And, you know, if I had . . . if I'd asked you to dance, would you have?"

Lailu wasn't sure what to say. For a second, she pictured Greg asking her, pictured stepping onto the dance floor with him instead of Ryon, his hand on her waist . . . Her face burned like she'd been cooking over a stove in summer. "I—" she began.

The horses in front whinnied and dug their heels in, and the cart screeched to a halt, almost throwing Lailu over. She and Greg exchanged glances, then peered out around them.

The edge of the horizon glowed a deep crimson red. Set against the sky, the sea of weeping willow trees stood forlorn and ominous, their leaves trailing into the murky waters of the swamp below.

"Looks like the place," Greg said.

Lailu's stomach clenched with nerves. The best time to hunt hydra was daybreak, since they were weaker right around sunrise.

But with hydra, "weaker" was a very relative term. They shouldn't have wasted so much time on the ride here. They should have been planning the whole way. Lailu wasn't ready for this; she'd never hunted hydra before.

There was something very eerie about a swamp trailing across the middle of the road. A swamp that hadn't been there a couple of weeks before. She could smell it, the foul rotten-egg odor reminding her unpleasantly of the last hunt she'd gone on with Greg, back when they'd taken down a dragon.

Greg removed a coppery boxlike object from under the driver's seat and hopped down.

Lailu shivered and adjusted her knife belt, checking that her blades were set. "I'm ready," she lied.

"Don't worry." Greg slung the box over his back, pulling the straps of it onto his shoulders. "Hydra are much easier to hunt than chickens."

Lailu blanched. "Why'd you have to bring that up?" She hated fyrian chickens, *hated* them. Their scaly feet, that awful scratching noise their talons made, the way their beaks opened just before they prepared to roast you. "You always bring them up before a hunt."

"I know. It's a terrible habit." Greg grinned.

Still shuddering, Lailu followed him off the safety of the road and into the heart of the swamp.

10

A Suitable Target

Moisture hung in the air, suffocating and stinky. Despite the sun creeping above the horizon, very little light made it through the fog and the old blackened branches of the trees around them. Even Greg, mere feet ahead, seemed to fade into the mist until Lailu felt like she was alone. Just her, the swamp, and her set of extra-sharp knives.

Lailu tried to ignore the feeling of mud sucking at her boots and water seeping into her pants. Instead, she searched under every willow for signs of a den, even as strands of her hair clung to her face and swamp flies buzzed around her head.

It was hard to believe that only a couple of weeks ago, this swamp had been a sparsely wooded area, the ground a mixture of dirt and leaves instead of this soft, stinking bog. Then hydra moved in and began nesting, their essence flooding the woods, churning the dirt, and transforming the whole area into the swamps they preferred. Of all the mystic creatures in Savoria, hydra changed their surroundings the most. And the only way to remove a hydra-made swamp was to find the Heart Hydra and relocate her. The rest of her swarm would move with her, taking the magic along with them.

But since that was usually a job for a whole troop of heroes, Lailu figured she and Greg could do their part and at least slim down the swarm a bit in the meantime—if they could even find the swarm. She'd had no idea hydra could infect such a large area of land!

Click-click-click, whirrrrrrrrr.

Lailu spun, a knife already in hand. Was something behind her? She narrowed her eyes, barely making out a shape in the fog. A human shape. And it wasn't Greg, either; she could hear him splashing just up ahead. Was someone else hunting hydra?

As the figure moved closer, bounding quietly from tree stump to fallen log, Lailu realized they were trying to avoid the water, and she began to wonder if they were even hunting hydra at all. But if they weren't hunting hydra, then what were they doing here?

She shivered and slipped another knife from her sheath. She felt better with a blade in each hand. Hydra were one thing. Suspicious, lurking people were something altogether different.

Someone tapped Lailu on the shoulder, and she spun, blades raised.

"Whoa," Greg said quickly, hands up. "Maybe put the knives down?"

"Shh," Lailu hissed, but she lowered her knives.

"What's the matter?"

Lailu shook her head, peering through the fog, but the figure was gone. Whoever was out here with them could be anywhere by now. Frowning, she put one of her knives away, but kept the other in her hand. "I thought I saw . . ." She stopped. "Never mind. Let's just find this hydra and get out of here."

"Okay," Greg said carefully. "Let's stay closer together, yeah?"

Lailu nodded gratefully. Even though she'd beaten Greg in almost all their knife fighting classes back at school, she felt safer having him next to her as they sloshed silently through the murk.

"Wait. You see that?" Greg dropped his voice to a whisper as he pointed at a mound looming out of the muck of the swamp. Once a basic wooded hillside, it was now an ominous lump that had been hollowed out by something large. Moss clung to it, and dead trees and branches formed a barrier around the opening. The surrounding weeping willows finished the décor, giving the nest swaying curtains of long, dangling vines.

Lailu's heart beat faster. "I see it," she whispered back.

"It's got to be a den," Greg said, studying the mound. "Got a plan?"

"Isn't this your hunt? Shouldn't *you* be the one with the plan?"

Greg wiped a hand across his face, leaving a trail of mud. "I mean, I *can* come up with a plan, if it's too hard for you to think of one—"

"I can think of a plan just fine," Lailu snapped. "I can think of a hundred plans."

"Great. I look forward to hearing them."

Greg's grin was wide and smug, and Lailu resisted the urge to punch him. She hated when he tricked her, but there was nothing for it; she'd have to think of a plan now, or there would be no hearing the end of it. She chewed her lip, concentrating, ignoring the taste of sweat and the tang of bitter swamp water. "Well, first we want to find out how many heads we're dealing with—"

"'Cause you know *that's* going to be easy."

"And then," she continued, talking over him, "we need to figure out how to stab it in the heart, so its heads don't multiply."

Greg stared at her. "That's it? That's your plan? Just count the heads and stab it in the heart?"

"I don't see you coming up with anything better."

"Well, I'm not the one who took down a mountain dragon."

Lailu turned on him. "So you admit it! Finally!"

Roooaaarrrrr!

Lailu and Greg froze, then slowly turned to look at the cave, the swampy ground beneath them vibrating with the approaching footsteps of something large.

"New plan," Lailu whispered. "Hide in the willow tree branches."

They sprinted through the knee-high water to the nearest tree. Lailu tucked her blade into her belt as Greg propelled himself up to the lowest branch, then gave her a hand up. Any other time, Lailu would have refused his help, but she knew that each vibrating step was bringing the hydra closer to spotting them.

She climbed after Greg, moving higher into the tree branches. With all the straggling leaves and vines around her, she felt like she was battling a kraken again.

Snap!

The branch Lailu was reaching for broke off in her hand. She froze, suddenly very aware of the creaking branch beneath her. Willow trees were known for having weak wood, a fact that she hadn't really considered until about two seconds ago.

"Er, I don't think we should go any farther up," Greg whispered next to her.

"I think you should actually climb farther down," Lailu corrected.

"Yeah, that's definitely not happening."

The hydra had stomped its way to the cave entrance below them, bringing with it the sickly stench of decay and a stronger burst of rotting eggs. Lailu breathed shallowly and shrank back against the trunk of the tree, grateful for the comforting curtain of weeping willow vines.

This beast was much bigger than she'd been expecting. It remained half-inside its cave, but she could tell its body was taller than Greg's wagon, the three heads doubling its height. As it extended those heads farther, Lailu suddenly realized they had climbed right to its eye level. She froze and caught her breath, praying to the God of Cookery that what she read about the hydra's poor eyesight was true.

Three pairs of tomato-red eyes scanned the ground, looking for them. The creature's gray-green skin glistened with moisture, the perfect color to blend right into the fog. On top of each head quivered a spiky red crest, which told Lailu that this was a prime male, full-grown and ready for roasting.

With one last roar, the hydra backed up, vanishing inside the den.

Lailu let out her breath. She was relieved it hadn't spotted them, but a little disappointed it hadn't come all the way out so she could get a better look at it.

"Oh, butter knives," Greg breathed. "It's *huge*!"

"I know. Think of the feast we can prepare." Lailu already had the perfect seasonings, spices, and sauces in mind for each part of it, and she had mentally noted what parts she would want to tenderize with a good dry rub.

"Are you thinking what I'm thinking?" Greg asked.

"That we can make the world's largest and tastiest hydra tri-tip?"

Greg frowned. "I'm more of a rib eye fan, personally."

"That's only because your cooking lacks subtleties."

"Subtleties!" Greg sputtered. "That's way harsh coming from someone who is obsessed with lebinola spice."

"I am *not* obsessed with lebinola spice. I just think most recipes call for a pinch of it."

"*Anyway*, I was thinking that maybe, just maybe, we might have bitten off more than we can chew with that one."

"No way," Lailu said.

"Way."

"But we're already halfway to taking this one down."

"Just how are we halfway done with taking it down?" Greg demanded, running a hand through his hair. The humidity made his curls wilder than normal, and they puffed around his head in a tangled cloud.

"Easy." Lailu swatted away a bloodsucking fly that was trying to dine on her like a fine wine. "We needed to know how many heads we were dealing with, and now we know. So, we are halfway done with taking it down."

"Okay, maybe according to your two-step plan, we are," Greg grumbled. "But somehow I think stabbing it in the heart is going to be a bit harder than counting heads."

"I'm surprised at you, Greg. I never took you for the cowardly type."

"I'm not the cowardly type. I'm the 'don't want to die mangled by a hydra' type. And you know what? I don't think that's a bad thing."

Lailu shrugged. "If you say so."

Greg narrowed his eyes. "Fine. Fine. If you can come up with a good plan for taking this guy out, and I mean *good*, then I'll be all for it. But if you can't, then I say we find one a little smaller."

That felt too much like defeat to Lailu. She'd already failed to get her target once this week during that disastrous griffin hunt. She was not about to fail a second time. She just needed a plan . . . something that wouldn't get her killed. Or get Greg killed either, she decided reluctantly. She'd need his help carting the hydra back to the carriage.

As she stared at the vines dripping down around them, a plan slowly formed in the back of her mind. "Help me braid and twist these vines into a strong rope," she said, pulling some of the weeping willow vines toward her.

"Why?"

Lailu grinned. "Because we're going to lasso the three heads together and trip this hydra in one fell swoop."

A slow smile spread across Greg's face. "Now, that's the kind of plan I'm talking about."

Lailu lay across a branch of the willow tree, waiting. Her breeches were soaked, her boots each felt like they held a gallon of water, and her clothing clung to her like an extra layer of skin. But none of that mattered. All that mattered was the hunt, and it would all be over soon.

The lasso she and Greg had made was tied loosely to the branch beneath her. It should pull tight as a noose around the hydra's three necks. Once the beast tripped over the second rope strung tight below it, the noose should break free from the branch.

"Are you sure this is completely necessary?" Greg asked. He stood just on the other side of their trip line so he wouldn't accidentally fall when trying to outrun the hydra.

"Of course it's necessary," Lailu said. "The hydra has to hit our loop dead-on, or else it won't work. That's why you get to be our bait."

"What happens if our trap doesn't work?"

"Run. Real fast. Almost like a hydra's chasing you."

"Not funny." Greg ran a hand nervously through his hair again.

"Don't worry, I'll be here to take the hydra out whether our trap works or not, and if I fail, I guess you can call us even for that whole fyrian chicken hunting trip."

"Really?"

Lailu took a deep breath, remembering the sound of chicken feet scraping the stone behind her, the feeling of intense heat, and suddenly her scar hurt. "I take that back. We'll never be even for that."

"I figured as much." Greg grimaced. "Even though it was just an accident—"

"An 'accident,' my butt."

"So it *is* true about the scar." Greg smirked.

Lailu shifted impatiently on her branch, eager to change the subject. "Are you just going to stand there all day?"

"Says you who gets the easier job." His eyebrows drew together like a pair of anxious caterpillars clinging for safety. "O God of Cookery, protect me from this most foolish of plans."

"It's not that foolish," Lailu grumbled. "Now quit stalling."

"Easy for you to say." Greg took a deep breath, then called out, "Here, hydra, hydra! Here, hydra!"

Long seconds passed, and then they both felt it: the vibrating steps of something massive moving quickly. The hydra poked its heads out of the den, the crests on each head quivering in rage.

"Yeah, that's right, you ugly beast," Greg said loudly.

Roooaaarrrrr!

The heads reared back, front legs lifting off the ground and slamming down hard enough to shake the earth. And then it charged.

"Now!" Lailu yelled at Greg.

He turned and sprinted through the bog. Lailu swung her lasso, preparing to toss it, when she saw a snag in their plan. A huge snag. A snag of epic and disastrous proportions. And she knew even the God of Cookery might not be able to get them out of this stew.

Because this hydra didn't have three heads.

No—it had seven.

IN THE HEAT OF THE BATTLE

Lailu threw the lasso, slamming three of the heads together. The hydra stumbled forward, hitting the trip line exactly as she'd hoped, but already Lailu could see her plan crumbling to pieces in front of her.

The beast's massive neck split in two near the base, just like a great redwood tree, the front half separating into the three familiar heads while the back half divided itself into four more, each angrier-looking than the last as they tore easily through Lailu's homemade lasso.

Lailu spared a quick glance at Greg, who was already doubling back, heading straight toward the hydra. "Butter knives," she swore. Didn't he notice the extra heads? Didn't he see their plan was dissolving faster than sugar in water? Was he *trying* to get himself killed?

Already the hydra was struggling back to its feet, the lasso nothing but scraps of vine. With a quick prayer to the God of Cookery, Lailu ripped a few more vines free and leaped from the safety of her willow tree. She landed with her knees bent and immediately launched herself into a forward roll, coming up mere feet from the largest head, her knives in her hands.

The hydra snapped at her, those tomato-red eyes glowing with anger. Lailu fended it off with one of her knives, then ducked past it. She knew her only chance was to be small and quick, to dart straight into the center of the tangle of heads and count on the hydra's own confusion to buy her the precious seconds she'd need.

Another head lunged at her, so close she could feel its hot breath against her skin, but she was already moving past it.

Smack!

Two heads collided above her, and another got itself tangled with its neighbor. The hydra roared in frustration. It lifted its massive front legs and slammed them down, shaking the ground.

Lailu stumbled, caught herself, and moved in closer, so close she could reach out and touch the beast's chest. All around her, the air was alive with snapping, snarling heads. She could hear someone yelling her name, but she ignored it. She ignored all of it because now she could see the spot where the front of the hydra's leathery skin came together in a big, ugly seam, and just under that . . .

Lailu lunged, driving her knife down just before another head slammed into her. She managed to twist at the last minute, avoiding the teeth, but the force of the impact threw her back.

She hit the ground hard and tumbled feet over head before sliding to a stop. For a long second she couldn't move; she could only gasp as spots danced in front of her eyes, her ears filled with the roaring of her own blood. She managed to struggle to her side, the world swimming around her. The hydra stomped closer, closer, and she could see teeth, so many teeth, and all those red eyes. She knew she needed to run, but it was like she was moving through gravy, every movement slow and painful.

The hydra roared, its largest head lunging straight at her, and there was nowhere to run, no way to avoid those razor-sharp teeth.

She was going to die. She was going to die, and she'd never complete her apprenticeship. Slipshod would be stuck running Mystic Cooking without her.

She would never cook again.

Lailu lurched to her feet and staggered back. The teeth snapped inches in front of her face, another ravenous head closing in from the other side.

And then Greg was in front of her, shoving her backward, a knife in each hand as he fended off the heads.

Lailu sucked in as much air as her bruised lungs would take.

"Run away, you idiot!" Greg screamed as he dipped and ducked, staying just one second in front of the heads. His movements were growing sluggish, though, his shirt soaked with sweat. As he twisted too slowly, one of the heads managed to graze his left shoulder, blood blossoming and dripping down his arm. He kept fighting, but Lailu knew it was just a matter of time. Just as she knew he was trying to buy her time to get away.

As if she would run and leave him there.

She looked past him and saw it: her knife stuck up to the hilt in the hydra's chest, just next to its heart.

"Lailu!" Greg yelled. "Go!"

The hydra reared back, all heads pulling together in a wave of fury, its front legs lifting off the ground. Lailu recognized that posture from her textbooks: it was preparing to charge.

They'd never be able to outrun a charging hydra, not in the swamp, not at this close distance.

Lailu looked down at the forgotten vines still clutched in her hand. Without stopping to think, she tossed the end of the vine to Greg. "Catch!"

He dropped one of his knives and caught it. "Lailu, what—" he began, but she was already moving, racing around the back of the hydra, fear spurring her to move faster than she'd ever moved in her life.

The hydra stopped, confused by the sudden movement behind it. It lowered its feet to the ground, its heads writhing in and out to follow Lailu, the red flap on top of each head standing straight up in extreme agitation.

Lailu sprinted full circle, racing past Greg, the vine tightening around the legs of the hydra.

Greg finally caught on and raced in the other direction, both of them running and pulling with everything they had.

The hydra shrieked as its legs were yanked together. It wobbled, and Lailu changed course, running flat out at the hydra and charging it shoulder-first.

It wouldn't have worked, except that Greg caught up to her just in time to launch himself at the hydra with her. Together they managed to knock it off-balance enough to send it crashing to the ground.

Lailu didn't waste time celebrating, her eyes focused the whole time on her knife. She lunged for that handle, her fingers wrapping around the slippery hilt and yanking it out, then slamming it as hard as she could directly into the heart of the hydra.

The hydra's roar seemed to go on and on and on . . . and then it was over, the red eyes in all its heads rolling up.

Lailu dropped to her butt, not even caring about the mud squelching up her pants and into her boots. Her body ached everywhere, but she was alive.

Greg slumped down next to her. "You look terrible," he said.

"Yeah, well . . ." Lailu was too tired to think of a comeback. "You have mud on your face," she said.

"You do too. Only I can't see it underneath the layer of blood."

Lailu halfheartedly wiped a sleeve across her face, but it didn't really help; her sleeve was just as bloody as the rest of her. Pushing herself to her feet, she carefully stepped around the fallen heads of the hydra, then put her foot on the beast's chest. Bracing herself, she yanked her knife free.

Lailu studied the blade that had saved her life. It was disgusting; she needed a clean patch of cloth to wipe it down. Her clothes were completely drenched and filthy, but Greg's sleeve looked clean enough. Reaching forward, Lailu grabbed his arm and pulled it toward her.

Greg's eyes widened. "What are you doing?"

Lailu pinched the cloth of his white shirt and folded it over her gory knife, scraping it clean.

Now Greg's eyes narrowed. "You're cleaning your knife."

"Yep."

"On my shirt. You're cleaning your bloody, disgusting knife on my shirt."

"You catch on quick. No wonder you were near the top of our class." Lailu glanced up. "Why did you think I was grabbing your shirt?"

Greg's face reddened. "I don't know what I was thinking," he mumbled, adding something about the heat of the battle under his breath, or some such nonsense, but he wouldn't look at her, and Lailu decided to ignore it. After all, they had much bigger fish to fry—or rather, hydra to cook.

Speaking of large hydra . . . Lailu frowned. "Um, I don't suppose you've thought of how we're going to get this thing back with us?"

"As a matter of fact . . ." Greg picked up the box he'd been wearing on his back earlier and flourished it. "I did."

It wasn't that big, maybe twice as wide and thick as a large book, with weird levers and buttons on the sides, the whole thing gleaming a burnished copper. Greg looked so proud of it, Lailu almost felt bad letting him down.

"That's . . . that's really nice, Greg. It's a nice, er, box. But I'm not sure the hydra will fit in it."

"You doubt me?"

"All the time."

Greg laughed. "I set myself up for that one, didn't I? Well, watch this." He set the box down in the mud, pulled one of the levers, and stepped back. With a series of clicks and whirls, the metal contraption unfolded, then unfolded again, the sides sliding down until it formed into a sturdy-looking cart. Greg pressed a button on the side, and a handle popped out. Another button revealed wheels folded into the base. Greg adjusted them, then stood back. "Still doubt me?"

Lailu looked at the cart, then back at him. "Definitely," she said, but she couldn't help smiling. "Where did you get that?"

"Starling had it delivered last week. I think she's trying to curry favor after that whole . . . well, the whole Mr. Boss thing."

"Yeah, I think so too," Lailu mused. "I still don't trust her."

"Oh, me neither, absolutely not—but I have to admit, this thing is pretty amazing." He tapped his cart.

"It sure is," Lailu agreed. Maybe some of the noncooking inventions were okay after all.

12

SURPRISES IN THE SWAMP

"I take it all back," Lailu huffed. "This cart . . . is the worst."

"Oh, it's not that bad," Greg panted.

"The worst," Lailu repeated, slogging another step, then another. It felt like she'd been pushing this hydra for hours. Days, even. She'd be an old woman by the time they reached Greg's carriage. An old, broken, mud-covered woman.

"It's better than that donkey cart we used last time for the dragon," Greg said.

"I disagree." Lailu shifted her grip on the handle. "That cart came with donkeys. I would kill for a donkey to help us." She glanced sideways at Greg.

"Don't say it," he said. "I know what you're thinking, and I am *not* a donkey."

"Well, I wasn't going to phrase it quite that way," Lailu said sweetly.

"I know exactly how—*oof!*" Greg lurched to the side, tipping the cart.

Lailu yanked back on the handle, overcompensated, and ended up dumping the full weight of the hydra on herself. She staggered, falling into the muck. "What the spatula are you doing?" she spluttered, pushing at the carcass until she could free herself.

No answer.

"Greg?"

Greg was kneeling in the mud nearby, his eyes wide and white in his dirt-streaked face.

"What is it?" Lailu asked, climbing to her feet.

"I . . . I tripped."

"Are you hurt?"

He shook his head.

"So . . . you're just kneeling in the mud for fun?" Lailu pushed her wet hair back from her face.

"I thought I tripped over a log." Greg's voice was strangely flat. "But it wasn't a log. It was . . . It was . . ."

Lailu moved closer. She could see something large in the shallow, muddy water, could see how it might look like a log from farther away, but as she got closer—

"O God of Cookery," she breathed.

Greg looked at her solemnly. "I don't think Chushi is going to be much help here."

Lailu couldn't argue. Because it wasn't a log at all, but a dead body. And worse, Lailu knew him, had seen him alive just two nights ago.

She watched the water drip off the man's bald head and felt like crying. True, Carbon hadn't seemed like the best scientist, and his invention had almost killed her. But still, he didn't deserve this. Nobody did.

"What happened to him?" Lailu whispered.

"I'm not sure," Greg said. "I . . . I don't really want to, uh, inspect him."

Lailu couldn't blame Greg for that. And with all the mud, it was impossible to see what had killed him.

"What should we do?" Greg asked, his voice high-pitched, uncertain.

Lailu blinked, surprised. Even Greg—aristocratic, arrogant, confident Greg—didn't know what to do. It made her feel somehow stronger. "Well, first we need to get him back to the carriage," she decided.

"Are you sure we should move him?"

"We can't just leave him here." Lailu shuddered at the idea of touching him, but it had to be done. "No, we'll take him to the carriage, then come back for the hydra. And then . . . then I think we need to take him to Lord Elister's."

"Elister the Bloody?" Greg's face grew even paler. "Are you sure?"

Lailu nodded. "He needs to know first. The scientists are supposed to be under his protection. We'll drop you and the hydra off first at your restaurant, then I'll take Carbon myself."

"That's not fair. I can come with you."

"You need to get started on the hydra prep work. You know there's only a limited amount of time before it'll go bad." She narrowed her eyes. "Just make sure you don't mess anything up."

"When have I ever messed anything up? On second thought, please don't answer that," Greg added quickly.

"Are you sure? Because I can write you a list. It might take all day, but . . ."

"Ouch. Way to stab a guy when he's down."

"It's the only way to make sure he'll stay down." Lailu forced a smile.

"I'm going to take that as a hint." Greg stood and brushed uselessly at his muddy pants. "What will you tell Elister?"

Lailu stared down at Carbon's face. His eyes were wide, mouth open. He looked like he'd been terrified. But of what? She remembered again that sound she'd heard, the figure moving through the swamp, then pushed that memory away. "Just the facts," she said aloud. "Just the basic facts." She would keep it simple.

Unfortunately, she knew that when dealing with Lord Elister, nothing was ever simple.

13

The New Butler

No matter how many times Lailu stood outside Lord Elister's mansion, she never got used to it. Maybe it was the statue in front of a man swinging an axe. Or maybe it was the fact that she'd seen Elister kill two different men right in front of her. It was ridiculous; she'd faced almost certain death just that morning, and yet she was more nervous now, staring down Elister's doors, than she'd been in that swamp.

Lailu took a deep breath, wiped her sweaty palms on her shirt, then lifted the heavy metal knocker on the iron doors and slammed it down twice.

The door opened. "What do you want?" a large man with a dainty mustache demanded. He eyed her muck- and blood-covered clothes disdainfully. If he recognized her, he gave no sign of it.

"I—I'm here to see Lord Elister." Lailu stood up taller, fighting the urge to shrink beneath that gaze.

"He's busy." The door began to close.

Lailu lunged forward to stop it. "Wait, it's important! It's about the scientists—"

"Lailu, is that you?" Wren's voice came from somewhere behind Mr. Mustache.

The door stopped threatening to shut on Lailu's fingers, and Wren's head poked around the opening. She wore a pair of funny glasses covered in gears and gadgets, her eyes magnified alarmingly.

"Ah, it *is* you! Come in, come in," she said happily, pushing her glasses up and pulling the door all the way open.

"Wait a second," the guard said.

Wren looked at him, her eyes narrowing. "Excuse me?"

Mr. Mustache actually took a step back. "Just . . . just don't track dirt on the carpets," he told Lailu.

Lailu looked down at her mud-caked boots, wondering how that would be possible.

The guard sighed. "Don't track too much dirt on the carpets," he amended. "And hurry up. I don't want to stand here all day."

"There are worse places for you to stand," Wren said coldly. Then she turned back to Lailu, all smiles. "Come inside."

Lailu carefully stepped past the guard and followed Wren down the hallway.

"I was just installing a new alarm system so guys like Gordon won't be necessary, when I heard your voice," Wren said. Lailu noticed that in addition to the strange glasses, Wren wore a heavy-duty leather apron, thick gloves, and a tool belt that jangled mysteriously as she walked. "What do you need to tell Elister?"

Lailu bit her lip. Wren *knew* Carbon. How could she tell her he was dead?

Wren's face filled with worry. "Is it something that will get my mom in trouble?"

Lailu shook her head.

"Oh good. Elister just finished meeting with her now. He wasn't too happy about the automaton not working for her the other night in front of his guests."

"I thought your mom was just building up the suspense."

Wren laughed. "And people say *I* take things too literally. No, that wasn't supposed to happen. One of Mama's scientists messed something up. It didn't want to listen to any of her commands. But it came around. Eventually."

"Oh." Lailu thought of Carbon, looking so frantic that night, and wondered . . .

"Here we are," Wren chirped, stopping in front of a polished door. She knocked twice, and the door opened almost immediately.

Lailu's jaw dropped.

Starling's automaton stood in the doorway, the burning blue lights in the smooth metal plate of its face aimed straight at Lailu. It wore a bowl of a hat, which somehow made it look even more inhuman with its torso full of wires and gears and its spindly legs.

Lailu backed up, bumping into Wren.

"Lailu?" Elister called. "Walton, let her in."

Walton cocked its head like a well-trained pup, then took a step back with a gentle whir of movement.

"Precious, isn't he?" Lord Elister smiled at Lailu from behind a large wooden desk. Walton glided over to his side and crouched down, and Elister patted its head, careful not to dislodge the thing's hat. Lailu could only stare in horror. "Starling gave me one of her automatons to test out."

"Is that the one from your party?" Lailu asked, eyeing it uneasily.

"Oh yes. The very first one made. He's the best butler I've ever had."

The thing wagged. It actually wagged. Truly terrifying.

"Now, what is it you need, Lailu? Have you received my payment yet? I sent it to your restaurant yesterday morning."

"Oh, it's not about that. It's . . . well . . ." There was no easy way to say it, not with Wren standing just behind her, so Lailu blurted out, "I found a dead body. In the swamp. By the hydra."

"A dead body." Elister's eyebrows lifted. "Go on."

Lailu shot an apologetic look at Wren. "It was Carbon, sir. I recognized him."

Wren gasped.

"This is very . . . upsetting news." Elister drummed his fingers on the top of the automaton's head. It stared at Lailu the whole time, those blue lights flaring with an intensity like a couple of miniature suns. Could it actually see? Lailu shivered.

"Where is the body now?" Elister asked. "Is it still in the swamp?"

"No, I—I didn't think it was right to leave him. I brought him back. He's in a cart in the loading area behind your house."

"Good. Good." Elister sighed. "I shall have to inform Starling, of course."

"Inform me of what?" Starling asked, stepping out from behind a door in the back of Elister's spacious office.

Lailu jumped at the scientist's sudden appearance, but Elister merely inclined his head in her direction.

"Hello, Lailu," Starling said. She glanced at Wren. "Shouldn't you be working?"

"I . . . I was, Mama," Wren began, her face turning as red as her hair. "I needed to show Lailu in."

"Hmm." Starling strode forward, her leather apron creaking, the tools in each of its pockets clinking together.

"I regret to inform you—stop that, Walton," Elister said as the automaton straightened and moved to stand between him and Starling. It held its arms out from its body, as if it were trying to look larger, and made a *whirrr* noise that sounded an awful lot like some kind of mechanical growl.

Starling frowned. "I thought I had corrected that." She pulled out a small metal box from one of her apron pockets and pressed a button. Immediately the automaton powered down with a wail like a kettle turning off, its shoulders slumping and head listing to the side before the lights in its faceplate flickered and went out. The bowler hat slipped off, drifting sadly to the floor, and rolled to land near Lailu's feet.

"You really didn't have to do that." Elister looked devastated.

"I can't have it challenging me." Starling fiddled with the remote. "The voice commands are faulty too. It doesn't respond to mine at all. I need to use a remote." She shook her head. "I have several more models ready to go. I'll bring in a replacement for you this evening."

"I'm rather attached to this one, actually."

"Don't be silly. They are all identical models."

"Silly?" Elister raised his eyebrows. "It's been a very long time since anyone has referred to me as . . . silly."

Starling looked up, her face coloring. "I did not mean . . . Forgive me. My word choice was poor. I'll have this model back to you soon."

Elister said nothing, his silence as heavy and suffocating as a prime male hydra carcass.

"This *exact* model," Starling added.

"Good," Elister said, some of the tension leaking away.

Starling tucked the remote back in her pocket, her eyes finding Lailu frozen near the doorway. "What did you need to tell me?"

Lailu swallowed hard, the words sticking in her suddenly dry throat. "I . . . I f-found . . ."

"She found Carbon," Wren cut in. "Dead. Left in the swamp for the hydra."

Starling visibly started. Was that fear snaking across her angular face? A second later and it was gone, replaced by cold fury. "My scientist . . . dead. Dead!" She turned to Elister. "You *know* who's behind this."

"I have some ideas, yes. But no concrete answer yet," Elister said, his voice calm.

"No concrete answer?" Starling threw her hands in the air, more animated than Lailu had ever seen her. "Elister, I have been warning you for weeks. Those elves are targeting me and my people, and this is their work. This *has* to be their work."

"As I have told you *repeatedly*, while you are under my protection, the elves cannot kill you."

"And as *I* have reminded *you*, they are experts at weaseling their way out of their promises. They must have found a way out of your treaty."

Elister tapped his chin thoughtfully. "It's not impossible," he admitted. "Still, this was carelessly done. And why dump the body in the swamp? No, this does not sound like them. I would need more information before—"

"Before what? Before they can kill again?"

"Before I can make any conclusions." Elister's voice was ice. "I would think you, being a believer in science and logic, would appreciate not jumping to a conclusion based on circumstantial evidence."

Starling drew herself up. "Need I remind you that one of my own is now dead? This will set me back weeks, if not months, in my research. I cannot work in such conditions. Either those elves leave this city, or . . ." Starling took a breath. "Or *I* leave, and I take the rest of the scientists with me."

Lailu and Wren exchanged wide-eyed glances.

Elister let the silence build around him. Lailu was reminded suddenly of her brother Lonnie, the way he would pack snow in a fort and hide inside when he wanted to be alone. He always did that when their mother left for one of her unpredictable trips. Sometimes he would let Lailu crawl in with him, and they would huddle together in their room made of ice and snow and watch their breath freeze. . . . Lailu gave herself a shake, her bones feeling as chilled now as they ever felt inside Lonnie's snow forts.

"You could leave," Elister said finally, the room somehow growing colder still. "But where would you go? Do you really think you'd be any more welcomed by our neighboring countries? Perhaps you thought to visit the Krigaen Empire?" His hands reflexively twitched like they longed for those two curved blades hidden beneath his dark vest. Any mention of the Krigs, Savoria's lifelong enemies, seemed to make him long for a weapon.

Starling paled. "Of—of course not."

"Then where? Would you return to Beolann?" Elister leaned forward. "Do you think you would be safe returning there?"

"You know they would not take us back," Starling said. "We would be seized and executed as traitors the moment we set foot on Beolann soil. It's the price we would pay for sharing our science with you."

"The moment you chose to leave Beolann, you were branded traitors," Elister said. "Do not pretend this consequence is because of your scientific generosity. Now, I have offered you asylum from the country you fled, I have offered you the protection of my own home, and I will have my best man look into this . . . *unfortunate* death. But I am warning you, do *not* challenge me, Starling. You will not like me as your enemy."

Wren clutched at Lailu's hands. Elister seemed to loom larger and larger until, even seated, it felt like he overshadowed the whole room.

"I understand," Starling said at last, but the words came out strained and bitter as lime.

Elister turned back to Lailu like the showdown never happened. "Leave the body here. Someone will be by Mystic Cooking to investigate this case shortly. And I trust you understand this is very sensitive, so keep this news to yourself."

Lailu bowed, noticing Walton's fallen bowler hat. She picked it up, her eyes landing on a smudge on the rim.

A smudge that looked suspiciously like swamp mud.

"I'll take that, Lailu," Starling said.

Wordlessly, Lailu handed it over and left the room.

14

CAREENING THROUGH THE CITY

Lailu didn't relax until she'd stepped outside Elister's front door, her skin still crawling. Between the muddy hat, that creepy automaton, and Elister and Starling's argument, it felt like the start of something serious. Something ugly. Something . . . bad for business.

"Lailu!" Wren called, jogging over. She was weighed down by a huge leather sack that bulged in mysterious ways. "Whew, I'm glad I caught up."

"What's all that?" Lailu jerked her chin at the sack.

"Oh, it's some of my tools. Mama wanted me to come with you and check on those harnesses, see if I could find out what went wrong with them. You know, the ones Carbon gave you." She ran a hand across her face. "Sorry, got something in my eye."

Was she crying? Lailu shifted uncomfortably. Wren had come here with Carbon. She was probably devastated.

"I'm really sorry about Carbon," Lailu began.

Wren looked up. "What? Oh. Yeah, it's too bad."

Lailu blinked. Wren sounded so calm. "I thought you were crying," Lailu said carefully.

"Why would you think that?"

"Because usually when people say they have something in their eye . . ." Lailu shook her head. "Never mind."

Wren shrugged. "I'm not about to cry over it, but I *am* sorry he's dead. He wasn't so bad. Not as smart as he pretended to be, though." She drummed her fingers on her bag. "Anyhow, he was old." She waved a hand like that made his death okay.

Even dressed in her leather apron and boy's clothing, there was something very delicate about Wren. Maybe it was the dusting of freckles across her tiny button-nose, or the way her red hair curled around her head like a halo. It made her callous words even more surprising, but Wren had always been very direct. Lailu could appreciate that, even if she felt like Carbon deserved a little more sympathy.

"Let's take an auto-carriage," Wren suggested.

"A what, now?"

"You know, one of those." Wren pointed at a large metal monstrosity with four wheels, an open top, and two glowing lights in front.

"That's one of those horseless carriage things, isn't it?" Lailu asked nervously. She glanced at Greg's cart parked nearby. "Shouldn't we just take Greg's?"

"No, no," Wren said. "Elister still needs to have the body removed."

"But it looks like someone else is taking the auto-carriage, see?" Lailu tried not to sound too relieved as one of the scientists climbed up into the front of the metal contraption.

Wren frowned. "That won't do." She hurried forward. "Neon," she called.

Neon turned, his round face twisting into an insincere little smile. "Ah, Wren. How lovely to see you." He glanced at Lailu. "And you," he said politely.

"You never collected on the feast I owe you," Lailu said. She hated to remind someone that she owed them food, but a debt was a debt. In her experience, it was best to get them taken care of as soon as possible, and several months back, Neon had taken her picture for an advertisement in exchange for a free meal at Mystic Cooking.

"I've been quite busy." Neon glanced again at Wren. "All of us have been. Working hard. Happy to be, of course. Very happy to be kept busy."

"Speaking of busy, I need this carriage," Wren said.

Neon fiddled with his vest. Lailu noticed it hung more limply on him than before, his ball of a stomach deflating. She could see shadows under his eyes too. Maybe he really was too busy to eat. What a terrible thought. "Well, miss, I actually was under the impression that it was my turn with the carriage. You see, I need it for, uh . . ."

Wren crossed her arms and tilted her chin, looking like a mini version of Starling, and Neon's words dried up. He hung his head, then stepped out of the carriage.

"Of course, I'm sure whatever Starling has asked you to do is more important. I'll just, er, I'll just walk. The exercise will do me good, I'm sure." He attempted another sickly smile.

"While you're at it, go take care of Carbon's body," Wren ordered, hopping into the driver's seat.

Neon froze. "B-body?"

"Oh yes, someone killed him and dumped him in the swamp. Coming, Lailu?" Wren lowered her goggles and pulled a lever, and the carriage roared to life. The sound reminded Lailu uncomfortably of a charging hydra, but she climbed in anyway. As Wren pressed a button and they shot away from Elister's mansion in a rush of steam, Lailu had one last glimpse of Neon, his face gray in the midday light.

Lailu gripped the side of the auto-carriage as Wren carelessly tore down the street. She could feel the carriage rumbling beneath her, and it felt more precarious than riding on the back of a griffin.

"Ah, that was fun," Wren giggled.

"F-fun?"

"Mama has all the other scientists terrified of her, so they're extra nice to me. They shouldn't bother. It's not like Mama actually cares. But I like being able to boss them around."

"H-how are things with you and your mom?" Lailu remembered the way Starling had criticized Wren in Elister's office, and how the two had been fighting just months ago over Wren's desire to be an actress and not a scientist.

"Things are okay," Wren said. "I told you I've been working on my own inventions, right?" She took a sharp turn, and several people had to leap out of the way. Lailu clutched at her seat. "Well, I've been enjoying that work, and Mama appreciates it. I mean, she hasn't said so exactly, but she did tell me I could work on Walton for her."

"Elister's automaton?"

Wren nodded happily. "He *was* Carbon's pet project, but now he'll be mine. I'm supposed to get him to listen to Mama's commands. He doesn't really respond to her, but I think he likes me better."

Lailu wasn't sure how something made of metal could "like" anyone, but she decided not to bring that up. "So Carbon . . . made that thing?" she said instead.

"Whoops, almost missed the bridge." Wren spun the wheel, and their carriage made a screeching U-turn, Lailu's side lifting off the ground for a second before slamming back onto the road in a shower of sparks. Lailu concentrated on breathing deeply and trying not to fall out.

"Yeah, he had his moments of brilliance. Occasionally," Wren said as they drove across the bridge and away from Gilded Island.

Lailu frowned.

"Wow, I just realized how mean that sounded. I know I should be sorrier about him," Wren said quickly, "but before we left Beolann, scientists died all the time. I guess I just got used to it."

"Was it really that bad?" Lailu hadn't heard much about Beolann, except for the well-known rumor that Starling and her people had disguised themselves as fishermen to escape, the first group to leave that country in living memory.

"Anyone who didn't fall in line with what the General wanted was let go. Permanently." Wren drew a finger across her throat, and the auto-carriage wobbled until she grabbed the wheel with both hands. "I'm not supposed to talk about it. Anyhow, I was young when we left. Things are better here." She smiled. "And Mama's going to make sure they stay that way." Her smile turned cold and brittle, and Lailu noticed a tall figure leaning against one of the buildings, holding a small stack of masks. She raised a hand mockingly as they roared past.

Was that Gwendyl? Lailu thought she recognized the female elf's sneer and the way she wore her chestnut-brown hair twisted into an elaborate knot on top of her head, showing off her pointed ears.

"Elves," Wren muttered, her shoulders hunching up toward her neck. "They have it in for us, you know."

"Well, you did kidnap their people," Lailu said.

Wren flinched. "We were being forced to do Mr. Boss's dirty work. It's hardly our fault. And it's not like we really hurt them."

Lailu gaped at her. "You were draining their blood."

"But it's not like they feel pain."

"What? Why wouldn't they feel pain?" Lailu could still vividly picture the female elf trapped in that weird coffin, her eyes sunken, her strawlike hair tangled around her face, her dry, cracked lips pulled back in a silent howl of anguish. Was it possible that Wren never saw that?

"Because they're creatures. They're not human." Wren turned her wide green eyes on Lailu, so matter-of-fact. "They're not like us at all."

Lailu's skin prickled. She knew Wren wasn't the only one who thought like this. It was a common attitude among the wealthy of Twin Rivers, those who could afford to stay separated from the rest of the city's "riffraff" and never interacted with the elves. "They're still *people*," Lailu said firmly. She might not like those pointy-eared tricksters, but she'd been around them enough to see that. "They still— Eyes on the road, eyes on the road!"

Wren glanced back, adjusting the wheel just in time to avoid two men and a cart.

"Anyway, the elves aren't that important," Wren said. "What's important is getting ourselves well established—that's what Mama says. And that's why I wanted to talk to you."

"Me?"

"Yep. We—my mom and I—want to make you an offer." Wren turned down the industrial district, zooming past metal buildings with large smokestacks. Lailu noticed that a few of them seemed to be working, the smoke drifting hazily up to mingle with the clouds hanging overhead.

"What kind of offer?" Lailu asked.

Wren smiled, a perfect Vahn-type smile, all pearly whites and dimples. "We want to set up a power generator in your restaurant."

"A what?"

"A power generator."

"No, I meant, what *is* a power generator?" Lailu asked. "Is that like some kind of new stove or something?"

"No, it's *way* better."

Lailu seriously doubted that. What could possibly be better than a stove?

"Just imagine this." Wren turned toward her, her green eyes sparkling. "Lights that can be turned on at the flick of a switch, running water—either hot or cold—*inside* your restaurant, and all our newly tested cooking gadgets installed for you, working with your generator."

"People. Up ahead," Lailu said nervously.

Wren slammed a button on the wheel, and a honk that sounded like an angry pack of chickens split the afternoon. A couple of men in worker smocks and bowl hats leaped out of the way, shouting angry curses as the carriage zoomed on by. "This is why I love this thing," Wren admitted happily. "So? What do you think?"

"What's the catch?" Lailu asked. "What do you get out of it?" After her time working for the vicious Mr. Boss, Lailu no longer trusted anything that seemed like a good deal. He'd promised her and Slipshod a loan . . . and then nearly took their restaurant and their freedom.

Wren slowed down, her shoulders slumping. "I thought," she said in a small voice, "that we were friends."

"Of course we are," Lailu said, surprised.

"Well, isn't that what friends do? They help each other out?" Wren turned large, teary eyes on Lailu. "I just wanted to help you revolutionize your restaurant."

Lailu felt a sharp pang of guilt, like a knife stabbed into her gut. "Oh."

"I mean," Wren sniffed, wiping a hand across her eyes, "you're actually my only friend."

The knife twisted. "R-really?"

Wren nodded. "Mama doesn't usually approve of my 'fraternizing with children.'" She emphasized those last three words in a way that showed she'd heard them often. "She's afraid their immaturity will rub off on me. But she likes you well enough. I'm allowed to be friends with you."

"Oh, uh, thanks." Lailu hadn't realized she was Wren's only friend. Back home in her village, Lailu didn't have many friends either, but at least she had her brothers, and Hannah. Poor Wren. "I'm glad we're friends," Lailu added.

"Do you really mean it?"

"Of course."

"So . . . you'll do it? You'll let us install a power generator?" Wren asked, all trace of tears gone. "Mama will be so excited!"

"I'm not sure—"

"She's always said you have the eyes of a true chef. She'll be happy to see your restaurant really thrive," Wren said, turning down the road that led to Mystic Cooking.

Lailu stopped. She remembered Starling saying that to her. Lailu had once really looked up to her, the brilliant scientist who had revolutionized the cooking world with her stoves the same way Lailu wanted to change the world with her restaurant.

As they pulled up in front of Mystic Cooking, Lailu tried to picture it fully revolutionized. Lights on, people laughing on the patio that she could have built out back where her current water pump sat . . .

"I have to make sure Master Slipshod agrees," Lailu said.

"Oh, he already said it was fine, as long as you were okay with it," Wren said. "He told me that you got final say."

Lailu felt a burst of pride. First Master Slipshod sent her to hunt hydra without him, and then he gave her final say in such an important decision? He must really trust her judgment. "All right," she decided. "I'll do it."

15

UNEXPECTED VISITORS

Hannah flew outside Mystic Cooking in a whirl of scarlet skirts and long black hair. Her eyes widened as she took in Lailu's transportation. "Wow, Lailu! You came home in style!" She ran her hands along the sides of the auto-carriage reverently. "This is the newest model, the wood-paneled Steamer Model S. It's a shame you had to ride in it so dirty."

Lailu frowned. She *was* dirty, but Hannah made it sound like she'd somehow insulted this ridiculous carriage with her appearance.

"You really know your automotives," Wren said, impressed.

"Well, it's important to stay on top of things." Hannah gazed up at Wren. "Are you a scientist?"

"Almost." Wren sat up taller. "I've been working with my mother lately. You know, Starling Volan?"

Lailu was surprised by the pride in Wren's voice. It was so

different from how she'd reacted a few months back when Lailu had asked her about Starling. Back then Wren had seemed reluctant to discuss her mother and the work she was forced to do for her. She really must have embraced her role as her mother's apprentice. For the first time, Lailu wondered what had made her change her mind.

"Wren, I have to ask you," Hannah began, with an apologetic look at Lailu, "what was up with your mom's hair at Elister's party?"

Lailu groaned. "Would you stop with the ponytail already?"

"No, it's a good question." Wren hopped down from her seat, closing the door carefully behind her. "Mama is hopeless with hair, and she fired her hairdresser that morning. Said she suffered from 'an abundance of stupidity.'" She shook her head. "It's the third one she's let go this month."

"See?" Hannah beamed at Lailu. "I knew Wren would understand. She has great hair."

"Really?" Wren touched her red curls.

"Oh, definitely. And I have an eye for such things. I studied at Twin Rivers's Finest." Hannah neglected to mention she'd been kicked out of that school recently.

"You know, Mama will probably be looking for a new hairdresser soon. Are you looking for a job?"

"Of course not," Lailu said, at the same time that Hannah said "Maybe."

Lailu felt like she'd just been smacked with a frying pan. Hannah was looking for a job? What about working with her? What about Mystic Cooking?

"I'll mention it to Mama. It's Hannah, right?"

Hannah nodded, not meeting Lailu's eyes.

"Well, I should get to work." Lailu tried to keep her voice even. "The harnesses are right behind the building." She pointed them out, then retreated inside her safe, warm restaurant, waiting until the door closed before turning on Hannah. "A job?" she demanded. "What's wrong with the one you have here?"

Hannah twined her hands together. "I like helping you with your restaurant, but this might be my one big chance to get back into doing what I love, and what I'm good at."

"You're good at *this*!" Lailu waved her hands to indicate the restaurant around her.

Hannah sighed. "Look, I'll still help you. And I'll still be living here. . . . I mean, if you let me. And you'll *still* have Slipshod. Don't look so abandoned."

Lailu flinched.

Hannah's eyes widened. "Sorry," she said quickly. "Bad choice of words. But I'm not going anywhere, I promise. It's just a job, Lailu."

"Ah, so you *did* find a job," Ryon said.

Lailu whirled. Ryon leaned against the wall, his sleeves rolled up to his elbows, his navy coat thrown over his shoulder. He looked way too relaxed, like it was his own house.

Lailu crossed her arms. "We're closed to customers."

"Oh, don't worry, I'm not eating. I was just visiting your light-fingered friend here." He inclined his head toward Hannah.

Lailu's stomach churned like she'd just gulped down curdled milk. "Why are you visiting Hannah?" she asked as calmly as she could. As if it didn't bother her at all. Because it didn't.

"Well, technically, she owes me a meal." Ryon smirked. "You know, on account of our dance?"

Lailu wanted to crawl inside her cellar and hide in the icebox.

"You don't have to look so embarrassed. You only stepped on my feet twice." He paused and rubbed his chin. "Maybe three times."

"I did not!"

"I have the bruises to show for it."

"I'll give you bruises," Lailu grumbled.

"Speaking of bruises," Ryon said quickly, "I notice you've picked up a couple more. Not to mention a shirt full of blood. I take it you had a successful hunt?"

Lailu thought about giving Ryon a vague answer and winking in his face to see how he liked it for once. But instead she found herself telling him and Hannah about the hunt. And then, despite Elister's command to keep the news to herself, she couldn't help describing the way she and Greg found Carbon's body and the scene in Elister's office afterward. "Starling claimed it was the elves," Lailu finished, staring hard at Ryon, but his face was the same careful mask it always was, telling her nothing.

"Hey, I think I've found the problem." Wren burst into the restaurant, then stopped at the sight of Lailu, Ryon, and Hannah all clustered together.

Lailu stood up. "You've fixed the harnesses?"

"Not yet," Wren said slowly, her eyes lingering on Ryon. "I have to take them to the shop. I'll bring them back when I'm done."

"Sure. And take your time. Really." If Lailu never saw those blasted things again, it would still be too soon.

"Well, ladies, it's been a pleasure, but I'd best be on my way." Ryon pushed off the wall abruptly, nodded at Hannah and Wren, winked at Lailu, and disappeared through the front door.

"That was abrupt," Lailu said.

"Why was he here?" Wren asked. "Didn't he work for Mr. Boss?"

"I think he was working for Mr. Boss about as much as your mom was working for him," Lailu said. Both Starling and Ryon had temporarily aligned themselves with Lailu's old nemesis, but both were really there for their own purposes.

"You know, Mama always suspected he was up to something. She thought he had some sort of tie with the elves." Wren wrinkled her nose.

Lailu and Hannah exchanged looks. "Er . . . ," Lailu said, as noncommittally as she could.

"I think . . ." Wren stopped, then adjusted her tool belt. "I think I need to go now. I'll see you around." And she hurried out the door after Ryon. Moments later Lailu heard the roar of the auto-carriage taking off.

"Also abrupt," Lailu said.

Hannah slumped into a chair. "Do you think it's true?"

"What?"

"About the elves?"

Lailu hesitated. Eirad had been there at the feast, and he'd been "working." Ryon thought he was up to something, and after Eirad's strange, veiled hints in the Western Travel District, Lailu had to agree. And even though he'd said they were incapable of killing anyone under Elister's protection, she had to admit, they seemed to find ways around their promises. Still, to murder a scientist? And right after Elister's party? "I don't think it was them," Lailu said slowly. "They're smarter than that."

"So what do we do about it?"

"Do? We don't *do* anything," Lailu said. "Elister's looking into it, and I'm going to stay out of it . . . or at least as much as I can. I've had it with getting involved with those people."

"Good," Master Slipshod barked.

Lailu jumped, her heart hammering.

Her mentor stood in the kitchen doorway. "And while you're at it, quit lollygagging around. We need to prepare for the dinner rush," he said.

Lailu's jaw dropped, and she exchanged a glance with Hannah.

Master Slipshod's chef's hat was puffier than usual, his apron freshly pressed and whiter than egg whites. Even his hair had been brushed back into a neat ponytail, of all things.

"M-Master Slipshod?" Lailu whispered. He *never* looked presentable. Rumor had it he wore a stained apron and left his hair unbrushed even in the days he'd worked as the king's chef.

"What is it?"

"Nice . . . ponytail," Hannah said.

Slipshod ran a hand self-consciously through his hair. "Big nights ahead, big nights. Important to look our best." His eyes narrowed on Lailu's appearance. "So you might want to go wash up. Can't have a sloppy-looking apprentice. But first, go greet your guest."

"Greet my what?" Lailu asked, confused.

Master Slipshod stepped to the side to reveal a short, curvy woman with auburn hair held back by a vibrant scarf, her skirts a swirl of color around her. The woman smiled, her large hazel eyes taking in Lailu's appearance, from the dirt and blood on Lailu's clothing to the bruises underneath. "It's nice to see that some things never change," she said, her voice as warm and welcoming as a large pot of homemade stew. "My little Lailu. How I've missed you."

Lailu's breath caught. It was her mother.

16

Rumor Has It

As Lailu bustled about the kitchen, she could feel her aches and pains drifting away on a minty-fresh breeze thanks to her mother's salve. Lianna Loganberry might not have been the most reliable mother, but her healing ointments never failed. Still, Lailu had to wonder why her mother was there. She hadn't seen her in over a year; her mother hadn't bothered to show up to her graduation. So why now? It felt like hunting that hydra, as if she were seeing only the first three heads, the rest of the beast hidden.

"Your father sends his love," Lianna said from her perch on the counter. "And so do Lonnie and Laurent. They asked when you were going to come home for a visit."

"When I have free time," Lailu said, trying not to feel guilty.

She had a restaurant to run. She didn't have time for family visits. She knew her father understood; he had always respected those who sacrificed their time in pursuit of hard work. But Lonnie occasionally sent her whiny letters. "I'm surprised Lonnie didn't come with you." Lailu thought of the last letter he'd sent, where he'd threatened to move in to Mystic Cooking. She loved her brother. He was only a year older than her, and he was one of her best friends, but he could be a bit much sometimes. She didn't think she could handle him *and* run a business.

Lianna laughed. "Oh, he tried. I had to sneak out."

Lailu winced.

"What? He doesn't mind." Lianna waved her hands as if ditching her son was no big deal. And to her, it wasn't. It really wasn't.

Lailu took a deep breath. She wanted to tell her mother how much it hurt when she abandoned them, wanted to ask her how she was so sure Lonnie didn't mind being left behind. But when she looked her mother in the face, she couldn't do it. She was never able to do it.

Every time her mom came back after another random trip, Lailu pretended everything was fine, squashing her anger and sadness deep, deep down, covering them up like a lid over a noxious stew. This was her mother, who treated her wounds and told her stories when she was little. Her mother, whom she loved.

And Lailu could feel that tiny pinprick of fear buried beneath the anger and sadness. She was afraid that if she said anything, then the next time her mother left, she wouldn't bother coming back.

"Looks like you're getting low on lebinola," her mother said, peeking in the spice cupboard behind her. "Are you still using that in everything?"

Lailu sagged. Maybe she'd tell her mom later. . . . "Not in everything," she said, letting the words she couldn't say vanish like steam off her cream-of-griffin soup. "Just when it's needed."

"Which is often, I take it?"

"Did you really come out here to criticize my cooking?" Lailu stirred the soup cooking on the stove, her knuckles white on the ladle.

"I told you, I came out to visit. The criticism is just a bonus." Lianna smiled.

Lailu scowled.

"Oh, relax, Lailu. You're always so serious. I'm sorry I said anything about your cooking. It smells absolutely wonderful, and I'm sure it will taste even better."

"Greg always teases me about my use of lebinola too," Lailu grumbled, setting her ladle down.

"Ooh, Greg?" Lianna's eyes sparkled as she leaned forward. "And who is this Greg?"

Lailu's ears turned red. "He's just . . . Greg is just my rival."

"Just your rival. Interesting. Tell me more."

"There's nothing to tell," Lailu said. "Are you going to be here long?"

Lianna laughed. "At least through the Week of Masks. And don't try to change the subject. It won't work on me. Especially since I counted two *just*s there. Must be serious."

"Lailu, another family of five came in clamoring for the special, and Master Slipshod says to pull out the soufflé," Hannah said, bustling into the kitchen holding a tray loaded with dirty dishes.

"Hannah, be a dear and tell me about Lailu's Greg," Lianna said.

Lailu's blush spread from her ears to her cheeks like melted butter on a frying pan. "I told you, he's just—" She caught herself, cleared her throat. "He's a fellow chef."

"He leaped to Lailu's defense a few weeks back when we had to hunt dragon," Hannah added, setting her tray down. "He's a LaSilvian. A very *handsome* LaSilvian."

"Hannah!"

"What? He is—you can't deny it. Even if he does have too much hair."

"A handsome aristocrat, interested in my Lailu," Lianna purred. "Well, well."

"He is *not* interested in me," Lailu said, but she could tell her mother wasn't listening. Typical. Sighing, she pulled the soufflé out.

"He's always making excuses to hunt together. And aren't you cooking together tomorrow?" Hannah smirked.

"That's different. That's just cooking."

"Another 'just,'" Lianna remarked, exchanging knowing smiles with Hannah.

"Stop smiling so much!" Lailu said. This was almost as bad as the time her oldest brother, Laurent, caught her writing poetry about Vahn. "I need to go check on my customers."

"Go on, then. I'm sure Hannah will tell me everything while you're gone. Won't you, Hannah?" Lianna clasped Hannah's fingers.

"Of course, Mrs. Loganberry."

"I've told you, call me Lianna, dear. 'Mrs.' makes me feel old."

"Hannah, shouldn't you come with me?" Lailu asked, loading up a new tray with dishes. She couldn't leave her friend there unsupervised. Who knew what she'd tell her mother?

"Did you know Lailu actually danced with another boy on the First Night of Masks?" Hannah said.

"Hey, this tray is awfully heavy. I could use some help," Lailu said desperately.

"Another boy? How intriguing. Do continue."

"Well, he's a bit older, and mysterious. His name's Ryon."

Lianna dropped Hannah's hands so quickly, it was like she'd picked up a hot pan.

"Mom?" Lailu asked.

"Hmm?"

"Do you . . . Do you know Ryon?"

"Of course not. How could I possibly?" Lianna stood. "Now, I'll help you with this tray, shall I? We shouldn't be sitting around chatting when there are hungry people out there." She took the tray out of Lailu's unresisting hands.

"I can take that, Mrs. Loganberry," Hannah said quickly.

"Nonsense. I might be old, as you insist on reminding me, but I can still carry a tray. And I know you must be tired, Lailu honey, what with the hunt and then the excitement of discovering a body out there."

Lailu's jaw dropped. How did her mother know about that? It was supposed to be a secret.

"Don't look so surprised, you two. Word spreads fast in these parts, particularly when someone wants the word to spread."

"And what word would that be?" Hannah asked.

"Murder." Lianna looked hard at Hannah. "Murder . . . at the hands of the elves."

THE GREATER GOOD

Someone shook Lailu's shoulder.

Lailu rolled over, pulling her blankets tighter around her. "Skilly-wigs are for amateurs," she mumbled into her pillow.

"Lailu, you have to wake up. Lord Elister is here," Hannah said.

Those words were like a bucket of ice shattering Lailu's sleep into a million terrified pieces.

"What? Why? Now?" Lailu sat up, her hand going for her knife. She stopped herself. A knife wouldn't help her. Not in this.

"I'm not sure why," Hannah said, adjusting the robe she'd thrown on over her own nightclothes, "but he's definitely here now."

Lailu glanced at the darkened window. She felt like she'd just drifted off; sunlight wouldn't be breaking for another hour. What did Elister want? Was he there to question her? Had they found Carbon's murderer?

Or . . . had there been another murder?

Lailu's fingers were numb and clumsy as she changed out of her nightclothes and into a long gray shirt and a pair of brown trousers, then padded down the stairs. "You're staying up?" she asked Hannah.

Hannah sipped her tea. "I'm meeting Starling later this morning," she explained. "Who needs sleep, right?"

"Right," Lailu muttered grumpily.

"Good luck out there."

Lailu slipped into the candlelit dining room. And stopped.

Lord Elister was there, all right. And so was her mother. Both of them were sitting at a table in the corner, talking too quietly for Lailu to overhear. She remembered Elister saying he had met her mother once before. The comfortable way they sat made it look like he'd met her many times. But that couldn't be true. Surely Lailu would know if her mother regularly came to Twin Rivers.

No, you wouldn't, Lailu thought bitterly. Her mother never said where she was going, or where she'd been. She never told Lailu anything of importance.

Lianna glanced up, caught sight of her daughter, and immediately rose from her chair. "Good morning, dear heart," she chirped. "Eli—Lord Elister was just telling me all about the amazing dinner you recently catered for him. I'm so proud." She put her hands over her heart, the many rings on her fingers clinking softly together.

Lord Elister stood up. He towered over Lailu's mother but did not overshadow her. No one ever overshadowed Lianna Loganberry; Lailu wasn't sure what it was, but her mother always seemed like the brightest spot in any room, the person everyone noticed first.

"I thought we should discuss yesterday's events," he said. "Walk with me?"

Even though he phrased it as a question, Lailu knew there was only one answer. She nodded, too nervous to say anything.

"Here, honey, it's cold outside." Her mother shrugged out of her wrap and handed it to Lailu. "And it'll do you good to wear some color for once."

Lailu was sure her face was a bright enough red to qualify. It was embarrassing to have her mother fussing over her in front of the king's executioner, of all people. Still, she took the purple-and-green cloth and wrapped it around herself, breathing in the scent of incense and cinnamon.

"Oh, and don't forget this." Lianna grabbed Lailu's fancy griffin mask and handed it over.

"It's practically morning," Lailu protested.

"Until that sun peeks its little head over the horizon, you keep your mask on. You too, Lord Elister. You *especially*," Lianna said firmly. "We're only midway through the week. Still plenty of angry spirits hanging around."

Elister slipped a simple green domino mask from his pocket. "As you say."

Lianna smiled approvingly. "Have a pleasant walk." She curtsied in his direction, patted Lailu's cheek, then swept from the room.

Elister's green eyes crinkled at the edges in a genuine smile. "Your mother is an enchanting woman." Then his smile fell away, and it was all business again. "Shall we?"

Lailu pulled on her mask and followed him outside, the autumn chill enveloping her with the promise of rain to come. She tugged her mother's wrap more tightly around her shoulders.

Whirl, tick, tick.

Lailu spun, hand dropping to her hip. An automaton stepped into view around the corner of the restaurant, a bowler hat perched on its metal head. Its eyes glowed that same intense blue as before as it watched Lailu. Even though it had no expression, Lailu could tell it was glaring, could feel the animosity radiating from its metal core.

This . . . this *thing* did not like her.

But that was impossible. It was like a stove. Or a carriage. It couldn't like or dislike anyone. Could it?

"Ah, Walton, so good of you to wait." Elister smiled fondly at the automaton.

"Doesn't he have to?" Lailu asked.

"Of course he does, but that doesn't mean I can't be polite about it." As Elister walked, Walton fell into step behind him, trotting at his heel like some kind of metallic dog. "After all, his ability to do precisely what I ask puts him far above any person who has ever worked for me."

Lailu had to hurry to keep up with Elister's much longer strides, and she was very conscious of Walton's creepy blue eyes on her back the whole time.

"I'm taking him out for a test run this morning," Elister continued. "Starling's daughter fixed some of his bugs, and she also added a few new features. According to Starling, Walton here should be able to take pictures, storing images of the things around him. Isn't that marvelous?"

"Er . . . ," Lailu said. She wasn't sure how she felt about this new ability. It made her even more nervous about saying anything, if Walton was somehow going to trap her image forever.

Elister fell silent as they walked past his carriage. Lailu noticed it was the same auto-carriage Wren had driven earlier and not Elister's usual black affair. Clearly the king's executioner was enjoying all the newest inventions the scientists had to offer.

"You're probably wondering why I came here now instead of sending one of my agents," Elister finally said.

"No, sir," Lailu answered. "I just assumed you never slept."

Elister chuckled. "These days, that statement feels too close to the truth." They turned down a side road, passing a shabby brick apartment building. The candles in the nearest window had burned down to nubs. She recognized them as Nighters, created specifically to burn the full night before melting away with the dawn.

"I came personally because I don't want any more leaks. People talking about murder is bad enough, but when the deceased is someone who was under my protection . . ." He shook his head. "The fewer people involved in this, the better. We don't need any more damaging rumors."

Lailu fidgeted, feeling strangely guilty. She had told Ryon and Hannah. . . . Did Lord Elister know somehow? *Of course he knew.* He always seemed to. But Lailu also knew her friends would have kept quiet. It had to be someone else spreading rumors, someone who wanted the city to know about this death, who wanted people to worry about the elves.

"Now." Lord Elister stopped in the middle of the deserted street.

"Is there anything else you want to tell me about your hunt? Did you notice anything—anything at all—that might have been suspicious?"

Lailu hesitated, remembering that figure she'd seen moving quietly through the swamp. As she told Elister about it, Walton's blue eyes glowed brighter and brighter. He sucked in her words, his head tilted to the side.

Its head, Lailu corrected herself. It was a thing. It was not alive.

Lailu shuddered, trying not to look at the automaton. "Whoever or whatever it was, it moved like it didn't want us to know it was there," she finished.

"Whatever it was?" Elister asked.

Lailu bit her lip, but she had to tell him. Even with Walton standing right there. "Sir, I don't believe anything human could have moved through that muck without ending up in it, and I heard no splashing."

"Interesting," Elister said, running one hand down his chin thoughtfully.

They started circling back toward Mystic Cooking. Lailu thought longingly of her warm bed, and then of her even warmer kitchen. As her restaurant came into view, she had to fight the urge to run inside, away from the intimidating presence of Elister and his new butler.

"Your story certainly matches young LaSilvian's," Elister said, "but with more detail. Some creature moving through the swamp. That gives Starling's suspicions even more weight."

"I don't think it was an elf," Lailu said.

Elister stopped. His eyes narrowed on Lailu's face, and suddenly she found it hard to breathe, like she had swallowed an extra-large glob of peanut butter.

"I heard clicking noises. I don't think it was alive." She gulped, but she made herself say it. "I think it was . . . made." She thought of the hat again, that dirty bowler hat, but those words dried up in the face of Elister's stony expression.

"*I* think," he said quietly, "that there are a lot of noises in a swamp. I think," his voice grew louder, "that it would be hard for someone to distinguish among them. And I *think* that this is something a chef would be wise to *not* think too much about."

"But, sir—"

"Do *not* get involved, Lailu Loganberry. Sometimes the good of the country must take precedence over justice, or what might seem right to someone in your situation."

Lailu swallowed hard. It sounded almost like Elister was already choosing the scientists and their accusations over the elves, regardless of the truth. Like the truth was something that could just be decided.

"Do you understand me?" he asked.

"I . . . I think so," Lailu whispered. She could picture the axe hanging just above her head.

"Good. I'm glad we had this chance to chat. Come along, Walton," he said, striding to his auto-carriage.

The automaton cocked its head again, then leaned in closer to Lailu. She froze.

Click-click-click, whirrrrrrrrr.

"Walton!" Elister ordered.

The automaton turned and glided to the carriage, vaulting inside. Lailu remained outside her restaurant for a long time after the carriage drove off.

If she didn't know better, she'd think Walton had just threatened her. And although she'd dealt with threats in the past, both from Mr. Boss and the elves, this felt somehow worse. More terrifying. For how could she reason with a thing that had no heart? A thing that wasn't alive.

Times are changing.

Lailu shook herself, then headed inside. She had to get ready now if she was going to get to Greg's in time to help cook.

18

EXTRA HEADS

Lailu prodded the hydra meat with a long-handled fork, checking for any bright green streaks, the lingering signs of poison. Usually, the more *magic* a creature had in life, the more poisonous it could be in death—if not cooked and treated properly, that is. Hydra meat was almost as deadly as dragon meat. And sometimes poison from a mystical beast might cause strange side effects. Of course, this topic was widely disputed among chefs. No mystic chef worth her apron would ever admit to cooking anything incorrectly, so the few instances of magical poisoning that resulted in bizarre changes instead of death were always blamed on other things.

"How's it look?" Greg asked. He pulled a roast from the broiler, sweat glimmering on his upper lip.

"I don't think anyone will grow an extra head from this steak,"

Lailu declared, tipping the bottle of Greg's "special" dry rub.

"There's no proof that hydra meat does that."

"No, just theory." Lailu began delicately slicing the meat. "Although I know you're not really up on all your chef theories."

Greg narrowed his eyes. "If you mean up on all my theories from that dried-up, has-been Chef Gingersnap—"

"Hey! That's *Master* Chef Gingersnap."

Greg snorted. Master Chef Gingersnap had been one of the few teachers at the Chef Academy whom he hadn't been able to charm. He'd passed her class, but just barely.

"And she was right about the side effects of griffin meat," Lailu said.

"Well, even a tasteless chef can find spice if it's loaded onto her plate."

Gingersnap had theorized that griffin meat, if not treated and cooked properly, would cause extreme honesty in people who ate it. Then, about twenty-five years ago, that theory had been put into effect. Rumor had it, some of the tension between Savoria and the Krigaen Empire stemmed from a single failed banquet, when the Savorian diplomat insulted the Krigaen queen's nose . . . and worse yet, her fighting prowess.

"I still maintain that those diplomats wanted to insult the queen all along," Greg said. "And I'm just about done with my end. Have a look." He gestured with his knife. "The flaked mandrake and chopped scallops." They would be turning those into delicious steak rolls. Another dramatic knife gesture for "our spicy tahini and sesame chili."

Lailu's mouth watered at the thought of the tasty salad that these would be going into.

"The nuts for that are still marinating over by the oven." Greg pointed over his shoulder. "The peppercorn and *lebinola* is over there." He crinkled his nose at the lebinola.

"It will taste amazing, you'll see."

"Whatever. And finally, we have the gorgon's milk cheese, and orc bacon there." He gestured to the last bowls hanging onto the edge of the crowded countertop. "Am I missing anything?"

Lailu walked around, double-checking all their work and tasting the sauces. One could never be *too* careful with cooking. Especially for the Week of Masks parade. Practically the whole city turned out to watch all the students from the different academies show off, and to gawk at the royal family. There would be jugglers and dancers and music. But more important, there would be plenty of food booths set up along the main street.

Since everything served had to be finger food, easy to eat on the go, it was challenging to create a proper feast. And hydra was not as flavorful as mountain dragon, so extra seasoning and marinades were important. Still, Lailu felt they had done an excellent job.

She dabbed a final spoon into the peppercorn lebinola, letting the sweet and spicy taste linger on her tongue. "I think we've got everything." She beamed. "This meal is officially—*green!*"

"Officially green?"

"Look at that steak you're cutting." Lailu pointed to the faint green streak through the middle and shook her head. "No wonder Gingersnap almost failed you."

"She did *not* almost fail me."

"Oh yeah? Even Sandy did better than you in that class."

"Well, I . . . I did well in the classes that mattered."

"I think it matters if you accidentally give your customers extra heads."

Greg sighed. "For the last time, Lailu, they would not have grown extra heads."

"Why don't you eat some and find out?"

"I'm not even dignifying that with a response." Greg grabbed the purifying salts and rubbed them down his tainted knife to remove the poison.

"Ahem," Greg's uncle said from the doorway to the kitchen. His gaze slid past Lailu as if she were a stain in the kitchen, just a spill waiting to be mopped up. "A few important clients will be arriving shortly to enjoy a snack and our pleasant ambiance before the festival. I really must insist you send your . . . *guest* . . . home before they arrive."

Lailu's ears burned. Clearly the great Dante LaSilvian did not want his fancy diners to see her at his establishment.

"We just need a little more time," Greg said, but Lailu was already gathering her things. It shouldn't hurt, but it did. Every time she forgot how awful the aristocrats could be, one of them had to go and remind her that she didn't really belong in their world. This was why she loved Mystic Cooking. It was the one place in this whole city that actually felt like home, like it wanted her.

Dante left, closing the kitchen door firmly behind him.

"Think you can handle the rest of the steaks?" she asked Greg, her voice only shaking a tiny bit.

"Lailu, you don't have to go, really," Greg said.

"N-no, it's fine."

He sighed. "I can handle the rest of the steaks. And I'll get the decorations set too, okay?" He set down his knife. "Want me to send for the carriage to bring you home?"

"I'd rather walk." Lailu didn't want to ride in Dante's carriage. She didn't want to feel like she owed that man anything.

"I'm sorry, Lailu," Greg said sadly. "And . . . and for before, for ignoring you at the party. I understand now why that was so mean."

Lailu realized, for the first time, that she didn't hold his aristocracy over him. "It's okay. I mean, you were a total jerk—"

"A complete and total jerk," he agreed.

Lailu smiled. It wasn't her best smile, but the tightness in her chest eased some. "Well, as Master Gingersnap used to say, once you know the theory behind it, you can fix anything."

Greg's mouth twisted. "Are you sure she said that? Because that actually sounds almost useful."

"Of course I'm sure. But then, *I* actually paid attention in her class."

"Watch it."

Lailu grinned, then headed outside into the cool evening air. But as soon as the door to LaSilvian's Kitchen closed behind her, her grin dropped away.

She took a deep breath and started walking. She took the side streets, noticing that on Gilded Island, even the alleyways were so clean, they sparkled.

Click–click–click.

Lailu's blood froze. She scanned the street, searching the shingles on the rooftops.

Click–click.

Something was definitely there, watching her from the shadows.

19

SOMETHING IN THE SHADOWS

It's been following me all day," said a voice from right behind Lailu.

Lailu spun so hard, she fell over.

"Ryon!" Lailu picked herself up. "What are you doing here? And why do you always hide in the shadows like that? It's not nice." She brushed the dirt from her trousers.

"I never claimed to be nice." Ryon gazed past her.

The sky had turned into the slate gray of early evening, too overcast to see the sun. Lailu couldn't see anything out of the ordinary. Did being part elf give Ryon better senses?

"What is it?" Lailu whispered.

"I'm not sure, but whatever it is has been tailing me off and on since I left Mystic Cooking yesterday." Ryon ran a hand over his face. He had bags under his eyes, and his clothing was even more rumpled than usual. It looked like he'd slept in it, if he'd slept at all. "I did manage to lose it temporarily in the Industrial District at night, but it found me again this morning." He grinned. "Must be my animal magnetism."

"What are you going to do about it?"

"Do?" Ryon's smile was small and as brittle as a stale cookie. "Absolutely nothing."

"What?"

"I'm just going to go about the rest of my day like all the other mundane holiday celebrators and hope that whatever it is eventually gets bored and goes away."

Lailu scowled. "That sounds like a terrible plan. What if it attacks you?"

"I'll take my chances."

Click-click.

Lailu turned but couldn't see anything at all. She thought of the noises she had heard in the swamp and of Walton's disturbingly threatening glare that morning. Suddenly Ryon seemed very small, and very vulnerable.

"This is serious, you know. I heard something similar in the swamp before I found Carbon. It might be the same thing that killed him."

Ryon's eyes widened. "Interesting. Still, can't be helped. Errands to run and all that."

Lailu wanted nothing more than to get back to Mystic Cooking and grab a nap before tonight's street festival. Sighing, she pushed her warm, comfortable bed from her thoughts. "Let's go," she said.

"You're . . . coming with me?"

"Not that *you* seem to care, but *I'd* actually feel bad if you were murdered." Lailu glared at him. "Probably," she added. She didn't like the idea of being followed by some sort of creepy creature she couldn't see, but it bugged her even more that Ryon was taking the whole thing so lightly. Someone died, and if Lailu gambled half as much as her mentor used to, she'd bet that whatever was watching them held an important clue.

"You know, you really are my favorite chef." Ryon grinned broadly. "I won't even wink the rest of the afternoon."

"Wow, you're so generous."

"I know. It's my only real fault."

Lailu snorted, falling into step beside Ryon. "Where are we going?"

"We're paying a visit to Paulie."

Lailu froze. "Paulie? As in Paulie Anna, the witch?"

"That would be the one. I need something to take care of wormrot at my home."

Lailu wrinkled her nose. "Wormrot?"

"Yep. A mystical fungus that's quite common in these parts. Grows on wood, and can really damage the strength of a building if not treated soon enough," Ryon said. "You should scrape some off and try to make it into a salad or something."

"Ha ha."

It was hard to picture Ryon living in an ordinary house and taking care of domestic things. He was just so . . . sneaky. She tried imagining him doing dishes or folding laundry, and it made her head ache. And now that she knew he was half elf, she had to wonder if that changed anything for him. Did he have magic? Did he spend half his time among the elves? She realized she had no idea what he did when he wasn't busy skulking around and winking at people.

"Stop looking at me like that," he said.

"Like what?"

"Like you're trying to decide what kind of dish I could be cooked into."

Lailu smiled. "I wouldn't dream of cooking you. But if I did, it would be a delicious pot pie. I would call it Mystic Cooking's Skulduggery Special."

Ryon laughed. Still, despite how lighthearted he seemed, Lailu couldn't help but notice how he kept an eye on every shadow. And every once in a while, she'd hear the *click-click-click* of whatever was following him. It made her skin feel tight and itchy, and she was almost relieved when they reached Paulie's Potions.

Almost.

"Are those human skulls?" Lailu asked, eyeing the window in front.

"Don't worry, they're fake." Ryon peered closer at them. "I think," he amended. He climbed up the steps two at a time, leaving Lailu to either hurry after him or stand there feeling like a scared little kid. She shifted nervously. Back in her village, people tended to stay away from anyone who did magic. And after Lailu's experience with the elves, she didn't blame them. She could still remember the taste of sulfur, the hunger for blood, the way she'd begun oozing into a new shape, her old one as forgotten as a distant dream.

Loosening her knife in its sheath, she reluctantly tiptoed up the stairs to join Ryon.

From inside Lailu thought she could hear a woman laughing, and a man's voice. "Maybe we should come back? And by 'we,' I mean 'you,'" Lailu said. "She sounds busy."

"What's the matter? Chicken?"

"Don't call me that."

"Oh yeah, I almost forgot. You really don't like those creatures, do you?" He smirked. "Maybe Paulie might turn you into one. You know, just for an hour or two."

Lailu blanched and almost fell off the porch. "C-could she really do that?"

He shrugged, then knocked.

"You mean you don't know?" Lailu was feeling worse and worse about this.

"I'm actually not sure what the limits are when it comes to human magic. But I don't think so—"

The door opened abruptly. "Wait for me. I'll just be a moment," a young woman said to someone behind her.

Lailu gaped at her. She had long, wavy black hair and bright purple eyes, and she looked barely older than Ryon. Hands down, she was the most beautiful girl Lailu had ever seen . . . well, aside from Hannah. *This* was Paulie Anna? *This* was the witch of Twin Rivers?

"You're here about that wormrot, aren't you?" she asked Ryon.

"You read my mind."

Lailu felt sick. "She can read minds too?" she whispered.

Paulie heard her. The witch's elegantly shaped brows lifted, and she let out a peal of laughter that seemed to brighten the air around her. "Don't worry, sweet one. It was just a little joke. Ryon sent a message ahead."

"Oh." Lailu's face burned.

"Come in, come in," Paulie said, stepping back.

"We wouldn't like to interrupt your guest," Ryon said carefully.

"I'm sure he won't mind," Paulie said, urging Ryon and then Lailu inside. "I don't like to leave my front door open too long. The veil between is much too thin on a week like this."

"The veil between? Between what?" Lailu asked.

Paulie just smiled mysteriously.

Lailu wasn't sure what she was expecting when she followed Ryon inside, but Paulie's shop was small and very tidy. Surprisingly so, considering every shelf was full, and stacks of labeled jars and pouches covered every counter. Lailu could smell a hundred different herbs and spices, especially cinnamon. It reminded her of her mother's poultices.

A very familiar face sat at a corner table.

"Vahn?" Lailu said.

Vahn's eyes widened. "Oh, uh, Lil—er, I mean, Lailu." He grinned uneasily and ran a hand through his long golden hair. "I wasn't expecting to see you here." He stood up. "I should be on my way."

"This will just take a second, handsome," Paulie told him.

"No, no, I've taken up too much of your time as it is." He glanced at Lailu, then away. "Thank you, er, for your help." He stepped around Ryon and hurried outside.

"My help?" Paulie frowned. Then she shrugged and handed

Ryon a jar off the counter. "It's freshly cut and cooked. Just sprinkle it around the foundation at the next full moon, and that should take care of it."

"Thank you," Ryon said, sounding politer than Lailu had ever heard him before. "And . . . payment?"

Paulie cocked her head to the side. "The usual, I think."

Ryon nodded. "I'll see you around."

"Have a pleasant evening, the both of you," Paulie called as Ryon and Lailu left, the door closing softly behind them.

"This is where I leave you," Ryon said, hefting his jar. "Have a pleasant evening," he said, imitating Paulie's voice almost perfectly.

"Wait, Ryon." Lailu grabbed his arm. "What about that clicking creature?"

"Left us again at the edge of Gilded Island." He winked.

"Hey, you promised!"

"Sorry. Old habits die hard." He strolled down the street, practically whistling.

Wham!

Something about the size of two of Lailu's fists shot out from behind a building and slammed into him.

Ryon staggered, his jar of wormrot powder smashing to the ground. "Gah!" he cried, grappling with the thing. It came on relentlessly, scuttling up his arm and then latching on with its six long appendages.

"Ahh, get it off!" Ryon punched at it, then tried prying at its legs.

Lailu was by his side in an instant, her knife in her hand. She wavered. She couldn't use the blade, not without slicing Ryon. And anyhow, it was a thing of metal. How could she cut it?

It lifted its metallic head and hissed at Lailu. Just like the automatons, it had two glowing blue eyes. It also had a line slashed horizontally across its "face." That line opened into a crack, then widened until it revealed two sharp needles.

"Lailu!" Ryon yelled. "Don't just stand there!"

Lailu reversed her knife and slammed the hilt into the thing. Its head dented, but it wasn't enough; it sank its needle-teeth deep into Ryon's arm.

He cried out, falling to his knees in the street.

"Get off my friend!" Lailu used her knife hilt again, bashing it on the head as hard as she could. Again. And again.

Finally it fell backward, its legs twitching, its head a ruined crumple of metal. But before Lailu or Ryon could do anything, it flipped back over and scuttled away.

"What . . . the spatula . . . was that?" Lailu asked.

Ryon held his arm against his chest. "I have no idea. But—and I know this might just be the blood loss speaking here—I don't think it wished me well." He winced.

Lailu shook her head, smiling despite her fear. "I don't think so either." She sheathed her knife.

"Caught me the moment I got distracted . . . let down my guard." He staggered to his feet, swaying. "Gonna . . . see Paulie. She'll . . . patch me up." His words slowed, then slurred into nothing. He wobbled, and Lailu caught him.

"Ryon? Ryon!" Lailu slung his good arm over her shoulders, then half walked, half carried him back to Paulie's door.

"Oh my," Paulie said as she let them inside. "You didn't make it very far, did you? Here, lay him in back."

Lailu told Paulie what happened as the two of them moved Ryon to a cot in the back of the small shop.

"Needles?" Paulie's purple eyes widened in alarm. She brought out a small jar and smeared a pungent poultice on Ryon's arm and forehead, then muttered a few words under her breath.

She sat back. "Oh good," she breathed. "It doesn't look like he was injected with anything. Whatever that thing was, it just took a bunch of his blood."

"And that's . . . that's good?" Lailu asked.

"That means he'll recover just fine if he gets enough rest and fluids. I'll keep an eye on him for you."

"Are you sure?"

Paulie nodded. "I know you don't know me or trust me, and I respect that. But Ryon is one of my oldest friends. I'll keep him safe."

Lailu didn't realize they were friends. But then, there was a lot about Ryon she didn't know.

As Lailu walked home, she whispered a quick prayer to Chushi to protect her friend. She knew Ryon could take care of himself, but she kept seeing Carbon's terrified face, frozen forever in death, and the way that metal thing had come sailing out of nowhere, relentless and unstoppable.

It just took a bunch of his blood.

Lailu bit her lip. It had to be something the scientists had created. Did it attack Ryon on Starling's orders? And if so, why?

20

What's in a Name

*L*ailu tugged on her black vest. It flared out gently like a skirt, giving the whole ensemble a more feminine touch that she actually liked.

"Do my eyes deceive me, or is that a faint smile I see on your face?" Hannah looked pleased as punch. "Does this mean that the outfit meets your approval?"

Lailu spun in a slow circle. "I think it will do." She actually loved the eggplant color of the blouse, how fresh it looked, with lace that ended at the hands. Plus the sleeve cuffs had pearly shell buttons. The whole thing felt practical—practical *and* beautiful.

"You think? You *think*?" Hannah threw her hands up. "After all the effort I went through to get this for you."

"And how did you get it for me?"

"Don't sound so suspicious," Hannah scolded. "I didn't *re-home* it, if that's what you think. Starling gave me the cloth. I'm working on a design for her, and thought I'd test it out on you first."

Lailu suddenly didn't find the color or cut so appealing.

Hannah laughed. "Stop making that face. She's not so bad. Besides, I thought you admired her."

"I did, before. But I don't trust her." Lailu flopped down on the bed next to Hannah.

"Easy there. That'll wrinkle."

"I told you about the attack, right? That invention really had it in for Ryon."

"Well, maybe he was sticking his nose somewhere he shouldn't have been," Hannah said, studying her nails. "This was probably supposed to scare him off."

"Maybe." Lailu hedged. "Do you think it will work?"

Hannah sighed. "Of course not. That boy is beyond nosy." She narrowed her eyes. "And I wish I could've done something about your boots."

"My boots?" Lailu blinked at the sudden change in topic. "Why? What's wrong with them?" She studied her well-worn boots. They had served her well throughout her Academy years.

"Lailu, hon, they look like you've battled a mountain dragon in them—"

"Well, I did. You were there—"

"And a hydra," Hannah continued. "I don't think you'll ever be able to get all the swamp gunk off them."

Lailu frowned, kind of seeing what Hannah meant.

Hannah stood and stretched. "I guess I'd better be off." She gathered her brushes, hair combs, and other items from her night-stand and stuffed them into a bag. "I don't want to be late for my appointment with Starling. She's not a fan of tardiness."

Lailu bit her lip. "Just . . . be careful, okay?" She hesitated, then added, "I think Starling might have been behind Carbon's death."

Hannah looked up. "Why? He was working for her."

"He wasn't working very well."

"Hmm," Hannah said, zipping up her bag.

"Do you know what happened to the other hairdressers? The ones Starling fired?"

Hannah laughed. "Oh, Lailu, you act like maybe Starling had them murdered."

"Maybe she did."

"Pishposh." Hannah waved a hand. "I'll ask around, okay? *Carefully*," she added. "Good luck with Greg tonight." She grinned, then sashayed down the stairs.

Lailu did one last check of her supplies, then left her bedroom. As worried as she was about Ryon, she still helped with the festive dinner rush and managed to snag some sleep once she got back. And good thing, too—it was promising to be a long, long night.

Slipshod was in the kitchen when she walked in. "Evening, Pigtails," he said gruffly.

Lailu stared at him. His long, thin hair had been twisted into a low braid. "Y-your hair . . . ," she began.

Slipshod ran a hand over it. "Just something I'm trying out. Never you mind about it."

"And is that my Cooling and Containment cart?"

"Technically, I believe it's Greg's cart."

Lailu flushed. Greg had loaned it to her months ago, and she'd forgotten to give it back. Truthfully she'd gotten kind of attached to it. It wasn't Mr. Frosty, her old Cooling and Containment cart, but it was a close substitute.

"You don't need it today, do you?" Slipshod asked.

"No. Greg has all the food at his place."

"Okay, then." Her mentor closed it up and wheeled it out of the kitchen, with Lailu hurrying after him.

"What do you need it for?" Lailu asked.

"Just . . . testing something out. Oh, and Wren will be here tomorrow morning to begin installations."

"You're okay with that, right? I mean, I don't mind telling her no if you're not sure."

Slipshod laughed. "No, I think this can be a good thing for Mystic Cooking. We can't stay still when times are changing. And good luck at the street fair. Maybe I'll come by and sample some of that hydra of yours." He pulled the cart out of the restaurant.

"Be careful with Mr. Icy!"

Slipshod winced. "You have got to work on that, Pigtails. A chef should be a little more creative when naming things." Shaking his head, he closed the door and was gone.

"What's wrong with Mr. Icy?" Lailu wondered.

Pink and purple clouds blew across the sky as the sun dangled low, like an orange on a branch, the last of its light engulfing the city in a rosy glow. Lailu weaved through all sorts of masked people, rubbing elbows with the rich and poor alike. During the Week of Masks, those differences melted away. She hated crowds and how she could never see over them, but the festive mood was contagious as Lailu watched jugglers and acrobats twirling through the streets, scientists offering rides in horseless carriages, and much more.

Lailu accepted a caramel apple on a stick from a boy with a monkey mask, then continued on toward the bridge, passing tables covered in brightly colored trinkets and booths full of exotic scents. She noticed Melvin's Marvelous Masks was doing brisk business as well, with a whole line of people eagerly waiting to replace their handmade masks for something more exciting. It was hard for her to focus when so much surrounded her, but before she knew it, she was crossing onto Gilded Island, her feet carrying her through the tide of people over to LaSilvian's Kitchen.

Lailu studied the long table out front, admiring the gauzy black-and-gold tablecloth, the silver platters all covered with elegant silver lids, and the gorgeous displays of mystic beasts molded out of porcelain. She especially appreciated the hydra charging down the middle of the table.

"It's about time, assistant," Greg called, grinning behind his fancy phoenix mask. It was truly marvelous, the feathers so realistic that she almost believed it might burst into flames. "Everything is prepped and ready to go. We just need to finish bringing it all out."

Lailu's smile stuck to her face like the caramel on her apple. "Your banner," she whispered.

"You like it?"

Lailu was speechless. Stretched across the front of his restaurant, the banner for their street festival feast proudly proclaimed: *Mystic Cooking and LaSilvian's Kitchen special: Hydra!*

He had put her restaurant's name first.

21

Parade of Mayhem

"I love it," Lailu said, ignoring the crowd shoving past her. She beamed at Greg. "It's perfect."

He put a hand to the back of his neck. "Perfect, huh? High praise coming from you."

Lailu laughed, still staring at the banner. "Your uncle was okay with the restaurant order?"

Greg shrugged. "Honestly, he didn't even want me to include Mystic Cooking at all. But as he's always telling me, LaSilvian's is *my* restaurant. And despite what all the papers are sure to say, you did help take down that hydra. A little."

Lailu narrowed her eyes.

"I mean, a lot. A lot," Greg said quickly. "Besides, I honestly like your restaurant's name better. Of course, I'll never admit this again. But I can tell you tonight." He grinned, and even behind the mask, Lailu could see his eyes crinkling. She realized she'd started to like his grin. Then the rest of his words caught up to her.

"Why do the papers always leave me out?" she demanded.

Greg adjusted his mask. "It's . . . my uncle is friendly with the press." He sighed. "It's his influence. I don't even know what they're writing about me. They don't ask me at all."

"Your uncle sounds like a big fan of mine," Lailu said drily.

"He'll come around. I know I did." Greg froze, the words hanging awkwardly between them. "Uh, let's go get the rest of the food, yeah? Don't want to miss the parade."

The entire street was lit up bright as day, with candles in all the windows and large torches set up every few feet to fight off the chill and the night. Lailu and Greg stood on a broad wooden box set behind their table so they could see over the tops of everyone's heads.

"There're all the Chef Academy students," Greg pointed out. "Oh, and look, Master Sanford!"

Lailu cheered and waved as her former classmates marched past, the seniors in front doing fancy knife-tossing tricks. Behind them strode the teachers, led by Lailu's favorite—a stout, grizzled man in an eye patch. He turned his good eye on Lailu and lifted his knife in a salute as he strode past.

Lailu beamed. "Did you see that? Did you?"

"I saw," Greg said. "He was totally saluting me."

Lailu scowled. "He was saluting *me*."

"Maybe he was saluting both of us?" Greg suggested. "You're missing the heroes, you know."

Lailu turned back to see the heroes marching in formation. At the front strode the younger students, the firelight reflecting off their fancy uniforms. No one in the parade wore a mask, even tonight; this was their chance to be seen by the city, and some of the older students were truly enjoying it, doing flips and spinning their swords in complicated patterns.

Lailu noticed several of the already-graduated heroes marching behind the students, including Vahn. His long blond hair made him impossible to miss, especially when he kept tossing it behind his shoulders and blowing kisses at all the girls.

Lailu frowned. Vahn wasn't the only one preening out there, but it just seemed kind of . . . tacky. She turned away, catching Greg staring at her. "What?" she asked.

Greg shrugged. "Still think he's the most amazing ever?"

Lailu sighed. "I don't know what I think," she said, watching the scholars follow the heroes, their students marching solemn-faced, like they would much rather be indoors studying than parading through cobblestones and crowds. She couldn't help remembering the conversation she'd overheard between Vahn and Hannah, and it filled her with a sick, prickly feeling. Embarrassment? Shame? She'd liked him so much, looked up to him, and this whole time, he thought she was just some annoying little kid. "Anyhow, it doesn't matter. He's interested in Hannah. I think . . . I think they might be dating already."

"Really?" Greg's eyebrows shot up.

"I don't know. Hannah hasn't really told me anything," Lailu admitted, and the thought of actually asking Hannah about it made

Lailu feel like she'd just swallowed a griffin whole. Ryon was right: Hannah really *was* good at keeping secrets. *Maybe she thinks I'm just an annoying little kid too*, she thought sadly.

"Well, I'm shocked. Here I thought Hannah had taste."

Lailu scowled, so distracted that she barely noticed the artists bringing up the rear of the Academy parade. But even her bad mood couldn't hold up when the entertainers jumped in. Jugglers hurled fire into the night sky, masked dancers twirled and spun, and acrobats did flips, tossing each other into the air. One of the dancers laughed and threw her head back, her auburn hair catching the light.

"Mom?" Lailu gasped.

"Seriously?" Greg leaned in beside her, and they both watched Lailu's mother as she sashayed and spun with a group of other women, all wearing brightly colored skirts that sparkled and flowed around them.

Boom!

Lailu almost fell off the box, and Greg put an arm out to steady her.

"Look! It's one of those fireworks!" His teeth flashed white in the darkness as colors raced across the sky in intricate patterns.

"Hannah's show was better," Lailu decided, remembering the time Hannah had used a firework to distract a mountain dragon, saving Lailu from being turned into a fine roast.

"Definitely."

Lailu was suddenly very aware of Greg's arm still around her shoulders. She decided she didn't mind so much. But just because it was cold out. "Do you think the king will really be here this year?" she asked.

Ever since the last king had succumbed to his lifelong illness, it had always been either the queen or Lord Elister representing the royal family at these events. That did nothing to stop the rumors that the young king suffered from the same unnatural weakness as his father, a weakness caused by a curse from the depths of Mystalon, the queen's home country. A curse, it was whispered, brought by the queen herself.

People around here didn't whisper it very often though, or very loudly. Lord Elister did not tolerate that kind of gossip, and he had a way of shutting it down quickly and quite permanently.

"You mean you don't know?" Greg smirked.

"Like you do." Lailu shifted, and his arm fell away from her. It was suddenly colder.

Click-click, whirr, click.

Silence spread over the waiting crowd as everyone craned their heads to see.

"I see Starling has been very busy," Greg said.

"She's been wha—*oh.*" Lailu's chest tightened because now she saw what he meant: Starling had created a whole pack of automatons.

Four of the metal creatures marched in front of an enormous horseless carriage, its front lights illuminating their brassy features, while four more marched behind.

Lailu shivered. She knew Starling had planned on making more of them, but this many? And so quickly! It was like an army. And the carriage itself was much larger than any other Lailu had ever seen, with six wheels on each side so close together, they were nearly touching as they rolled gracefully over the cobblestones. Steam shot out of the large pipes in back, and in front, a scientist with a shock of white hair spun the controls from his perch. Next to him on the raised front bench, Starling beamed and waved. Lailu noticed that the scientist wore a similar flared vest outfit, her red hair twisted into a practical-yet-elegant bun and pinned in place with a starling-shaped comb. Clearly, Hannah was already working her magic.

The carriage itself had an open top, so the passengers were all visible. Lailu noticed one of them was a boy not much older than she was, with blond, curling hair falling to his shoulders. She stared at him, leaning forward so far that the box under her feet wobbled.

Was that the king? It had to be. He was sitting next to the queen, and the resemblance was impossible to miss, with his delicate features and small, slim build. Lailu could understand the rumors of him being sickly; he looked almost more like a pretty doll than a king. Lord Elister sat on the other side of the king, with his two bodyguards sharing the row of seats behind them with . . . Walton? Lailu narrowed her eyes. Yes, the automaton butler was definitely sitting inside the carriage. She'd recognize that bowl of a hat anywhere.

"Do you think the king will be back to try our cooking?" Lailu asked as the auto-carriage rumbled past.

"Doubtful," Greg said. "Even if he did come back, the crowd is looking hungry, so I don't think we'll have much left for him."

Indeed, the people around them were starting to eye their silver platters with interest. Once the royal family had finished driving past, the parade would be officially over, and all citizens would be free to sample the different cuisines. Lailu could hardly wait to share their hydra feast.

The automatons stopped suddenly a few feet down the road, and the auto-carriage rolled to an abrupt halt to avoid running over them.

"This is different . . . ," Greg began.

Lailu's hand dropped to the knife at her hip because she knew from the look on Starling's face that this was not a planned stop. Something was wrong.

Click-click-click.

The nearest automaton cocked its head to look directly over at Lailu and Greg, who froze beneath that glowing blue stare.

Zing!

Four-inch blades appeared out of each metal finger.

"Oh, butter knives," Lailu breathed, as the blue of the automaton's eyes flashed, changing into a sharp, blazing red.

22

AUTOMATON ATTACK

Lailu barely had time to think as the automaton sprang unnaturally high into the air, launching itself right at her. Greg shoved their table over, the automaton's blades embedding themselves into the thick wood as all their food crashed to the ground.

"No!" Lailu cried out, seeing all their dishes spilled, ruined. The expertly seasoned hydra tri-tip, rolls, and finger foods. The elegant platters of—

"Focus, Lailu," Greg hissed. "We still have more hydra. We can make more food . . . if we survive this."

Lailu nodded. Greg was right. Still, it truly hurt her to see good food wasted like that. Especially food that *she* helped make. These automatons had a lot to answer for.

The crowd screamed, people running in all directions. Over it all Lailu could hear Elister shouting, "The king and queen! Protect the king and queen!"

"Look out!" Greg pulled Lailu down as the automaton wrenched its hand free from the table and swiped at their heads. Lailu drew her knife, but the blade was no use against a metal creature. All she could do was fend off its attacks, and just barely; the thing moved impossibly fast, and Lailu knew it wouldn't ever get tired.

"Pans," Lailu gasped, ducking under the automaton's arm and then kicking the table. It slammed into the thing's legs, toppling it. "Grab frying pans," Lailu ordered. She flipped the table and jumped on it, crushing the automaton beneath. To her right, another automaton grabbed a fleeing man by his vest and flung him over the heads of the crowd. Lailu had just enough time to see a woman lunge in with a metal staff before her automaton struggled out from under the table, blades flashing.

Wham!

Greg nailed it with a cast-iron frying pan, hard enough to dent its head.

Pop! Pop! Pop!

Starling stood on top of the carriage, firing shot after shot from a metal, pipelike weapon. With each loud *pop*, the advancing automaton jolted back a step, but it didn't stop. Lord Elister had his infamous curved blades swirling as he stood over the king and queen, his bodyguards standing back-to-back on the other side, and . . . Walton? Walton was fighting the other automatons.

Lailu blinked. Walton ducked a vicious swipe, then brought

its own metal hand up and smacked an automaton to the ground, stomping down on its head.

Crunch!

Lailu shuddered. Seven more to go.

"Lailu, it's not stopping!" Greg's yell brought Lailu back to her own battle. He tossed her a spare pan, and she caught it, spun, and slammed it into the automaton's torso with a very satisfying *clang*.

Click-click. WHIRR.

The metal beast rose up, its legs and arms extending, its body dented and twisted but still going strong. Lailu backed up. How could she kill something that wasn't even alive? How could she stop it?

"Cut the wires!" Starling yelled. "Cut the wires in back!"

Lailu's automaton twitched at the sound of Starling's voice, then jerked back to face Lailu, but it ended up with a face full of skillet instead. As its head spun around from the impact, Lailu used the opportunity to slip her knife in between the metal plates on the creature's neck and rip her blade through the barely exposed wires.

Whirr. Tick-tick . . .

Scalding hot steam shot out from under all the metal plates and joints on the automaton, and with a screech like a dying teapot, it fell over and was still.

Lailu saw the other heroes and chefs fighting the automatons around her. Despite being outnumbered, those creepy metal contraptions were holding their own. They never got tired, they never slowed down, and they had no mercy in their mechanical hearts. Still, Lailu was proud to see Master Sanford battling two at once, slamming a tray into one's face and then slicing through the wires of the second with a meat cleaver. Even her mom was helping—

Lailu's heart rose in her throat. Her *mom* was helping. Lianna didn't have a weapon, but she spun and twirled around an automaton, confusing it, distracting it, then dancing away before it could attack. She was keeping it focused on her long enough for someone with a knife to sever the wires. Only, she was slowing down, and the automaton wasn't.

It managed to backhand her just before a hero cut its wires.

Lianna went sprawling.

"Mom!" Lailu leaped over fallen automatons and moaning people, ducking between two heroes to get to her mother's side. "Are you okay?"

"I'm fine, I'm fine. Help me up." Lianna reached a hand out, and Lailu hauled her to her feet.

The street around them emptied and grew silent as everyone who could get away cleared out. All the automatons had fallen.

All except two. One more rogue automaton . . . and Walton.

The unnamed automaton lunged toward Elister, and Walton sprang forward, knocking it back. They circled each other, metal joints clicking, their movements fluid and much too fast. Walton feinted left, then darted right, managing to slip behind its opponent and tear through the wires in back with one violent swipe of its hand.

The automaton fell, smoking and twitching. Walton stared down at it for a few seconds, then moved to stand at Elister's side, its hat askew, its metal scratched and dented. It cocked its head toward Elister as if awaiting judgment.

Lailu couldn't help but feel sorry for Walton. It had fought bravely against its own. She wasn't sure why it was the only one that hadn't turned on them, but she knew it would still be destroyed. It didn't seem fair.

Elister slowly, deliberately lifted his hand, the crescent blade he held catching the lamplight along its razor-sharp edge. Lailu tensed, but Elister merely leaned forward, and Lailu swore she heard him say something to Walton before the automaton turned and fled through the streets, vanishing into the night.

"It's not like you to be so sentimental, Eli," Lianna said, limping to his side.

"I know. But . . . he's the best butler I've ever had." Elister slid his knives back into their sheaths.

Lailu stared openmouthed between the two of them, her earlier suspicions solidifying like quiche in the oven. Her mom and Lord Elister definitely knew each other far better than they let on. How else would her mother get away with calling the king's executioner *Eli*?

Elister instructed the bodyguards to see the king and queen safely home, then ordered the remaining chefs and heroes to help the wounded.

As Lianna limped back, Lailu's furious questions died in her throat. A nasty gash split her mother's cheek, a purple bruise already forming around it. "Will that scar?" Lailu asked. She didn't know why the idea of her mom carrying a scar bothered her so much, considering how many scars Lailu herself had.

Lianna probed her face, wincing. "No, I don't think so," she decided. "But a small scar is always good to carry as a reminder to be more careful. It would have been a lot worse, except for this." She held up the shattered remains of a lynx mask. "I'll have to get one of my sisters to make me a new one."

"Your sisters?" As far as Lailu knew, her mother was an only child.

"My caravan sisters. The ones I was dancing with. I traveled here with them," Lianna explained.

"And why is that again?" Lailu asked suspiciously.

"Because I wanted to see my beautiful, talented daughter."

That proved it; her mother *had* to be lying. Lailu's eyes narrowed. "Mom, why are you *really* here?"

"Hush, sweetie. Now is not the time to talk about this. Now is the time to be silent. Observant." Lianna jerked her chin in Elister's direction.

He had rounded on Starling, his eyes glowing nearly as brightly as the automatons'.

"How did this happen?" The anger in his voice was enough to make Lailu bite her tongue. But she wasn't going to forget her questions.

Starling quailed. "I—I'm looking into it."

"Your creations endangered my citizens—endangered my *king*!"

"To be fair, the king was never truly in danger while he was at your side," Starling began.

"Do not seek to flatter your way out of this." Elister's hands made a tiny, almost imperceptible move toward his hidden blades.

The scientist paled. "I wouldn't dream of it, my lord. It's not flattery to state a truth we both know." She straightened, composing herself. "And I agree, this was a travesty, and one I will personally get to the bottom of. Allow me a few minutes to examine the automatons, and I'll have some answers for you."

"Make it quick—my patience is rapidly diminishing. As is your future in our country."

Starling flinched. She kneeled over one of the automatons, muttering something to herself as she looked it over.

Lailu inched closer, curious despite her fear.

Starling grasped the faceplate of the automaton and yanked it open, then gasped as something tiny shot out. Something about the size of her finger, with vivid orange wings.

Something that looked suspiciously like a pixie.

23

A CLUE

So that's how they want to play," Starling whispered, watching the tiny speck of orange disappear into the night sky. Her hands curled into fists so tight, Lailu wondered if her skin might burst.

Starling turned, her eyes meeting Lailu's.

Lailu caught her breath, pinned beneath that wall of fury like a bug in a downpour. She had never seen anyone so angry. Even Elister's rage just moments before paled in comparison to this.

Starling blinked, and the anger was gone, swallowed into her clear green eyes as if it had never been. Lailu wasn't sure what to think. Maybe she had imagined it?

The scientist stood and brushed off her pants. "Lord Elister," she called. "I may have found something."

"Yes?" Elister asked.

"This was no mistake in my programming. This was caused deliberately. This was"—she paused dramatically—"magical interference!"

Elister ran a hand over his face. "Starling, if this is about the elves again—"

"I have proof. Irrefutable proof. Will you at least hear me out?"

"If you have proof, then show me," Elister said.

"Perhaps we should go elsewhere first, away from prying ears and eyes." She looked pointedly at Lailu.

Elister sighed. "Dante!" he called. Greg's uncle limped over. "Ah, there you are, good man. Glad to see you are . . . well. More or less." Lailu could understand his hesitation; Dante's long dark hair had come loose and straggled around his head, emphasizing the shadows in his unnaturally pallid face, and his suit jacket hung in tatters from his arms. Lailu almost felt sorry for him.

"Do you have an office we could use, somewhere Starling and I can discuss this incident in private?" Elister asked.

"Of course, my lord. Right away." Dante walked past Lailu, then stopped and looked her up and down. "Sweep this up, would you?" He indicated the spilled platters and tables in the street.

"M-me?"

Dante sniffed. "Unless you think you're too good for that kind of work."

Lailu gaped at him. Of *course* she didn't think she was too good for it—anything related to food, including cleanup, was well within her circle of responsibilities—but his attitude was exactly what she hated about the aristocrats. Before she could think of a good response, Dante had swept past, followed closely by Elister and Starling.

"What an unpleasant man," Lianna decided.

"He's Greg's uncle." Lailu knelt and picked up a shard of pottery.

"Oh, honey, don't hold that against Greg. You can't choose your family." Lianna smiled sadly, taking the shard from Lailu.

Lailu froze. Was her mother referring to Lailu and her father and brothers? Or was Lianna referring to *herself*?

"Can you believe this?" Greg shuffled over. "Not a single bite eaten."

"Are those tears?" Lailu leaned closer. "Are you seriously crying?"

"No," he sniffed. He sniffed again. "Maybe a little."

"It really was an impressive feast." Lailu nudged him with her shoulder. "We'll have a proper funeral for it later, okay?"

"If you two are done crying over spilled food, come see this— *ah!*" Lianna stumbled backward, an automaton faceplate coming loose in her hand. Something small and green flew at her face. She snatched it before it could escape into the sky.

"Are you okay, Mom?" Lailu hurried over.

"I'm fine, just fine," Lianna said, studying the tiny pixie in her cupped palm. "Starling wasn't kidding about magical interference."

"You really think the elves are behind this?"

"Probably."

"But how? I thought they couldn't do magic in the city," Greg said, eyes wide.

Lailu bit her lip, thinking of Eirad and his not-so-veiled hints.

"They can pour magic into a pixie," Lianna said. "So, technically, the pixie is doing the magic for them." She opened her hands wide. The pixie stood up and shook itself like a dog out of water. It put tiny hands on its hips, glared at all of them, and launched itself up into the sky. "And you know how the elves love their sneaky little technicalities," Lianna finished, watching until the small green form had disappeared.

"Mom . . . how do you know all this?" Lailu asked.

Her mother widened her eyes. "Why, honey, you pick up things when you travel a lot. That's all."

Lailu wasn't buying it.

"Can I borrow a knife?" Lianna asked.

Lailu frowned. "Why?" she asked slowly. Borrowing a chef's knives was like taking bites of food off another person's plate. It just wasn't done.

"There's something in here. . . ." Lianna riffled around in the nest of wires inside the automaton's head.

"Here, I'll do it," Lailu said, pushing past her mother. She used the tip of her blade to pop out a small black piece of plastic. "Is this it?"

Lianna took it from her, studying the strange cylinder.

"What is it?" Greg asked.

"I have no idea, but it looks like something important." Lianna's hazel eyes glittered with excitement. "It looks like a clue."

24

THE FUNERAL

*L*ianna managed to slip away before Lailu could get any answers out of her. "Not surprising," Lailu muttered. Her mother had always been good at leaving.

As Lailu and Greg cleaned up their sadly destroyed street feast, Lailu tried pushing the images of the pixies and that strange cylinder out of her mind, aware that too many things were happening. It felt like a huge vat of soup just about to boil, everything simmering and mixing and waiting for just a little more heat. And then what? What would happen?

What was it all leading to?

By the time the last shattered plate was picked up, it was nearly dawn, and Greg insisted on using his uncle's carriage to drive her home. "I'd be just fine," Lailu grumbled, but secretly she was glad about the ride; she felt exhausted, like a wrung-out dish towel.

"Don't forget, one of those automatons escaped," Greg said, pulling the carriage around.

"You mean, *was let go*," Lailu corrected. She climbed inside, enjoying the comfortable seat beneath her and the gentle rocking motion as the horses trotted along. And the quiet. It was so much quieter than the scientists' auto-carriages. She closed her eyes, just for a second.

The carriage stopped.

Lailu woke suddenly and completely, images of automatons with bladed fingers flashing in her mind.

"Relax, sleepyhead. We just arrived at your restaurant," Greg said.

"Oh!" Lailu took a deep breath, her heart still charging. "I'm sorry I fell asleep."

"Don't be. You snore so loudly, I think you chased away all the bad spirits."

"I do not snore!"

"How would you know?"

"Hannah would have told me by now."

"Maybe she's just too nice to say anything."

Lailu opened the carriage door and stomped out.

"What, you're not even going to thank me for the ride?" he asked.

"Thank you for the ride. The carriage was very nice, although the company left something to be desired. Also, I do not snore."

Greg laughed. "Okay, maybe you don't snore—but you do drool. I mean, look at that puddle! Right on my uncle's fine leather seats, too."

"I don't—" Lailu stopped, took a deep breath. He was just

trying to annoy her. And doing an awfully good job. "It's a shame you aren't as good at cooking as you are at being irritating," she said finally.

"I must be amazingly irritating, then, because my cooking is superb." Greg grinned. "And it's a good thing your cooking is better than your insults."

Lailu thought that through. "Thank you? I think."

"Don't mention it."

An awkward silence fell over them. Lailu shifted from foot to foot. Why wasn't Greg leaving? Should she just go inside? Was he waiting for her to leave first? "So . . . ," she began, at the same time that Greg said, "I was wondering . . ."

They both stopped.

"Go ahead," Lailu said.

"Did you want to bake a pie?" Greg asked.

"A . . . pie," she said slowly.

"LaSilvians always make apple pies for funerals. Something comforting to cheer everyone up, you know? Old family tradition."

"Funeral?" Had someone else died? What had she missed? She'd just been asleep for a second!

"You know, for our poor feast?" Greg reminded her. "It's the least that meal deserves."

Lailu hesitated. The idea of baking with Greg seemed like it was crossing some kind of line. Sure, it was fine to hunt and even cook together, but *bake*?

"But I mean, only if you want to. I'm sure you're tired." His shoulders slumped.

He looked so defeated that Lailu decided she'd do it. Plus she was hungry. "Why not?" she said.

"Really?"

"I think I have everything we'd need inside." She smiled. "We'll have pie for breakfast."

"Last apple." Greg tossed Lailu a freshly peeled apple.

She yawned as she sliced it.

The door to the stairs opened, and Slipshod poked his head in. His eyes widened at the sight of Lailu and Greg in the kitchen. "What the blazes are you both doing at this hour? Shouldn't you be resting? We'll be prepping for the dinner rush this afternoon, and you look like you haven't slept in days."

"I slept yesterday," Lailu protested.

"Hmph. Well, I need to go run some errands. Do something about that hair, would you?" Slipshod's own hair was still slicked back in a low braid, his clothing freshly pressed and laundered.

The bell above the front door chimed as he disappeared into the morning.

"Wow," Greg said, wide-eyed. "What the spatula was *that*?"

"I have no idea. He's been really weird for a while now." Lailu frowned. Actually, *everyone* seemed to be weird lately: Slipshod, Hannah, Ryon. Even her mother was acting stranger than usual. The only one who hadn't changed was Greg, who was as obnoxious as ever. It was strangely comforting. "And don't say 'what the spatula,'" she added. "That's my thing."

"I've decided I like it. It can be my thing too," Greg said.

Lailu narrowed her eyes. "Don't you dare. You already took my restaurant idea—"

"We were brainstorming it together!"

"It was *my* idea and you know it."

"I still think I helped," Greg muttered.

Lailu sniffed. "You could help more with this pie."

She worked in silence for a few minutes before Greg burst out, "I've got it!"

"What?"

"He's in love."

"Who?" Lailu asked.

"Master Slipshod." Greg leaned back in his chair. "It would explain all the weirdness."

"No way." Lailu mixed the apple slices into the bowl of cinnamon and sugar until they were well coated, then glared at Greg. "Are you *resting*?"

Greg stood up hurriedly, almost falling over. "Nope. Not at all."

"Good. Then start making some dough balls." Lailu pointed at the ingredients piled up on the counter.

"Don't change the subject," Greg said. "Why can't your mentor be in love?"

"Well, because . . . because he just *can't*, okay?" The idea of Slipshod in love . . . yuck! Lailu shook her head.

"Oh, because you know so much about love." Greg smirked.

Lailu scooped up a handful of flour and chucked it at him, smacking him right in the forehead.

"I can't believe you just did that." Greg's face was full of shock, flour clinging to his hair like a dusting of snow around her mountain village.

"Oh yeah," Lailu laughed. "And I'd do it again."

"I'm so getting you back for that." Greg reached into his own bowl and grabbed some flour. Lailu managed to duck just as white powder burst onto the cabinet above her, showering down into her pigtails.

"Your aim is as terrible as ever," Lailu taunted as she ducked another flour ball. "No wonder I always beat you at knife throw—*gah!*" She tripped over the chair, laughing as Greg smashed a handful of doughy flour right into her hair. "That doesn't count! It was the chair!"

"So I had an accomplice. Still counts."

"My, my, isn't this fun?" Lianna surveyed the scene through the kitchen curtain.

Lailu froze, her face burning. "We were just baking." She looked away from Greg.

"*Just* baking, huh?" Lianna's smile widened. "I see."

"Er, I'll go put those pies in the oven, shall I?" Greg's face was nearly as red as Lailu's felt, but he was still smiling when he turned away to work with the oven.

Lailu brushed the flour from her hair as she followed her mother into the dining room. "Are you going to stick around long enough to answer some questions?" she demanded.

"Absolutely," Lianna said. She reached into her pocket and pulled out the plastic cylinder they'd found inside the automaton. "I think it's time we all had a few answers."

25

A Few Answers

"D o you know what that is?" Lailu asked.

"Watch this." Lianna ran her thumb along the side of the cylinder and pressed down, and the top popped up. She dumped out its contents: a small roll of translucent paper. "See?" She peeled an edge off the roll and pulled it straight. Now Lailu could see a series of tiny pictures in perfect detail, just like the pictures in the newspapers, only much smaller.

"Whoa," Lailu whispered. She remembered how Elister had told her about this new trick.

"It looks like it somehow recorded important moments. Like this one." Lianna tapped a tiny frame. In it, a series of automatons in various stages of creation stood in front of Starling. A few were missing arms or legs, and one had all its limbs, but wires were sticking out all over the place. "I think this was the First Day of Masks, after Starling unveiled these . . . things. I'm assuming she rushed their production after her demonstration didn't go as planned."

Lailu glanced through the other pictures. Most of them were of Starling, but a few were of her scientists. One picture showed Carbon in his signature bowler hat in a huddle with Neon and two other scientists Lailu didn't recognize: a man with amazingly tall hair and a tiny woman. In the background, Lailu could just make out Wren crouched on the floor, watching them. There were no more pictures of Carbon after that, but there was another of Wren, this time working on an automaton. Walton? Probably.

Lailu skimmed the rest of the pictures, pausing at the sight of a very familiar wooden sign, a sign that featured a black splotch of ink below tiny, red writing. Lailu couldn't read the words, but she'd never forget that image: the Crow's Nest, Mr. Boss's old not-so-secret hideout. Why would that be an important moment for the automaton? Frowning, she scrolled through the rest.

Near the end of the roll, the pictures fizzled, the colors running together and turning black. Just before they did, one face was very clear. A face with bright blue eyes and hundreds of blond braids. Eirad, his lips parted, teeth bared in a ferocious smile, caught for just a second before the automaton could record no more.

"It was definitely the elves who sabotaged the automatons for the parade, then," Lailu said, handing the roll back to her mom. Had Eirad killed Carbon, too? She shivered. She knew she couldn't trust him at all, knew he was capable of murder, but still, she just didn't believe it. She looked at her mother and decided it was time to ask other questions. More personal questions. "Mom, why are you here? Really?"

Lianna brushed some of the flour off Lailu's face.

Lailu batted her hand away. "I'm serious. I think I deserve to know."

Lianna sighed. "Look at you, so grown-up, so quickly." She tucked the cylinder out of sight. "Eli asked me to come out here."

"Eli?"

"Lord Elister. He and I . . . we're old friends. Sometimes I see things in my travels that are useful to him. And sometimes . . . sometimes I travel to places that are also useful to him."

Lailu stared at her mother, at her familiar hazel eyes, the crow's feet that had just started to creep out at the corners, her auburn hair twisted back from her face with a bit of colorful cloth. "Mom . . . ," Lailu said slowly, carefully. "Are you a spy?"

Lianna laughed. "Oh, honey, don't be ridiculous."

Lailu relaxed.

"Of course I'm a spy."

Lailu's jaw dropped. The front door chimed, and Hannah waltzed in. "Oh! Mrs. Loganberry! And . . . Lailu? Is that flour on your face? And that expression is really not flattering."

Lailu snapped her mouth shut.

"Pies are in the oven." Greg poked his head through the kitchen curtain.

Wren burst in. "Hi, Lailu! Ready for me to start on the installations?"

"Wow, it's like a regular party in here," Hannah said.

Lailu rubbed her head. She didn't have time for this. She wanted to ask her mother so many questions. How long had she been a spy? Who was she spying on? Who was she spying *for*? Did she just work for Elister? And the question that bothered her the most—why was she so willing to come to Twin Rivers when Elister asked, but she couldn't be bothered to come out for her daughter's graduation? *Does she even care about me at all?* Lailu wondered.

"Lailu?" Hannah said, waving a hand in front of her face.

"Just a minute, everyone. First, Mom—" But when she turned, her mother was gone. "Mom?"

"Oh, she slipped out the back," Hannah said.

"When?"

"Just now. I saw her leaving. . . . I thought you noticed?"

"I was a little distracted by all of you." Lailu sighed. She'd just have to ask her mother later. If she even bothered to show up again.

At least the pies looked was good.

Lailu managed to clean up and get a couple hours of sleep before it was time to prep for their dinner crowd. Slipshod seemed uncharacteristically jumpy. Twice Lailu caught him almost using sugar in place of salt, and once he managed to leave an entire griffin bone embedded in the casserole.

"Is everything all right?" Lailu asked, rescuing the dish and doing what she could to save it.

"Fine, fine. Everything's fine." Slipshod ran a hand down the length of his braid, and Lailu began to wonder if he really *was* in love. He kept glancing into the dining room like he was expecting someone. And she did remember that woman at Elister's party, the one who'd been smiling right at him. . . .

Lailu was relieved when the first customers came piling in. She needed a distraction from her thoughts.

Despite the disastrous street fair, as the evening wore on, Lailu realized there were a lot of new faces coming into her restaurant. Maybe not such a disaster after all, then. Even if their feast had been destroyed, people must have remembered Mystic Cooking and wanted to try some of her cuisine.

"Going back to Starling's tonight?" Lailu asked Hannah as her friend loaded up a tray.

"Yes, after your diners leave. You know, she really appreciates my work. It's been extremely rewarding. I mean, not that this isn't rewarding work here too," Hannah added quickly.

Lailu grunted and loaded up her own tray, then marched out of the kitchen. She tried not to feel betrayed. Still, it was obvious to her now that Hannah couldn't wait to leave Mystic Cooking. It was just a matter of time before she got tired of sticking around and left Lailu behind entirely.

Lailu swallowed hard, her vision blurring. She paused at the edge of the dining room and took a few deep, shaky breaths. It wasn't like her to be so sad so quickly, but she felt like ever since her mom showed up, she'd been off-balance, like she was trying to create a new meal with only half a recipe.

As she forced herself to move forward and serve her customers, she couldn't help noticing how many of them were happy families, complete with parents who showed no signs of running off suddenly. The couples obviously out for a date weren't much better; every time Lailu looked at them, she thought of Hannah and Vahn, and her chest ached. She didn't care about Vahn anymore, but she hated the thought of losing her friend. Between Vahn and Starling, would there be any Hannah left for her?

Lailu was so distracted that she didn't notice the familiar figure sitting at the table in the back corner until she was practically on top of him.

"Mr. Mustache?" Lailu gasped, recognizing one of Lord Elister's bodyguards. Mr. Mustache and someone who looked like his clean-shaven twin sat together, with a slender boy nestled between them. Lailu scanned the room for Elister, but he wasn't around. So what were his bodyguards doing here without him?

Hannah strode past.

"Wait," Lailu began, but it was too late; Hannah had already gone right up to the table.

"And what can I get you fine gentlemen?" Hannah asked, and Lailu realized her friend had no idea who they were.

Mr. Mustache narrowed his eyes at her, completely impervious to her charm. "Nothing." His twin grunted in response.

"I see," Hannah said slowly. "You came to our restaurant for the fine atmosphere and comfortable seating arrangements only, is that it?"

"I wanted to eat here," the boy sitting in the middle said. Lailu hovered behind Hannah, peeking out at him. He had a long, narrow face with high cheekbones, a delicate nose, and thick eyelashes framing large amber eyes. His hair was a pale blond that curled slightly at the ends where it brushed his thin shoulders. He reminded her of a bird, all hollow-boned and ready to fly away at a moment's notice. And he looked so familiar . . . but he couldn't possibly be . . .

"Wonderful!" Hannah turned the full force of her smile on him, and he seemed to melt under it, his cheeks burning. "One special, then?"

He nodded, and Hannah sashayed away.

Lailu remained frozen, staring at him. There was no way he was . . .

She was absolutely sure the king would not be eating in their tiny restaurant crammed in the bad side of town.

Would he?

"Move along, chef," Mustache barked. "There's nothing to see here."

Lailu moved along. Her heart thumped painfully against her rib cage as she went to find Slipshod.

"Are you sure?" he asked her when she told him. His face had gone the color of unbleached flour.

"No, but I think so," Lailu said.

"This is it. This is my chance," Slipshod mumbled. "He said he might . . . but I wasn't sure . . ."

"What do you mean?" Lailu asked. Her mentor did not look like himself, his eyes glazed, his hands held curled up at his chest, almost like a puppet being lifted from a box.

Slipshod took a deep breath, collecting himself. He adjusted his fluffy white chef's hat, straightened his apron, and tucked his braided hair back. "How do I look?"

"Um," Lailu said, "fine, I guess?"

Slipshod shook his head. "The one time I need Hannah," he grumbled. "Okay, Pigtails, I'll handle him myself. Go see to the other customers."

Lailu nodded, relieved. The other customers, she could handle.

26

GENERATOR ON!

Lailu flipped the sign over to CLOSED and sagged against the door. She could hardly believe the king—the *king!*—had eaten at her restaurant.

"That went about as well as I could have hoped," Slipshod said, rubbing his hands together.

"Did you know he was coming?" Lailu asked.

"I . . . er—"

Crash! Bam! Smash!

Lailu jumped. What was going on?

"Is that Wren?" Hannah asked. "Do you think she's almost done installing the generator?" Wren had started working that morning and had been down in the wine cellar banging away ever since.

"That, or possibly smashing all our wine bottles." Lailu flinched at the sound of another crash. She bit her lip. "Maybe I should go and check on her."

"Good idea, Pigtails," Slipshod said. "I'm going to go run a few errands. Make sure she doesn't destroy everything in my absence."

"Errands? Again?" Lailu asked. "Do you need my help?"

"No, no, better that you stay here."

The floor shook with another crash.

Slipshod winced. "Yes, definitely better. Keep an eye on things." And he headed out before Lailu could stop him.

"Do you really think he's gambling again?" Lailu asked Hannah.

"I don't know. None of the money has gone missing, and he says he isn't, but . . ." Hannah shrugged. "He's definitely up to something."

Wren burst through the kitchen curtain, almost knocking Lailu over in her excitement, her red hair a tangled cloud around her face. "I did it! I installed it! Quick, blow out all the candles." Then she dashed back inside the kitchen, vanishing beneath Lailu's trapdoor into the cellar.

Lailu hesitated. You weren't supposed to extinguish all candles during the Week of Masks. A house without candles was a house inviting in the darkness and ghosts. Feeling uneasy, Lailu moved through the room with her candlesnuffer, until only one candelabra was lit.

Hannah clapped, her eyes wide and gleaming. "This is it, Lailu, we're in the big leagues now. Slipshod is going to be sorry he missed this. Here, let me help you." And she blew out the remaining candles, plunging them both into darkness.

"Hannah!" A slow trembling began beneath Lailu's feet, like

she was standing near a charging hydra. She put a hand to the knife at her waist and spun, waiting for her eyes to adjust to the darkness.

Flash!

The dining room exploded in a burst of light. Lailu blinked rapidly to clear the floating blue spots in her vision.

"She did it!" Hannah grabbed Lailu's hands and twirled her around in a circle. "Oh, Starling is going to be *so* pleased! She wasn't sure if Wren would be able to manage this on her own." She dropped Lailu's hands and picked up a mask off the table near her.

A fox mask.

"Isn't that Ryon's?" Lailu stared at it. But no. Ryon's was a reddish-brown color, whereas Hannah's was silvery white, the eye sockets lined with sparkles. Lailu's stomach filled with a mix of guilt and worry. She hadn't seen him since he was attacked. She had barely thought of him in all the excitement lately.

Hannah adjusted the mask over her face, then shrugged into a matching white coat. "Ryon doesn't get to be the only fox in the city," she said, winking.

Lailu shuddered. "Don't do that."

"What?"

"That whole winking thing. It's too creepy coming from you."

Hannah laughed. "Well, I'm off to tell Starling how it went. Don't wait up!"

Wren danced back into the dining room. "I did it! I really did it!" Her smile stretched from ear to ear, and despite her misgivings about all things new and scientist-related, Lailu couldn't help but smile too. Plus she had to admit, her restaurant looked pretty amazing with several orbs descending delicately from the ceiling, casting their glow over everything.

"I'll add a switch inside so you don't have to go downstairs to turn them on and off," Wren said. "And I think I can rig up a dimmer, so you won't need to have them so bright all the time if you don't want."

"Thanks, Wren. You did a great job. I'm sure your mom will be proud."

Wren's smile wilted. "I hope so," she said. "She's been in a terrible mood lately."

"Oh yeah?" Lailu thought of Carbon again, and the automatons going haywire. "I can see why. How's Hannah been working out for her?"

"Oh, she's been great," Wren shrugged. "Mama only laughs when she's around." She scuffed her foot against the hardwood floor. "I mean, I like Hannah, I do, but does she always have to be so much in the center of everything?"

"What do you mean?"

"Like, when she's standing there, Mama doesn't notice me. She does it to you, too. I've seen it."

Lailu opened her mouth to argue, then remembered Vahn's words. "She doesn't mean to," she said instead.

Wren shrugged. Then she brightened. "Are you free now?"

"Not exactly," Lailu hedged. True, she didn't have any parties to go to or dinners to cook, but their supplies were running dangerously low. "I need to go hunting tonight. I'm just waiting for Slipshod to come back."

"Oh, he's going to be out all night," Wren said offhandedly.

"What? Why?"

"He didn't tell you?" Wren blinked her wide green eyes. "He received a Royal Invitation."

"H-he did?" And he hadn't taken *her*? "He just told me he was running errands," Lailu said. She felt like her lungs were missing air, like a griffin had just tossed her. She was his apprentice. She should have gone with him. Or at least he could have told her about it. Did everyone know but her?

"Oh, sorry. This might have been one of those things I was supposed to keep to myself." Wren sighed. "I never know which things are secret and which aren't. Mama is always telling me to keep my mouth shut, but it's hard to do all the time."

"No, I'm glad you told me." She wasn't, though. *Slipshod* should have told her. Suddenly she was angry. "I guess I'm going hunting alone."

"Oh good," Wren said quickly. "I'll come with you."

"Er, what?"

"I want to test out those harnesses, make sure they're working properly for you. This is a perfect night to try them out, right?"

"Um, maybe we should wait?" Lailu's stomach ached just thinking about going back in one of those death traps. "I mean, Slipshod would want to be here. Plus it's dark out."

Wren drooped faster than a cake in the sun. "I understand. I know I got the generator to work all on my own, but I don't blame you for not trusting me with the harnesses."

"It's not that."

"Really? So you do trust me?"

"Of course."

"Then let's go! I mean, unless you're just scared." She frowned. "I hope you're not scared. I told Mama you were the bravest person I know."

"Really? You really said that?"

"Of course." Wren's smile was back. "So, what are we hunting? Griffins again?"

And Lailu knew she was trapped as surely as if Wren had thrown a net around her. "No," she sighed. "Not griffins. If they're smart, and they usually are, they'll have moved farther from town. But when griffins abandon a nesting spot, often raptierols will move in. They're not as dangerous, but if left alone, they breed like mad." And they tasted delicious panfried, baked, broiled, or mixed into a good pasta. Lailu realized she was already mentally planning a menu around them. Maybe hunting with Wren at night in a harness wouldn't be so bad after all.

27

HUNTING IN HARNESSES . . . AGAIN

*I*cy wind beat at Lailu and Wren as they dangled in their harnesses from the side of the cliff. The chill air felt like thorns on exposed skin, a feeling Lailu was no longer used to. Back at home in her mountain village, this would have been a warm night, but here in Twin Rivers, this cold air promised an early, bitter winter.

"O God of Cookery," Lailu whispered, "what was I thinking?" Hunting at night in a harness with only a young scientist for backup? This had to be her stupidest idea yet. Even worse than bargaining with elves . . .

Well, maybe not quite that bad. And certainly not as bad as owing Greg a favor.

"This was my third-stupidest idea yet," Lailu decided.

"What's that?" Wren called, her voice snatched away by the howling wind. "You're ready to go?"

"What? No, I'm no—*ahhhhhh!*"

Wren slapped a button on the front of Lailu's harness, and Lailu shot down the cliff. All the flailing of her arms did nothing to slow her down.

Wren fell next to her, her laughter tearing through the night.

The harness jerked and thrummed like a living thing, and then it finally caught, slowing Lailu's descent, then gradually stopping. Lailu hung there for several long seconds trying to teach herself how to breathe again. She could feel the straps digging into her thighs and around her waist and tried to take comfort from that. She was secured. She wasn't going to fall out. The rope that looped through the front of her harness and attached to the box on top of the cliff was thick and sturdy and not going to break. Probably. Which was a good thing because they were hanging about halfway down the cliff, just above the first of the old griffin caves.

The moon wasn't quite full; it would be on the Seventh Night of Masks, two nights away, but it was large enough to bathe the landscape in light. Nothing stirred except for a gentle breeze.

"Ready to lower?" Wren whispered. Her hair was a giant red tangle around her face, her green eyes wide behind her magnifying goggles. "Ready to hunt?"

"Just about." Lailu loosened her knife in its sheath. "I don't hear anything, so there's a chance the raptierols haven't moved in yet. But if they have, they can be dangerous, okay? They have sharp claws, and they move quickly."

"Okay," Wren said.

Lailu paused. Wren looked so young. "Maybe you should wait here."

"No, I want to come." Wren smiled. "Don't look so worried, Lailu. I'm prepared. Now, you just tap this button when you want to lower, and you should be able to manually let yourself down. If you start falling fast, it has an auto-lock that should stop you, like what happened when we first jumped." Wren indicated the button on the front of their harness belts.

Lailu bit her lip. There were an awful lot of *should*s in that explanation. She eased back in her harness and put her feet against the wall, like she was sitting in a chair. Gripping the rope firmly in one hand, she carefully pushed the button, then walked her feet slowly down the cliff as the box secured to the top spooled her rope out a few inches at a time.

This was definitely better than the free fall she'd been doing earlier. Lailu still didn't like it, but at least her heart wasn't leaping out of her throat. Clearly Wren knew what she was doing when she fixed these.

Lailu dropped down until she was peering into the caves.

Empty.

A few griffin feathers and a pile of bones were the only indication that these caves had ever been occupied.

"Hey, I'm not sure there's anything here," Lailu said.

Wren frowned at the cave, then began fiddling with her harness.

"What are you doing? Wren? Wren!"

But it was too late. Wren's harness lowered, the rope developing enough slack to drop her to the cave floor. "I just want to look around," she called, pulling something out of one of her bulging pockets. She shook it, and light streamed out, illuminating the long cave. The left side veered out, disappearing into blackness, and Lailu hoped nothing hid in that tunnel.

Lailu looked down at the ground far, far below. So far it was impossible to see it clearly. She thought she caught a gleam from the river twisting below, and she shivered. "I think we'll need to hunt elsewhere. There are lots of things in the Velvet Forest."

"Nah, the elves are in there, and they've already told me what they'll do if they catch me in their territory. Besides . . ." Wren grinned. "This is much more interesting." She held up a skull.

A human skull. Picked completely clean of flesh, the bone blackened.

Lailu's stomach plummeted faster than any harness. A griffin wouldn't have been able to do that. There were only a few creatures that could achieve that level of destruction and would find an abandoned griffin home an acceptable den, and none of them would be good to face here, unprepared.

She had to get Wren out of there, now.

Scratch. Scratch. Scratch.

The sound of heavily taloned feet scraping against stone echoed down the recesses of the tunnel. Each noise was like a knife sawing at Lailu's nerves. "Wren, get out of there, now."

"Just a minute," Wren said, tucking the skull away in her pack.

"Wren!" Lailu hissed, already fumbling with her harness, but it wouldn't work. The lock mechanism had jammed so she couldn't lower herself.

She popped the leg straps open and undid the belt, leaping into the cave just as the creature turned the corner.

28

REFLECTION

The second Lailu's feet hit the cave floor, she dove at Wren, knocking her backward. A blast of white-hot fire fizzled through the air, just barely missing them.

White-hot fire . . . combined with the scratching sound of chicken feet.

Lailu went cold. She knew exactly what they were dealing with: a cockatrice.

A distant relative of the fyrian chickens Lailu hated and feared so much, the cockatrice was something no chef would hunt without months of preparation and reliable backup. One look directly into a cockatrice's bloodred eyes meant instant death. Not looking meant risking a blast of fire so hot, it could melt rock.

Wren started to turn.

"Don't look!" Lailu grabbed her and pulled her to the cave entrance. "Its gaze can kill."

Wren's eyes widened behind her goggles. She flicked a switch, and her goggles went completely dark. Lailu didn't have any sort of magic goggles, but even without looking, she knew the cockatrice was close. She could smell it, the musty stink of chicken mixed with the sulfuric smell of bad eggs.

These beasts were extremely rare, as one of the few things that could kill a cockatrice was the gaze of another cockatrice, so they avoided each other's company and did not often breed. A mixed-up combination, they had the body and teeth of a small, sinewy dragon with the head and legs of a giant, vicious chicken.

Lailu wrapped herself around Wren like a backpack and pulled her off the cliff edge.

The air sizzled above them as another white-hot blast of fire missed them by inches. Lailu punched the button on the front of Wren's harness to belay them back up the cliff, the harness buzzing angrily beneath the weight of two people. But it had to work. If it could hold Slipshod, it could support the weight of two girls.

"Can you make it go faster?" Lailu panted as they inched up.

"Not safely," Wren said. "And where's your harness? You're choking me."

"If I was choking you, you wouldn't be able to say that I was choking you," Lailu said, but as they left the cave entrance below them, she adjusted her hold on Wren. Just a little, though. She was very aware of the fact that only her grip on Wren saved her from the very long drop beneath her. "And I had to jump out of my harness. I couldn't get the button to work."

"Oh no!"

"What? What?" Lailu frantically looked around.

"That means I didn't get something right when I fixed it." Wren sighed and pushed off against the wall with her feet, guiding them up. "I'll have to take another look. At least it didn't burst into flames on you."

"Was that an option?"

"Well . . . sometimes my inventions have a tendency to explode."

"Good to know." Lailu made a mental note to never again use one of Wren's inventions. Then she thought of the power generator in her wine cellar, and her blood ran cold. "Er, that power generator thing you made? Should I be concerned?"

"Oh no, that's pretty solid. I barely tinkered with Mama's design at all."

Somehow that was not completely comforting.

"Also, I think it's coming after us."

"What?" Lailu twisted around, almost losing her grip on Wren as the cockatrice launched itself from the cliffs below them. "O God of Cookery," Lailu breathed, turning away from it. She'd been counting on the fact that they rarely flew after prey. But she knew there would be no escaping it by going back up. Wren would have to unclip from her harness, and cockatrices were notoriously fast over short distances. They'd never be able to outrun it—or its fire.

Her mind moved at breakneck speed. Only blades made from forged iron heated by phoenix fire and doused in the western fairy springs of Mystalon were able to slice through a cockatrice's scaly hide; Lailu's chef's knives wouldn't stand a chance.

No, the surest way to kill a cockatrice was with its own formidable weapons. Get it to somehow roast itself, or trick it into seeing its own reflection.

Lailu thought of the river down below. In most parts, the water would be too rough, too choppy. But there was that one little outlet, the place where Slipshod had fallen. Maybe that would be calm enough to act as a mirror. But would the sky be light enough? The sun wouldn't rise for another hour.

It didn't matter; the cockatrice was gaining on them, and they were out of other options. "We need to go down." Lailu reached around Wren and switched the lever.

They dropped immediately, dropped without any resistance at all, dropped like they were free-falling and would never stop. Lailu didn't even have time to scream. She could feel the heat of the cockatrice as she and Wren shot past it.

Wren flicked another lever, and the harness clicked, then slowed gradually until they were only a foot off the ground. Lailu hopped down on shaky legs, the river roaring behind her.

"That worked perfectly." Wren beamed.

"Now is not the time, Wren," Lailu said, searching the sky for the cockatrice. "Hurry and get out of that—"

The cockatrice landed behind them. Lailu could feel it, could smell it, could practically taste it. She froze. If she turned, she risked looking it in the face. If she ran, she left Wren tied up in the harness like a tasty pre-dawn snack.

The beast gave a strangled cry, the roar of a dragon forced through the throat of a rooster. Lailu clapped her hands over her ears. She had to do something. She had to run and hope it followed her.

Stumbling forward, Lailu raced along the river, the cockatrice right on her heels. She darted erratically from side to side, avoiding blasts of fire so hot her clothing sizzled and the ends of her pigtails were singed.

Lailu gasped and ran harder, changing direction as often as she could. She felt like she'd never reach the spot. She turned, darting sharply to the side, and it was there, right in front of her. Past the rocks and the foam-topped waves where the curve of the river created a natural swimming hole, the water looked pristine and smooth as a mirror.

A blast of heat raced toward her, and she leaped into the river, plunging into its icy depths. She clung to a rock underwater and waited. The shape of the cockatrice loomed over her, and she peered up at it carefully. It was mere feet above her, so close she could have reached out and touched it, too close for her to escape. It was staring at the calm pool, at the hint of its reflection in it.

And it was still very much alive.

29

MAL-CANTATION POWDER

Lailu's lungs burned, and she knew she'd have to come up for air soon. And when she did, the cockatrice would be waiting. There'd be no escape.

She should have known this was how she would die: at the talons of a chicken.

And then she noticed another silhouette moving toward the cockatrice. A Wren-shaped silhouette.

The cockatrice started to turn, and Lailu reacted. She shot up to the surface, her knife already in her hand. Caught between Wren and Lailu, the cockatrice had a brief split second of hesitation.

Wren tossed some sort of glittery powder at it just as Lailu threw her knife, the blade soaring straight into the beast's left eye.

It roared and collapsed onto the riverbank, its healthy eye rolling up into its head.

Lailu and Wren stared at each other. "What did you do to it?" Lailu asked.

"I knocked it out."

"With what? What *is* that stuff?"

"This stuff?" Wren held out the pouch to Lailu, who took it carefully. It was a simple leather pouch, the powder inside one moment black as pitch, the next bright as the stars in the sky. "General Tori created it out of particles he discovered on Beolann. We call it mal-cantation powder."

"Mal-cantation powder." It sounded familiar, but Lailu couldn't remember where she'd heard that name before. "What does it do?"

"It neutralizes magic."

"Wow! Really?" Plenty of mystic chefs had searched for a way to neutralize magic, but as far as Lailu knew, all of them had failed. "That sounds really useful."

"It is, but its effects wear off in about an hour. You can keep that, if you'd like."

Lailu tucked it away in her vest. It certainly couldn't hurt. "Thanks, Wren."

"Well, Mama might not be pleased. I mean, we're running low, but I think I've found a good replacement substance that works even better."

"So, if the effects wear off in an hour, that means it's not dead?" Lailu prodded the cockatrice with her boot. She wanted to pull her knife out, but she was afraid to.

"Not unless your knife to the eye killed it."

"I don't think so." Lailu hadn't realized she could even wound a cockatrice. Maybe their eyes were their weakness? Or more likely, it was the combination of the knife and Wren's powder that did the trick.

"Then I guess we'd better take care of that." Wren put her foot against the unconscious creature's head and yanked out Lailu's knife. Then she rolled back the other eyelid and jammed the blade in to the hilt, twisting it.

Lailu gasped.

The cockatrice shrieked and gurgled, flailing for a few seconds, and then was still. And this time, Lailu was sure it was dead.

"Wren . . . ," Lailu began, her stomach filling with dread at the sight of Wren standing there so calmly, her hands covered in blood.

"What?" Wren asked. "It's not a successful hunt if you don't actually kill your target, is it?"

"But . . . it was unconscious." Lailu had killed plenty of beasts, and she had no love at all for the cockatrice, but there was something very disturbing about the way Wren had killed it while it was so defenseless. Emotionlessly, mercilessly, like it was any other task. Like she was turning off a machine, and not taking a life.

30

Mother's Intuition

*L*ailu cut and separated the cockatrice meat while Wren hummed happily behind her. Wren had been in an exceptional mood ever since the hunt, and as soon as they got back to Mystic Cooking, she had insisted on working on more improvements for the restaurant.

"This is going to change everything for you," Wren had said before drilling a hole through the kitchen floor, where she had explained the pipes needed to go. She swore that Lailu would have running hot and cold water no later than tomorrow.

While the idea of running water in her restaurant was fantastic, Lailu kind of wished that Wren would just leave. Morning light had already warmed the city, and Lailu really wanted to get some sleep before Mystic Cooking opened that evening. Plus . . . Wren made her uncomfortable. Lailu wasn't sure why she was so bothered by the way her friend had dispatched the cockatrice. It had just seemed so cold.

As a mystic chef, Lailu had an obligation to take out those beasts that threatened the citizens of Twin Rivers. Or sometimes she would thin out a herd, or a pack, or a swarm, so that the rest of the creatures in it would be better able to survive.

It's not like they feel pain.

Lailu remembered Wren's words about the elves, how they were just creatures, and shivered.

"Are you going to be serving the cockatrice tonight?" Wren asked. She looked quite bizarre in her goggles, one eye magnified much larger than the other. A blue light glowed above the smaller of the lenses, reminding Lailu eerily of Walton—who was still running free, somewhere in the city. . . .

Lailu gave herself a mental shake. "No cockatrice tonight. It won't be safe to serve until tomorrow."

"Aww, too bad. What are you serving tonight?"

"Apparently Master Slipshod caught some freshwater carper fish the other night. I saw them marinating in the icebox."

"Interesting. I didn't realize he did so much hunting without you."

"He doesn't. . . . Not usually."

"Does it make you sad, being left behind so much?"

"I'm not left behind," Lailu said, annoyed.

"Uh-huh. So . . . where is your mentor now?" Wren smiled brightly.

"I don't know." Lailu thought of the Royal Invitation he'd gotten, the one she apparently wasn't supposed to know about. Maybe he was still at the palace. Her irritation turned to hurt, and she put down her knife. Maybe Wren was right, and she *was* being left behind. There was no denying that Master Slipshod had been distracted lately by . . . something. *Something he isn't sharing with me*, she thought sadly.

"It's okay, Lailu." Wren patted her on the shoulder. "I understand how it feels. First Hannah, and now your mentor, too."

Lailu had almost forgotten about Hannah and her new job, but Wren was right. How long before Hannah moved back out to Gilded Island? And it wasn't just Hannah and Slipshod. Ryon had vanished for months before coming back. Her mom would leave, of course. Everyone would go on to bigger, better things until Lailu was left here alone. Just her and her cooking.

She pictured herself alone in the kitchen of Mystic Cooking. She used to think that was all she needed, but it seemed lonely to her now.

"I can stay, if you'd like? To help you with the restaurant today?" Wren pushed her goggles up onto her forehead. "I wouldn't mind. It's fun to cook with you."

Lailu hesitated. Wren made her uncomfortable, but she was also the only one who *hadn't* left her yet. Greg's face flashed through her mind, and she realized she could count on her rivalry with him, too. *He* wasn't going anywhere. The thought made her smile. "I think I'm okay," Lailu began.

Lailu's mother yanked back the curtain, a newspaper tucked under one arm. She wore her most colorful scarf and matching orange, yellow, and red skirt. It almost distracted the eye from the large purplish bruise across her face, a reminder of her fight with the automatons. "Why, hello, girls." Her warm gaze seemed to take in Lailu, Wren, and the entire kitchen. "Isn't this nice? Must have been a successful hunt."

"Oh, it was amazing, Mrs. Loganberry," Wren gushed. "Lailu took out a cockatrice."

"She did *what*?" Lianna's head whipped around, her eyes searching Lailu intently. Lailu recognized the look: her mom was checking her over for injuries.

Lailu grimaced. "I'm not hurt, Mom. Just a couple scrapes and bruises. And it wasn't really me—"

"Yes, right through the eye with a knife throw. Can you believe it?" Wren continued, talking right over Lailu. "The cockatrice went 'Bleh!' and fell over dead."

"That's not exactly how it went," Lailu began, with a sideways look at Wren.

"Yeah, it didn't actually say 'Bleh,'" Wren agreed.

Lailu frowned but didn't correct her again. Maybe Wren felt bad about killing it.

"That's surprising," Lianna said. "I didn't think you could kill a cockatrice with a normal knife." She glanced at Lailu. "Don't look so shocked, honey. You've been talking about strengths and weaknesses in these beasts for years, and I pay attention."

"When you're around, maybe." Lailu wasn't sure why she said

it; she just knew she was tired of the way everyone found it so easy to leave her behind, and the words escaped her lips like noodles slipping off a spoon.

Her mom's eyes widened.

"It was my first real hunt," Wren continued, oblivious to the way the temperature in the room seemed to drop. "I learned so much and—"

"That all does sound exciting," Lianna cut her off. "It also sounds like Lailu could use some rest before the dinner crowd arrives. Can I help you pack up your stuff, Wren?"

"Oh, that's okay. I can pack it myself." Wren went right on working.

Lianna pursed her lips, and Lailu realized her mother had no idea how literally Wren took people's words.

"Wren, I think my mother was trying to politely ask you to go."

"Really?" Wren asked.

"Some quality mother-daughter time," Lianna said. "I'm sure you understand."

Wren flinched. "Maybe someday I will," she said sadly.

Lailu's heart ached. "Or, you know, if you'd like to stick around—"

"You can come back and visit us later," Lianna finished quickly. "But we need some time alone now. I'm sorry."

Wren packed up her tools and left, promising to return tomorrow to finish the installation.

Lianna waited until the front door was shut and Wren's

auto-carriage had roared away before turning back to Lailu, her expression solemn.

Lailu braced herself. This was it. This was the moment when she would tell her mom everything. All those mornings back home when she would slip out of her bedroom and feel the stillness of the house and know that once again, her mother had left. The way her father would retreat into his workroom, the sound of her brother Lonnie crying softly, while her oldest brother Laurent acted like nothing was wrong at all. How her mother's absence created a hole inside their home, a cavity that kept the rest of them separated.

Lailu swallowed. "I—" she began.

"So what really happened on your hunt?" Lianna asked.

"Um, er, well . . . ," Lailu fumbled. It felt like the griffin hunt all over again—like she was poised to strike and just . . . couldn't. Instead the truth of the hunt came tumbling out, the use of mal-cantation powder and the way Wren had been the one to make the kill. And Lailu let the other truths slide back under the surface.

"Mal-cantation powder," Lianna mused, tapping the newspaper into the palm of her hand. "Hmm."

"Is it important that Wren was the one to kill the cockatrice?" Lailu asked.

"All details are important, my sweet." Lianna unfolded the newspaper and dropped it in front of Lailu. One headline jumped out immediately:

Elf Found Dead in Warehouse District

Lailu felt like all the air in her lungs had turned to jelly. She sank to the floor, clutching the paper, her eyes moving down the article automatically.

> Gwendyl, age 237, was discovered dead in the Warehouse District. Cause of death could not immediately be determined, although there does not appear to have been a struggle. As of this printing, there has been no response from the elves.

(story continued on page 3)

Lailu looked up. "What does this mean?" she whispered.

Lianna knelt in front of Lailu. "Oh, honey, you know what this means. The scientists have a powder that neutralizes magic. That knocks out magical creatures." She brushed a strand of hair from Lailu's forehead.

Lailu swallowed. "So they did this." Of course they did. But why? Were they experimenting on elven blood again? "If the elves find proof . . ." She couldn't bring herself to say it.

"Even without proof," Lianna sighed, "it will mean war."

War. Lailu thought of the Western Travel District, which had never recovered from the last war the elves waged. She dropped the paper on the floor, her fingers numb.

31

LAILU'S BAD MOOD

*L*ailu managed to get a couple hours of sleep, but her dreams were full of Eirad's chilly blue eyes and Wren's darkened goggles. The words *It will mean war* circled through her head over and over until finally she woke up. She lay there, the afternoon light stabbing in through her window, her whole body so tired and heavy she felt like a slab of meat.

A slab of meat that was tired of being dragged around, that was tired of all these things happening around her, pulling her in, taking her away from the one thing that mattered: becoming the best master chef in the land. Lailu scowled, suddenly irritated. Irritated with the scientists for starting all this drama with the elves in the first place, and the elves for being so sneaky and tricky, and Slipshod for not telling her anything, and her mother. Her mother most of all, for deciding to visit now, and only because Lord Elister asked her to.

Lailu closed her eyes, remembering her graduation day. Her family had traveled for days to make it in time. As Lailu walked across the giant dining room the Chef Academy used for their large ceremonies, she had felt so proud, she'd thought she might float. Master Sanford had shaken her hand and told her big things were in store for her. And then she'd turned and noticed her father. And her brothers.

But her mother was nowhere to be seen.

"She couldn't make it out," her father had told her. "You know how she is."

Lailu opened her eyes. She knew exactly how she was. She had to remember that. Her mom might be here now, but she'd be gone again the moment Lailu started to rely on her.

Being cranky felt better than being scared, so Lailu wrapped that around herself like a second skin and stomped downstairs.

She could hear Slipshod and her mother talking in the kitchen, and her foul mood grew even fouler. Apparently they'd both decided to actually stick around for once. Maybe today Slipshod would at least finally tell her what he was up to. She kicked open the door.

"Pigtails!" he barked. "Finally! Where the blazes have you been?"

Lailu's scowl deepened. He was just standing there in the kitchen, stirring a pot, acting like he'd never left. Like he hadn't been off cooking for the king and leaving her behind. "Where have *I* been? Where the blazes have *you* been?"

"Language," her mother said.

Lailu shot her a glare. "He said it first."

"He's allowed to, sweetie. He's an adult."

"I'm a master chef!"

"You're an apprentice still, dear," Lianna reminded her.

"Don't you have somewhere you should be disappearing off to?" Lailu snapped.

Lianna dropped the pan she was holding, and even Slipshod looked shocked. Lailu felt like swallowing those words back up immediately, but it was too late.

Lailu looked down at her feet. "I'm sorry," she whispered. Because despite how true those words were, she still felt terrible for saying them.

"It's okay. I know how you get when you're tired. I'll just . . . I'll be outside. If you need me." Lianna swept out of the kitchen.

Slipshod shook his head. "Very unlike you, Pigtails."

Lailu narrowed her eyes, remembering Wren's words. *He's been hunting without you. Didn't you hear? He got a Royal Invitation.* And suddenly she didn't feel bad anymore. She just felt angry. "Of course you'd take *her* side. You're also a fan of skipping out and leaving me behind."

Slipshod opened and closed his mouth several times. "Well, I can see *someone* is determined to have no friends today. And here I was about to invite you to come with me to the palace for dinner."

Lailu blinked. "You were what?"

"I got a Royal Invitation yesterday. I wanted us to hunt and prepare for it last night, but you were gone. Speaking of people skipping out." Slipshod's eyebrows drew together in a dark, disapproving line.

"I thought . . . I thought you were cooking for them yesterday." Lailu felt like the whole room had shifted on her.

"Without you?"

Lailu nodded.

Slipshod's expression softened. "Pigtails, I promise I was not cooking for the king last night without my favorite apprentice." Then his scowl returned. "Of course, today you're only the favorite by process of elimination."

Lailu couldn't argue with that. "Sorry."

"Apology accepted. And, truth be told, I have been a little . . . absent, as of late. I have some irons in the fire right now. But soon we'll have to sit down and have a good chat."

"About what?" Lailu asked, anxiety replacing her earlier surge of anger. Any time someone wanted to "sit down and have a good chat," it meant something terrible was coming. Otherwise they would just say it.

"We'll talk later. Right now, we have to finish getting ready for the king." Slipshod grinned, any trace of his earlier disapproval vanishing. "It's been a long time since I've been able to say those words, Pigtails. A very long time." He stood straighter, and Lailu noticed how clean his hair was, and . . . by the gods! He'd gotten it cut! She gaped at him. "But first, don't you think it's time you talked to your mother?"

Lailu's thoughts on Slipshod's hair vanished beneath a fresh wave of irritation. "I've *been* talking to her," she grumbled.

Slipshod sighed. "It's none of my business what you do, Pigtails, but I know there's only so long you can keep a lid on a boiling pot before it spills over. Think about it."

Lailu remembered all those times at home when she swallowed her words, choked down her anger. And then this past week, all the moments when she wanted to confront her mother but didn't, and then all the little bitter words that managed to slip out anyway.

Maybe he was right. Maybe she should just talk to her mother, *really* talk to her. After all, she'd gone deep into the heart of a swamp to take down a hydra. She should be able to handle a tough conversation. Right?

She found her mom sitting on the edge of the well in back, gazing out toward the Velvet Forest. "M-Mom?" Lailu called.

Lianna turned. For once she wasn't smiling, her hazel eyes very serious.

Lailu swallowed. She would prefer the hydra. She would prefer a *hundred* hydra. But it was time to stop putting this off. What could her mom do? Leave again? She was going to leave eventually anyway. "I'm sorry for what I said before," Lailu began slowly, her voice small and shaky, "but you *do* disappear. You leave all the time. And it hurts." She made herself look into her mother's eyes. "When you vanish without even saying goodbye, it hurts Lonnie and Laurent, and Dad. And it hurts me."

"Oh, honey." Lianna reached for Lailu like she wanted to hold her, but then dropped her hand. "But you know I'll always come back."

Lailu sniffed. "When I was little, I didn't want a mother who would come back. I wanted a mother who cared enough to stay in the first place. But you didn't." Her vision blurred, tears trickling down her face, but she let them fall and for once didn't try to pretend they were something else. "Coming back is not the same as being there."

Lianna was quiet for a long moment, her brow furrowed. Then she let out a breath. "I'm sorry, my little one, my Lailu. I've always had a restless spirit. I never planned to stay in one place or fall in love. I never thought I'd have children."

Lailu flinched. It was more painful than putting her hand on a hot stove. She shouldn't have come out here. All this time, and it *was* her fault her mother kept leaving. Because she didn't want her.

"I said that badly," Lianna said.

"N-no. You were honest." Lailu sniffed again. "For once, you told me the truth." She wiped a hand across her face. She couldn't see anything now, and she felt so heavy, like everything inside was breaking and turning to lead.

"No, sweetie, that was only half the truth. I never thought I'd have children, but then I met your father, and I had you and your brothers, and I'm so glad." Lianna took Lailu's hands in hers and squeezed them. "I'm glad I had you. But traveling ... it's part of who I am. I would never ask you to give up your cooking. That's who *you* are. You can love a dragon, but you can't make it stop flying."

Lailu pulled her hands free. "But maybe the dragon would be willing to stay on the ground if it loved you back enough," she said sadly.

Lianna's eyes filled with tears, but she didn't respond, and Lailu turned and walked back to the safety of her restaurant.

Once the door shut behind her, she sank to the ground, put her head in her hands, and cried. Each sob tore through her, leaving her weak and gasping and raw inside. She cried for her brothers, for her father. She even cried for her mother, who longed to be free but kept coming back to the cage her family had created for her. But mostly, she cried for herself, for all the times she'd been left behind, for all the nights she'd been abandoned, for every moment she'd wished her mother was there with her. Eventually, she had no more tears left.

Lailu stood, her joints achy, her eyes swollen. She took a deep breath, straightened her spine, and headed upstairs to get ready. It didn't matter if her heart was broken; she had a king to cook for. And at least cooking was the one thing that would never let her down.

The carriage bounded smoothly over cobblestones as it followed along one of the Dancing Rivers. Sunlight reflected off the water, all pink and golden, the promise of a few short hours of light left before the festivities would truly begin.

Lailu picked at the purple velvet of her seat. She wanted to enjoy the view, but her mind kept wandering around a maze of questions: Why did Wren tell her Master Slipshod was cooking for the king without her? Had she just gotten the details mixed up? Or . . . was she lying? But why? She had to know how abandoned and awful that had made Lailu feel. Lailu purposely avoided thinking about her conversation with her mother. She couldn't. Not right now. She didn't want to start crying again.

"You okay, Pigtails?" Slipshod asked.

"Yes," Lailu lied. Then she noticed how pale Master Slipshod looked, his forehead beaded with sweat despite the late afternoon chill. "Are *you* okay?"

"Me? Never better. Never better. Calm as a clam, that's me."

"Are you sure? Because you seem to be talking awfully fast."

Master Slipshod pulled a handkerchief out of his pocket and dabbed at his face. "I'm just worried about Mystic Cooking. We did leave your mom and Hannah in charge. Maybe that was a mistake. Maybe we should go back."

Lailu gaped at her mentor. Was he serious? He was thinking of bailing . . . on the *king*? He used to cook for the old king all the time. Why would he be so nervous now? "I don't think that's a good idea," she said slowly. "I think we need to see this through."

"You're right. Of course you're right." He looked out the window, his shoulders tense, and they rode the rest of the way in silence.

Eventually the tall stone towers of the royal castle rose into view. Even though the Academy shared the same island as the palace, Lailu had never been so close to it before. On all sides rose magnificent stone walls covered in ivy and blooming vines. As their carriage pulled up, a footman leaped forward to get their door.

Lailu helped Slipshod with the large Cooling and Containment cart, then followed him out. "Wow!" she whispered, spinning in a slow circle. The castle had presence, almost like it was a grand mystic beast, the stones very much alive and waiting. Watchful.

"Come on, Pigtails," Slipshod barked. "This way."

"Er, sir, I can show you—" the footman began.

"No need, I remember the way." Slipshod marched past, Lailu

at his heels as they went through an open side passage and into an empty stone hallway.

"This here is the servants' hall," he explained, the cart's wheels squeaking on the bare ground.

"Where are all the servants?" Lailu asked. A thin film of dust had settled on most of the surfaces, with the occasional faint footprint.

"Elsewhere," Slipshod said helpfully. "Since the last king passed, there hasn't been much need for servants here. Our current king, as you know, is still hard at work with his Scholarly Academy studies, so he spends little time here these days, and Lord Elister prefers to perform business at his Gilded Island estates."

"But what about the queen?" Lailu eyed a shabby-looking tapestry. The ends of the silver embroidery had been chewed away by mice. Her earlier amazement at the palace began boiling off like overcooked stew.

"Rumor has it she's been spending more and more time at her country estates, over near LaSilvian's vineyards."

They reached a spiraling stairway, and each of them took an end of the cart, hauling it up two floors before Slipshod had them set it down again in another hallway. *This* one looked more well-used, with bright, cheery tapestries displayed between wide-open windows. Lailu nodded her approval as their boots clicked across the freshly polished marble flooring.

"Wait until you see this, Pigtails." Slipshod's eyes gleamed with excitement as he threw open a large bronze door.

Lailu stepped inside a kitchen bigger than any room she had ever been in before, bigger than Lord Elister's kitchen—bigger, even, than all of Mystic Cooking combined. Her jaw dropped as she spun slowly, taking it all in.

"I see you both made it this time," a young man said.

Lailu turned too fast, tripped, and sprawled across the floor at the feet of the young king and his mother.

Master Slipshod sighed. "Way to make a good first impression."

32

The Offer

*L*ailu scrambled to her feet, then hovered in a kind of awkward half curtsy, her face scalding as Slipshod bowed next to her.

"Rise," the queen commanded, and Lailu straightened, keeping her eyes on her feet. She had just tripped in front of the king and queen. If Greg ever found out about this, she'd never live it down.

"Curious," the king said, his voice surprisingly deep for someone so delicate, and Lailu glanced up. She recognized him immediately as the ethereal boy who had eaten in her restaurant the other night with Elister's bodyguards. At fifteen, he was taller than his mother, but just barely, with similar Mystalon coloring. Rumor had it, the only thing he had inherited from his late father was the same tragic curse, a curse cast on him by the ruler of Mystalon and now doomed to carry over from generation to generation unless a cure was found.

Lailu didn't know all the details; the existence of the curse was not publicly acknowledged, but chefs were notorious gossips, and she'd heard all the whispers during her time at the Chef Academy. Apparently Old King Salivar had been betrothed to the heir of Mystalon but had fallen in love with her sister and married her instead. As a country, Mystalon was known for its higher concentration of magic and magic users, and when the heir took over as ruler, she crafted her magical revenge. Of course, she denied it, and Mystalon and Savoria were officially allies. But unofficially? Lailu didn't like to speculate. They were having enough trouble with the Krigs.

"What is curious, Your Majesty?" Lailu asked when it became apparent he was speaking to her.

"I would think one who hunts dragons and griffins would be more graceful."

Lailu wanted to dig a hole and crawl deep inside.

"Be nice to the poor girl," the queen said. "Look how red she's become."

Lailu realized there would be no hole deep enough for her. Maybe she could visit Old Salty the kraken at the bottom of the ocean instead.

"Sullivan, I'm so glad you could come again, and on such short notice. My son and I look forward to whatever wonderful feast you have planned this time," the queen continued. "I've asked Lord Elister to grace us with his presence as well."

"I am happy to be of service." Slipshod dropped into another bow. Lailu stood there, wondering if she should curtsy too. She glanced at the king. The corner of his mouth quirked up in amusement, and then he and his mother left.

Lailu buried her face in her hands. "I can't believe that just happened."

"Believe it. At least you got that out of the way at the start, eh, Pigtails?"

Lailu looked back up at him, the queen's words just now hitting her. "What did she mean by 'again' and 'this time'?"

"Er . . . I did used to cook here, remember?" He adjusted his puffy chef's hat. "From here on out, we have to do everything perfectly. There's a lot riding on this dinner."

"Like what?" Lailu asked, but Slipshod didn't answer.

And while Lailu may have physically landed on her face, Slipshod seemed to be tripping up in his own way, overseasoning the soup, slicing the vegetables so unevenly they didn't cook as well, and just generally making rookie cooking mistakes. There were only so many Lailu could fix.

"Master Slipshod, is everything all right?" she asked the third time she had to stop him from using the wrong seasoning.

"What? Oh, oh yes. Everything is going wonderfully. Couldn't have hoped for better." He lapsed into silence, studying his spice bottle. "This isn't pixie paprika, is it?"

"No, it's not," Lailu sighed. "It's really not." She had a bad feeling about this dinner. It was definitely not shaping up to be their best work.

Lailu eyed the king nervously as he took a sip of their cream of hydra soup. "Hmm," he said, setting the bowl down. Did he taste the extra spices that had been accidentally added?

She glanced at her mentor as the queen took a delicate bite of the griffin. Could she tell it had been overcooked just a tad? Enough to give it a hint of stringiness? Lailu had tried to add in a bit of hydra sauce to counteract that, but she wasn't sure if the flavors combined well enough.

Slipshod's face looked especially gray against the white of his chef's hat, and Lailu could see the sweat beading his upper lip.

Finally Elister patted his mouth with a napkin. "Still not your finest work, Sullivan," he commented. "But better this time."

The queen frowned at him, and he immediately quieted. *Interesting*, Lailu thought. Maybe Lord Elister *didn't* call all the shots. The queen certainly seemed more sure of herself here than she'd been at his party, a quiet confidence radiating out from her slender frame. "Don't listen to him, Sullivan," she said. Like her son, she also had a deeper voice than expected, low and beautiful. "I thought this meal was marvelous. The hint of hydra especially was a fine touch."

"Time is wasting. Let's get to the point." The young king put down his fork and turned to Slipshod. "Do you know why we asked you here today?"

Lailu frowned. Was there an ulterior motive?

Master Slipshod cleared his throat. "I . . . have some ideas. I know that this is Your Majesty's final year of Academy studies, and I know that . . ." He cleared his throat again, adjusting the neck of his apron. "That you'll be needing a fuller staff here at the castle."

"As future ruler, we . . ." The king glanced at Elister. "We *all* thought it best that I apprentice under Lord Elister and begin learning how the kingdom is run." His smile turned to a grimace.

If Elister noticed, he gave no indication.

"During my apprenticeship, I *will* need a more complete staff. Including a head chef." The king tapped his plate.

Wait, what? Lailu's jaw dropped. Slipshod wouldn't look at her.

"Someone loyal, experienced," the queen spoke up. "Someone who knows how to be discreet. Someone who can be of help in the days to come." She leaned forward. "We are inviting an ambassador from the Krigaen Empire to join us. Our two countries have much to discuss."

"And I told you, *Your Majesty*, that this will not be necessary," Elister said carefully, his tone respectful but annoyed. "Starling assures me her automatons will be corrected and enhanced. There's no need for us to make a new treaty with the Krigs."

"And I told *you*, I am no longer confident in Starling *or* her plans," Queen Alina said. "Not after this most recent fiasco. I don't believe we will be strong enough."

Elister's jaw clenched, but he remained silent.

"What about the elves?" the king asked. "Fahr has said if we banish the scientists, then he will—"

"*Never* trust the elves," Queen Alina snapped.

Elister sighed. "We're wasting Master Slipshod's and Apprentice Chef Loganberry's time."

Queen Alina pushed her plate away. "Sullivan Slipshod, you

served my husband faithfully for a number of years. I am willing to put some of your later indiscretions behind us both, if my son decides he would like you to join our staff." Her blue eyes flicked over to Lailu, who stood completely frozen in shock. Was this what Slipshod had been working on?

Had he been planning on leaving her all along?

The queen's eyes filled with something like pity, and Lailu looked away, her own eyes burning.

"What do you say, Sullivan Slipshod?" the king asked in his strangely deep voice. "Will you be my royal chef?"

33

GOING PLACES

Lailu crossed her arms and glared out the carriage window. At least everything finally made sense: Master Slipshod's improved appearance, his distracted air, his near panic when the king showed up at the doorstep of Mystic Cooking yesterday. He was trying to leave her, again.

Lit candles in windows grew fuzzy, and masked faces blurred as the carriage rolled on past. Lailu blinked rapidly, trying to keep the tears in.

"You okay there, Pigtails?"

"Yes," Lailu sniffed. "Fine." She wiped her eyes on the back of her hand. "So you *have* been cooking for the king without me. Why didn't you tell me sooner?"

Slipshod sighed. "I wasn't really expecting them to make me the offer tonight. This was just supposed to be the final test, and then I thought they would spend time deliberating. I thought—I thought I would have more time to sit down and explain things to you."

"But you *did* have time," Lailu said, turning on him. "You had lots and lots of time. You just chose to keep everything so secret!"

"You weren't there yesterday when I came back—"

"But that was just one time! You could have told me before our griffin hunt, you could have told me while we were preparing for Lord Elister's party, you could have told me today, even, in the carriage ride over. You had all week to tell me, but you chose not to."

Slipshod's face reddened in the dimly lit carriage, and he opened his mouth several times before fixing it into a grimace. "I'm sorry," he said finally.

Lailu shook her head. She wasn't ready to accept his apology. "What's going to happen to Mystic Cooking?" she asked. "What's going to happen to me?"

"Well . . ." Slipshod scratched his chin. "I imagine you'll go on to be a famous chef, one of the best in history. And as for Mystic Cooking, I'm sure it will blaze in history right along with you."

Lailu wanted to smile at that, but the dream felt lonely, like a cupboard with no pots. "And what about my apprenticeship?"

"It will be complete as soon as I take this position as the king's chef. I've already sent the Academy your papers."

Lailu blotted her eyes on her sleeve. This was what she'd wanted, though, right? She remembered what Master Slipshod had said when he'd taken her on: *You and me, Pigtails, we'll go places.* But he'd never said they'd go to them together.

"Can you . . . can you stop the carriage?" she whispered.

Master Slipshod hesitated, then had the driver pull over to the side of the street. Lailu drew her griffin mask down over her face, opened her door, and hopped out. "I'm going to walk."

Master Slipshod nodded. "I understand. I'll cover the rest of the dinner rush, and we can . . . we can talk more tonight. If you want."

Lailu closed the door and stepped back, waiting until the carriage moved on before she broke down crying.

She let her feet carry her where they wanted, ending up at the market. Her tears flowed hot and heavy, but under her mask, no one could see them anyway. All around her people laughed and talked and sang, celebrating and trying to give her food from their stalls, but she turned it all down. She felt like the world was a feast and she was nothing but an empty plate, stacked to the side, separate.

As she passed Paulie's Potions, she thought of the last time she was there, Ryon bleeding and half-conscious on a cot. She hadn't seen him since that afternoon. Lailu's misery turned to worry, and she bit her lip. Maybe she should check? Ask Paulie how he'd been?

Paulie's front door opened, and Lailu leaped back. That witch really could read minds!

But then Vahn stepped outside.

"—head back to the palace," he was saying. "They rely on me there these days." He tossed his hair back over his shoulders.

"I'll bet they do," Paulie purred.

Lailu frowned. What was Vahn doing at Paulie's again? It didn't seem like he needed a spell or a potion. But why else would he keep coming back to her shop?

Paulie glanced past Vahn, locking eyes with Lailu, and Lailu quickly moved on. It was none of her business, after all. But it might be Hannah's business.

Or it might be nothing.

She made a mental note to tell her friend. Just in case. Maybe then Hannah would actually admit she and Vahn were dating, and it would be one less secret between them. Lailu scowled. She was getting awfully tired of everyone keeping things from her.

Off to the side of the street was a brightly decorated wagon covered in cloths of every color imaginable. A large sign proclaimed: WE SELL DRAGON SILK AND WONDERS! The three women clustered around it wore clothing that was just as colorful as their wagon, favoring the same long, flowing skirts as Lailu's mother. Lailu's feet seemed to pull her the rest of the way over there.

"Why, hello! Aren't you adorable." A woman with reddish-purple hair bustled over. "Can I interest you in some silk?"

"Actually . . . I was wondering if you knew Lianna," Lailu asked. "Lianna Loganberry?"

The woman brightened. "Very well. She's been traveling with us."

Lailu idly ran her hands down a length of vivid, forest-green silk. Hannah would really love this, she decided.

"Ah, good choice," the woman said.

"Oh, I'm not buying. I'm just looking," Lailu said quickly. Much as she'd love to buy Hannah a present, all her money was tied up in Mystic Cooking.

"Well, if you change your mind, come find us. But don't wait too long! We're leaving as soon as the Week of Masks has ended."

Lailu felt those words like a punch. They were leaving . . . which meant her mom would be leaving with them. She was a dragon who cared more about the sky than staying with her daughter, and no matter how much Lailu told her that it hurt, it wouldn't change a thing. When the holidays were over, she would go, and Lailu would be all alone. No Slipshod, no Mom, and soon, probably no Hannah.

Her eyes filled with tears again, and she was grateful for her mask as she hurried off. What was wrong with her? It wasn't like this was the first time she'd been abandoned. She was going to be a full master chef. She'd hunted dragons and krakens and hydra. She would be just fine on her own.

During the Week of Masks, the nights came alive, so even as Lailu left the market behind, she was still surrounded by people.

"—from Melvin's," a man said loudly, knocking into her.

Lailu stumbled, then recoiled as a cockatrice glared at her. It took her a second to realize those were bloodshot human eyes behind a mask and not the red eyes of death. She let out a breath.

"I mean, have you ever seen a mask as realistic as this?" the man behind the mask continued.

"Sure scared the life out of that little griffin," his friend chortled.

They moved on, leaving Lailu to stagger in their wake.

As she approached the Industrial District, the crowds thinned. Maybe it was the flickering lights that kept people out. After the scientists left this area to do their experiments under Lord Elister's watchful eye, they'd stopped maintaining their fancy smokeless torches, and that lack of care showed. Something about those strange flashes of light bursting erratically into sudden darkness did not invite revelers, and by the time Lailu turned onto Iron Way, she was alone.

Good, Lailu thought. She had to get used to this.

She gave herself a shake. "Stop with the self-pity," she muttered. She wasn't some child. She needed to quit being a baby.

"L-Lailu?" Wren stepped out of a darkened alcove in one of the buildings.

Lailu wavered. She didn't want to get sucked into yet another conversation. She just wanted to get home. But then Wren took another step forward, the electric light of the Industrial District flaring brightly for a second, illuminating her face, and it was obvious she'd been crying, too. "Are you okay?" Lailu asked.

Wren nodded, then burst into tears.

34

TEARS AND FEARS

"What's wrong?" Lailu asked. She lifted her arms awkwardly, not sure what to do, and settled for patting Wren lightly on the back.

"Oh, n-nothing," Wren sobbed. "It's just, I work so hard. So hard!"

"I know you do."

"And she doesn't care! I th-thought"—she hiccuped—"if I embraced being a s-scientist"—another hiccup—"she would love me."

"Oh," Lailu said, sudden understanding dawning. "This is your mom you're talking about?"

Wren nodded miserably and blew her nose on her own sleeve.

Lailu took a step back. That was kind of gross, even by her standards. "I'm sure she loves you. I mean, at least she's never left you behind for months and months and didn't tell you she secretly spent a lot of time in the capital but still didn't have time to see your graduation."

"She . . . what?" Wren stopped crying. "How could my mom miss my graduation if I haven't graduated from anything?"

"My point is, she wouldn't miss it. She'd be there for it."

"Only to make sure I didn't screw it up," Wren sniffed.

"She's probably just hard on you because she knows how talented you are," Lailu suggested.

Wren sniffed again. "You think so?"

"Of course. Um, can I get you a handkerchief or something?"

"No, this is fine." Wren blew her nose on her sleeve again, then managed a small, tremulous smile. "Thanks, Lailu."

"You going to be okay, then?" Lailu didn't want to leave Wren here in distress, but she had her own problems to attend to.

"Yeah. I actually have a plan. Something I'm working on that will impress even my mom. I'm almost done with it, but one of the key components just exploded. Again."

Lailu sniffed the air. "That explains the smoke," she realized. Apparently, Wren was still using the Industrial District for her own experiments.

"It was a disaster," Wren admitted. "I thought I'd give up because it never seems to matter anyhow, but I feel better now. I'm going to try some more."

"That's great." Lailu smiled. "I hope you're successful. See you around?"

"See you around." Wren lunged in and hugged her. "Thank you," she said again, letting Lailu go. "Thank you for being my friend."

Lailu eyed Wren's snot-marked sleeve and knew she was going to immediately change shirts when she got home. Still, surprisingly she felt better as she waved goodbye and left Wren and the Industrial District behind. Maybe things weren't so bad after all. Maybe she would be all right too.

Lailu woke up late in the afternoon the next day, feeling rested for the first time all week. She'd returned home last night just in time to finish up the last of the dinner rush, then slipped upstairs and into bed before Slipshod could tell her any more bad news. After such an emotional day, sleep had hit her harder than a full-speed hydra, sucking her down into dreamless slumber.

"Hey, lazy bones," a familiar voice said by her bed.

Lailu sat up so fast she felt her back crack.

Ryon slouched against the wall next to her, his hands in his pockets, the sunlight streaming through the window and glinting off his dark hair.

"Ryon? What are you *doing*? This is my room!"

"I know. I like what you've done with the place. Simple. No distractions. Not sure about your friend's side, though. It's a little . . . extravagant."

Lailu couldn't help but see what he meant; there was a clear divide between Lailu's side—with her small bed, one dresser, and large chest full of hunting equipment—and Hannah's four-post canopy bed with nightstand, dresser, standing closet, and an entire shelf devoted to hair combs.

"Is she still re-homing things?" Ryon picked up a bronze hair comb in the shape of a dragon.

"Of course not!" Lailu eyed the towering stack of hair accessories. "Probably not," she amended. Then, "I hope not," she muttered under her breath. She shook herself. She had enough to worry about right now. "Stop changing the subject. Why are you here?"

"I thought you might be worried about me. I was attacked viciously right in front of you, and while I was under your protection, I might add."

Lailu's face flushed. "You told me you were fine," she spluttered. "You told me you weren't being followed anymore. That wasn't *my* fault."

"No, it wasn't," Ryon agreed cheerfully. "But I like how red you get."

Lailu threw her pillow at him. "Get out of my room."

He laughed and tossed her pillow back. "In a moment, grouchy one. I'm about to go on a fact-finding mission. I want to know who programmed that thing to come after me." His expression grew more serious. "And I want to know why."

"Are you hinting you need backup for this mission?" Lailu asked suspiciously.

Ryon shrugged. "Backup could be useful," he said casually, "if certain people and their very sharp knives were available."

Lailu debated. She should get up and help prep for dinner. But Slipshod would be leaving her soon anyhow; let him handle all the prep work for once.

"I'll go with you," she decided. "Give me five minutes. And we have to be back before the dinner rush."

"You got it." He stepped up onto the windowsill.

"Are you leaving through the *window*?"

"Same way I got in. It's like my own private entrance." Ryon climbed out, closing the window behind him.

Lailu made a mental note to get a window lock as soon as possible.

It was only after he'd left that she realized he hadn't winked the entire time he was there. *He must be more worried than he's letting on*, she decided. It was not a comforting thought. She got dressed, and after a moment's hesitation, she grabbed Wren's mal-cantation powder out of her top drawer. Just in case.

35

WREN'S NIGHTMARE WORKSHOP

The shift from buildings and houses with colorful edges and eaves to the blocky metal ones of the Industrial District was sudden. No matter how many times Lailu passed this way, she never got used to it. Glancing up, she read IRON WAY.

"Why the Industrial District?" she asked.

"When I was being followed, before I met you and was attacked, that monstrosity left me here." Ryon's voice echoed off the strange walls around them. "It's strange, though, isn't it? After all, the scientists no longer work here."

Lailu thought of Wren and her experiments. And her lab, still within the Industrial District. But no . . . Wren was just a kid. Why would she program something to attack Ryon? "Maybe," Lailu began slowly. "Maybe they haven't all left."

Ryon smiled, but there was no humor in it. "I don't think they've all left either. I think the scientist who programmed that thing to come after me is still here. And I think it's the same person who programmed the automaton to kill Gwendyl."

"An *automaton* killed Gwendyl?" Lailu hadn't realized that; the paper had just said the cause of death was unknown. "Are you sure? I read that there were no signs of struggle."

"And who printed that story?" Ryon asked, raising his eyebrows.

Lailu hesitated. The scientists had invented the press. Did that mean they controlled what articles were published in it? She remembered all the times Greg had gotten the credit for things she had done, and all because his uncle had a lot of influence. Of *course* she couldn't trust everything in the papers. She should have known better by now.

"You're catching on," Ryon said. "The truth is a slippery beast."

"It shouldn't be," Lailu muttered.

Ryon smiled. "Maybe not. But this is the world we live in. And I have it on good authority that in this case, Gwendyl was caught and eventually killed by an automaton. We don't know why it targeted her or what she told it before she died. All we know is that somehow it must have been impervious to elven magic, or she would have been able to stop it. Gwendyl was powerful."

Lailu thought of the mal-cantation powder, very aware of its weight inside her pocket. Something like that would stop elven magic. Was Wren the only scientist who had it? She couldn't imagine Wren programming anything to kill, even if her friend didn't believe elves felt pain.

Then she remembered the merciless way Wren had killed the cockatrice, and she went cold. Maybe she *could* imagine it.

"I know where a lab is," Lailu admitted. She didn't want to believe it, but all the signs were pointing toward her friend. She had to at least check it out. They weaved through gridlike streets as she led Ryon to the spot. "This is the place." She recognized the acrid smell of smoke that still tinged the air. This was where she'd met Wren last night, very close to the building that had housed the elven blood experiments months ago.

Lailu studied the giant bolted door in front.

"That does not look promising." Ryon rattled the lock.

Lailu scowled at him. "I'm sure there's a way in."

"Like, oh, with a key?"

"As if you always need a key to enter a place."

Ryon's grin was as sneaky as he was. "You're learning, my young friend."

"I'm learning," Lailu sighed. As Ryon bent to inspect the lock, she stepped to the side, idly tracing her hand down the wall. Her finger slipped along a groove, and she stopped, then peered closer. There was a perfect circle indented in the wall, and around it, the edges of something that might be another door, barely taller than she was.

"You know, this might be beyond my capabilities," Ryon was saying as Lailu traced the circle and a handle popped out. She twisted the handle, and the small door opened soundlessly, letting out a potent whiff of smoke. The smell reminded her even more strongly of the elven blood experiments, and she took a step back.

"I think I found our way in," she said slowly.

"Like I said, you're learning." Ryon tousled Lailu's hair, and she swatted at his hand. "Well, what are we waiting for?" He stepped past her and into the darkened room.

Lailu paused behind him. "Are you sure it's—"

Bam! Snap! Pow!

An arrow shot straight at Ryon's heart. He caught it, moving so fast he was practically a blur, just as a large blade hung above him swung toward his unprotected neck.

Lailu whipped out her knife, slamming it into the doorframe above Ryon. The hilt caught the swing of the deadly blade, pushing it away to clatter harmlessly to the floor.

"Safe?" Ryon finished, his mouth quirking to the side. "No, probably not."

Lailu's heart beat so hard she felt like she'd been punched in the chest. "No, probably not," she agreed. Then she squared her shoulders and stepped inside.

Lailu discovered a small light on the wall that flickered on when she tapped it. She and Ryon worked silently and quickly beneath its pulsing, eerie glow, riffling through the bizarre objects that filled the room. Lailu examined a shelf full of different tools: hammers, screwdrivers, tiny magnifying glasses, and plenty of other things she'd never seen before. Most of the tools were obviously second-hand but carefully maintained. Next to them lay a pile of metal limbs on a rusty table, screws and pins cluttering the space beside them. And hung over the chair nearby were Wren's goggles.

Clack–clack–clack.

Lailu caught her breath, then turned very slowly. The head and shoulders of an automaton leaned against the far wall, its metal spine dangling in empty space. The eyes were dull, but the mouth opened and closed, opened and closed. Lailu peered closer, noticing another head, this one missing the front paneling. It was attached to something larger, and it looked almost like there were wings strapped to its back. Wings made of twisted wires and full of gears. Pinned to the wall behind it was a hand-drawn diagram of a lake dragon. Lailu recognized it as a copy from Master Slipshod's book.

Click. Click. Click-click-click. Click.

Lailu spun, searching for the source of this new noise. Near the discarded automatons, something moved, something that scuttled back and forth below the bench. It was slightly smaller than her hand, with six legs that chimed softly as they struck the metal paneling beneath them.

Lailu leaned closer, noticing two more of the things made of the same glossy metal, with two shiny lights in front like eyes. They looked like smaller versions of the thing that had attacked Ryon. With another series of clicks, the three machines moved deeper beneath the bench and vanished into the shadows.

"Uh, Ryon—"

"Come look at this," Ryon whispered from across the room.

Lailu was happy to back away from the creepy metal spider things, although she kept an eye on them until she'd joined Ryon on the other side of the room.

The sight in front of her stopped her cold, all thoughts of mechanical spiders gone faster than a well-prepared feast.

Piled in neat stacks on a large table and labeled in a recognizable hand were several different mystic creature corpses. Lailu recognized the carefully sorted bones of a medusa fish; a long, curved tail that might have belonged to one of Beolann's merfolk; and the fangs and claws of a manticore. Vials of purple elven blood were carefully set in a stand beside them, a familiar blackened skull leaning against the wood frame. And next to that, stretched out on a flat piece of wood, was a blue pixie, a nail driven right through its heart.

Lailu walked as fast as her legs could carry her, like she could leave the image of Wren's nightmare workshop behind. She should have seen this coming—she *did* see this coming—but nothing could have quite prepared her for the sight of that blackened skull sitting among all those mystical corpses and the vials of elven blood. And worse by far was the dead pixie. Sure, Eirad had said it was practically an insect, but it looked humanoid. Why would Wren do that?

Who was she, really?

Lailu felt like she didn't really know her at all.

"Are you okay?" Ryon asked for the hundredth time.

"Do I look okay?" Lailu asked.

"You look terrible."

"Then stop asking me stupid questions." She had to get back to her restaurant, had to have some time to think. She knew those were Wren's things, Wren's inventions, Wren's . . . corpses. Lailu shook her head. She had no idea what Wren was up to. She just knew it couldn't be good.

And she also knew Wren had just installed something in her

restaurant, something big. Something that could possibly go horribly, horribly wrong, and take Mystic Cooking with it.

Lailu picked up her pace, shivering as the last rays of sunlight faded, taking the remaining warmth from the sky and replacing it with a clear, cloudless, chilly night. Automatically she pulled her griffin mask down over her face. Tonight was the Final Night of Masks, and it felt like a night for evil spirits and bad intentions.

As they left the Industrial District behind, the sounds of people celebrating washed over her. She could see flickering candles ahead and sped up. Usually she wasn't a fan of crowds, but tonight she welcomed the company.

"Wait," Ryon said slowly.

Lailu ignored him, intent on losing herself in the crowd and leaving that little laboratory of horrors behind.

"Lailu, wait—" he called again, but it was too late.

Lailu turned the corner, stepping straight into a crowd of roaring, cheering people.

People wearing masks of snarling dogs and grinning hyenas, and even one sharp-beaked griffin.

Only they weren't just masks.

Lailu staggered back as all those faces turned toward her. Faces that had melded with their costumes, changing people into the very creatures they'd dressed up to be.

The snarling dog closest to her lifted its snout in the air and howled.

36

MASQUERADE

The dog lunged at Lailu, who dropped instinctively to the ground. She swept its legs out from under it, then rolled to her feet, her knife unsheathed in her hand.

And stopped.

She had never seen anything so disturbing as these human-creature hybrids. Some of them looked almost exactly like beasts—the griffin had the full body, feathers, wings, and beak, but human eyes peered out from behind what had once been a mask; whereas some still had their human forms, with just their faces elongated and twisted, their hands curled into talons or claws.

These were all people . . . or they were *supposed* to be people. She couldn't just start slicing and dicing them like the evening's special.

The griffin flew at her, its beak snapping inches from her face.

Lailu fended it off as Ryon ducked around a pair of screeching batyrdactyls to catch up to her.

"This is the elves," Lailu gasped, blocking an attack from a three-horned anguay. "This is their magic."

Ryon didn't argue; he just bobbed and weaved next to her.

"Can they stop this?" Lailu asked, hitting one of the masked creations in the face, then shoving a girl in a unicorn mask into two boys charging up in matching panther suits. She hated to hurt any of them, but she had to use some force or they would rend her to pieces.

"Maybe."

"Then we need to get to them."

"Agreed." Ryon winced as the griffin managed a good swipe with its paw. "Let's go."

They darted through the crowd toward the Velvet Forest.

Wham!

Something huge and impossibly heavy landed directly in their path. Lailu skidded to a halt, nearly knocking Ryon over. "G-gargoyle?" she gasped, staring up into the wine-red eyes of the stone beast. "How is this possible?"

The gargoyle stomped forward, the ground shaking beneath it.

"This way!" Ryon grabbed Lailu's arm and tugged her back out of the street and down an alley.

Behind them, Lailu heard a chillingly familiar cry: the shrill, burbling call of a batyrdactyl on the hunt, joined by another, and another, this one much closer.

"Run faster!" Ryon said, ducking down another side street.

"I have . . . short legs," Lailu panted, struggling to keep up with him. She wanted to look over her shoulder, but Master Sanford had always told her to stay focused on what's ahead. *Sure, you can look behind you, but it'll probably be the last thing you see.* He'd tapped his eye patch for emphasis. It was a very effective way to make sure that the lesson stuck in all their heads.

Lailu pushed those thoughts away. She had no time for memories. Instead, she focused on her feet, the way they pounded the ground, the blur of people in masks and costumes as she tore past them. Screams erupted all around her, but as partygoers merged with their masks and costumes, those screams turned into shrieks and howls and hungry, blood-chilling cries. It was like the elven party all over again, but this time with humans.

Lailu didn't have the strength to pay attention to where she was going; she just sprinted after Ryon, her lungs on fire, as he led them down streets, through alleys, and even over a bridge or two, twisting and turning through a city gone mad.

Vaguely, she knew they were heading well away from Mystic Cooking, but she didn't know where until everything suddenly got quiet. It was as if Lailu had stepped inside a giant pot, the cries fading abruptly behind her.

"Where did everyone—" She stopped, her words dying as she looked at her surroundings.

All around her were the ruins of half-destroyed buildings, columns, and statues lying discarded like broken teeth. It was a graveyard without any bodies.

Ryon had led her clear across the city and straight into the Western Travel District.

Lailu shivered. "Why did we come here?"

"To find the elves." Ryon's eyes glittered.

"I thought they only used this entrance on the First Night of Masks?" Lailu searched the shadows around them. She thought she caught movement and the soft clicking of tiny metallic feet, but then it was gone.

"They use this space whenever they need to get in and out of the city quickly and without notice. It's not just a festival thing for them." Ryon moved closer to a decrepit wreck of a building, peering in through the gaping window.

"Why would they do this?" Lailu asked. "Why transform innocent people?"

"I'm not sure," Ryon admitted. "I know Fahr has been planning the downfall of the scientists, but he told me he's attempting to follow the letter of the law."

"What does *that* mean?" Lailu thought it sounded like sneaky elven doublespeak, but she knew Ryon trusted his half brother.

Ryon ran a hand through his hair. "I'm not supposed to say."

Lailu scowled. "Fine. Keep your secrets. I'm used to it." She wanted to sound like she didn't care, but it was impossible to keep the sting out of her voice.

Ryon sighed. "He's trying to see the king," he admitted. "He's been sending him secret correspondence."

"He's *what*? Behind Elister's back?"

"Now you're wishing I kept that secret, aren't you?" Ryon grinned.

"But . . . why? What does he think the king will do for him?"

"I don't know, but he'll be the ruler of Savoria in a few years, and Fahr has to do something. The other elves are really angry. I mean, look around." Ryon spread his arms, taking in the decay, the crumbled statues, the emptiness of this shattered spot of the city. "The elves don't forgive, Lailu. They don't forgive, and they don't forget."

His words seemed to echo between them, sending a chill up Lailu's spine. "Maybe they got tired of waiting, then," Lailu whispered. "Maybe tonight's masquerade is their way of getting revenge against the city."

"Masquerade, huh? I like that," Eirad said.

Lailu whipped around. Eirad leaned against a vine-choked building, his long blond braids pulled back from his face, his arms crossed casually over his chest.

"I should have known you were the one behind this," Ryon said.

"You know I'm not really the patient type." Eirad bared his teeth.

Ryon shifted into a defensive fighting stance. "Fahr worked very hard to restore peace after the last feud. It's a shame you had to throw that all away."

Eirad pushed away from the building. "Peace? Don't speak to me of peace. You and I both know that's nothing but false promises. Those scientists have been targeting us, and what has Elister, the 'city's protector,' done about it? *Nothing.*" His lip curled. "All because he's distracted by their foolish clockwork toys."

"And how is this riot going to change that?" Lailu demanded. "How is harming innocent people going to make Elister help you?"

"Ah, little chef, always so concerned with the pawns of this world." Eirad shook his head. "Fahr, with all his attempts at peace, has done nothing but convince you humans that we are weak. This is a reminder to Elister and to all the people who have forgotten: we used to own this land. We could take it back still." He curled his hands into fists.

"Your time has passed," Ryon said. "Fahr sees that. Why can't you?"

Eirad's hand moved so fast it was a blur, smashing into Ryon's face.

Lailu covered her mouth, horrified, as Ryon tumbled back. Swallowing, she gripped her knife and stepped in front of him. Eirad watched her, amused. "You're going to fight me, little chef?"

"If—if I have to." She'd lose, of course. She might be able to take down a hydra, but she was no match for an elf, and they both knew it. Still, Ryon was her friend.

Ryon put a hand on her shoulder. "It's okay, Lailu. I've got this." He wiped the blood from his mouth with the back of his hand and stepped forward, his eyes locked on Eirad's. "That," he said softly, "was a mistake, cousin." And then he launched himself forward.

RYON'S SECRET

Ryon moved with the same deadly speed as an elf, his attacks so fast they were impossible for Lailu to track. She blinked, and Eirad had staggered backward, purple blossoming on his cheek.

Eirad hissed, his braids whipping around his face as if he stood in the middle of a windstorm. He reached up and ripped two braids right off his head. Lailu winced and touched her pigtails in sympathy. The golden strands he held turned a bright, poisonous green, ballooning out until they became snakes as Eirad flung them at Ryon.

Ryon shrugged them off like oil sliding from a frying pan, and they coiled to the ground and became braids once again.

Eirad looked down at them. "I had forgotten about that annoying little trick of yours."

"I never forget," Ryon said, breathing heavily. "It comes with the ability to age that we mortals have."

Eirad's smile turned into an ugly snarl, and Lailu lunged between them, afraid that the elf would attack once more.

Eirad studied her, and Lailu was aware of how small and slow and weak she was. She raised her knife anyway and waited.

Eirad took a step back, then another, his hands in the air in a gesture of surrender. "Fahr weakened elven law when he kept *you* alive," he told Ryon. He pulled a black feather from his pocket and tossed it in the air. The air shimmered around it, forming a black mask with a long hooked beak that fell gently into his waiting fingers. "Those scientists killed Gwendyl, and if Lord Elister won't do anything about it, then it's time to remind him where the *real* power in this city lies. Enjoy the dance. It will go on until dawn."

He slipped into the mask, his features shifting into those of a large raven, his body shrinking, changing. He shrieked, then flew away into the night.

"Well, some help you were," Ryon teased.

"I tried," Lailu protested.

"I know you did. And I will be forever grateful."

Something nearby howled. Chills ran up and down Lailu's arms, and she tried to slow her breathing as panic beat its way from her chest. "Does this mean Eirad has gone rogue?" she asked.

"He must have. Fahr would never approve something like this."

"Can Fahr stop it?"

Ryon hesitated, then shook his head. "This is powerful magic. Eirad must have been planning it for a long time, hoarding magic in secret. Even *I* didn't realize how powerful he's become."

Lailu remembered the first time Eirad had tried to make a deal with her, months ago. He had offered her enough money to pay back Mr. Boss if she gave him the last years of her life. *The last five years you wouldn't even know you missed.* How many years had he bought from the people around him? "Then what should we—"

Grrr . . .

Lailu spun just as a man-wolf pounced forward, fangs bared. She drew her knife and dodged to the side, then slammed the hilt of her blade into the back of the beast's head. It crumpled with a high-pitched whimper. Ryon put a hand to its face, and the skin blurred, separating from the material of the mask.

Ryon slid the mask off and stomped on it. Immediately the creature turned back into a man.

"How did you—" Lailu began.

"Later," Ryon said. He helped the man sit up.

"Wh-what?" the former wolf groaned, rubbing his head.

"Get to your house. Now," Ryon told him. "And lock yourself in." The man's eyes widened and he scrambled away.

"We should take the same advice," Lailu decided. "If Fahr can't help us, there's nothing we can do here."

"Agreed." Ryon held out his hand. "Let's go."

Lailu took it, and they ran out into the wildness of the waiting city, dodging past claws and gnashing teeth in a sprint toward Mystic Cooking.

A man gave a milk-curdling cry as three large shadows descended on him. Their eyes glowed red, soft feathers speckling their bodies, and Lailu realized she couldn't run home like a frightened child. "Ryon, we've got to stop. We've got to help them." She tried to pull her hand free, but Ryon just tightened his grip and ran on as more people cried out in panic. Creatures attacked from all sides, creatures that had no place here in the city.

"Can't you do something for them?" she asked, thinking about how easily he had shrugged off Eirad's enchantments, and then the way he'd pulled the mask from the wolf-man.

Ryon's mouth formed a hard, sad line. "I can't."

"But—"

"Ask me later, when this is over."

Up ahead Lailu could see the shops, including Paulie's Potions. Could Paulie help? Lailu hated asking favors from a witch—she never knew what she'd have to give up in return—but these were desperate times.

Lailu caught a sudden movement from the side and lunged into Ryon, knocking them both over just as a blast of scalding fire hit the cobblestones. She scrambled back up, expecting to see maybe a dragon—or worse, a fyrian chicken.

Instead, a large, magnificent bird of red-gold circled them, its fiery feathers sleek aside from the unruly batch on the top of its head.

"Greg?" Lailu said. He had been wearing a phoenix mask before, a gift from his uncle. Had the mask been elven-made? She narrowed her eyes. Definitely Greg. She'd recognize that mop of hair anywhere, even transformed into feathers.

With a defiant screech, Greg flew at them. Lailu and Ryon dove in separate directions, and Lailu could feel all the aches from earlier as she rolled up to her feet. Something fell from her pocket: a pouch full of glittering powder. *Wren's* pouch.

Greg circled, then came back, tearing straight at Lailu.

She ducked, and Greg shot past just above her. As he turned and dove back at her, she lunged forward, snatched the pouch from the ground, and threw a handful of mal-cantation powder into Greg's open beak.

He screeched, the noise turning into a sputter, then a cough as he crashed to the ground, slowly morphing into his human form, then flickering back to a phoenix. Fire danced around his body, feathers sprouting and molting and sprouting again. The mal-cantation powder wasn't enough. The elven mask was just too strong.

Lailu tried to remove the mask, but she couldn't get close enough. The magical flames of the phoenix licked her arms in a wave of heat, and she jerked back.

Ryon darted in, the flames parting around his hands. He grabbed the mask and yanked it off, then stomped it to pieces.

Immediately Greg was Greg again. Lailu hated to admit how relieved that made her . . . until she saw the blood along the side of his head. "Greg?" She knelt down beside him, helping him sit up. "Are you okay?"

Greg groaned and touched his head, his fingers coming away bloody. "What happened?" His eyes darted around in confusion before focusing on Lailu like she somehow had all the answers.

Whirr, click, whirrrr . . .

Lailu turned to Ryon, whose own face mirrored hers.

"We've got to get out of here," she whispered.

"Sorry, sunshine," Ryon said to Greg. "Recovery time is over." He hoisted Greg up onto his feet, and they each took one of Greg's arms.

"Paulie's?" Lailu suggested.

Ryon's eyes widened. "Good choice," he said, and they began walking a barely conscious Greg toward her shop.

Click. Click. Whirr!

Lailu and Ryon moved faster, but Greg was slowing them down.

"Maybe it's time to lose the dead weight," Ryon suggested.

"Ryon!" Lailu snapped.

"Kidding, kidding." He stumbled along. "Well, mostly kidding."

They were almost to Paulie's door when the unmistakable sound of an auto-carriage split the night.

Lailu turned, jaw dropping. Starling had a machine resembling a large harpoon gripped in both arms.

Ryon staggered and almost fell. "Hey, don't let go like that. Your friend here is heavier than he looks."

Pop!

Starling fired her harpoon at the horde of beasts, launching a giant net. It spread open in midair, then swung closed, tangling three of the creatures inside. As they fought the metal net with teeth and claws, they slowly transformed, becoming human once again.

"Whoa," Lailu breathed, impressed.

Starling passed the weapon down to Wren, who eagerly took it and handed Starling another. Wren was positively beaming beside her mother, like this was the mother-daughter activity she'd always dreamed of.

Around them, automatons marched, firing their own nets at the transformed crowds.

"We've got to go," Ryon said.

"But they're helping—" Lailu began.

"Now!"

Lailu grabbed Greg's other arm and ran as fast as she could to Paulie's door. She wasn't sure why Ryon was more scared of the scientists and this newest invention than he was of the transformed people, but she trusted him. If he was scared, then it must be bad.

38

TRAPPED

Paulie opened the door just as they reached it. "In, quickly," she hissed, shutting the door behind them and locking it. She flicked the curtains back half an inch and peered out.

Lailu and Ryon helped Greg into a chair at the small corner table.

"You okay?" Lailu asked. Greg had crashed pretty hard in his transition from winged beast to boy, and she didn't like his color—or rather, lack of color.

"I've felt better." He touched the side of his head and winced.

"Aww, sweetheart, I'll patch you right up," Paulie chimed in.

Greg's eyes widened, and as soon as she had bustled over to the other side of the shop, he whispered, "I—I think I'm okay. I don't think I need any care."

"Don't be silly," Lailu scoffed. "You're bleeding all over the place. Besides, Paulie has all the supplies right here."

"But she's a—"

"Witch?" Paulie suggested coolly, her purple eyes glittering.

Greg and Lailu both jumped.

Paulie had snuck up right behind them, a small basket of bandages and healing salves over one arm.

"Er," Greg managed.

"The best witch in the city," Ryon said quickly. "Thanks for taking us in, Paulie. You know you're my favorite. Next to Lailu, that is." He winked.

Paulie pursed her lips but went ahead and bandaged Greg. She wasn't nearly as gentle as she'd been with Ryon, yet Lailu couldn't blame her. Especially when Greg kept flinching at her touch. Lailu had to admit she'd been scared of Paulie too—her experience with the elves had taught her to be cautious when it came to magic and those who wielded it—but Paulie had been nothing but helpful and kind since she'd met her, and it bothered Lailu to see Greg already passing judgment on her.

Bam! Bam! Bam!

Lailu felt each slam against the door like a punch to the heart. She looked around the room, but everyone else had frozen in place.

"Lailu!" Hannah yelled. "Let me in!"

Lailu scrambled to the door and unlocked it. Hannah flew in, her hair tangled, face red.

"Did you run here?" Lailu asked, shocked. Hannah was not really the biggest fan of exercise.

"I . . . came to warn . . . you," Hannah panted. She glanced back. "Close the door!"

Lailu slammed it shut.

"I saw you . . . come in here," Hannah managed, wheezing. "Been looking all over . . . for you." She looked at Ryon.

Ryon blinked. "Me?"

"Starling told me . . ." Hannah took a deep breath. "Starling told me they set a trap for you."

"What?" Lailu demanded. "Why? And why would she tell you?"

Hannah pushed her sweaty hair back from her face. "They got ahold of some of his blood, and it's been extremely useful to them, far better than the pure elf blood they had before. And she told me because she trusts me." Hannah glanced at Ryon. "I played up my dislike of the elves, like you suggested."

"Clever girl," Ryon said.

"Excuse me, but who are you?" Paulie moved out from behind Lailu, her purple eyes narrowed, hands on hips.

Hannah straightened.

"This is my best friend, Hannah," Lailu said quickly, not under-standing the sudden thickening in the air.

"Hannah. Is that right?" Paulie's smile was not warm or com-forting.

"Wait, I'm so lost," Greg spoke up. "Why would the scientists want Ryon's blood?"

Ryon frowned. "Because I'm half elf—"

"You're *what*?" Greg looked like he was going to fall over.

"How can I work in these conditions?" Ryon muttered. "As all the *intelligent* members of this room know, I'm half elf, so I have a few unique . . . abilities the scientists are interested in."

Greg scowled.

"You can neutralize magic," Lailu realized. "I saw you stop Eirad's magic, and you were able to fix Greg."

"Ah, and did I even get a thank-you?" Ryon stared pointedly at Greg.

Greg swallowed. "Thanks," he muttered. For some reason, he'd never really warmed up to Ryon.

"Greg's gratitude is not the point," Lailu snapped. "Stay on topic for once, would you? What else can you do?"

Ryon sighed. "Not much. Like you saw, I can neutralize elven magic. I can see through it, and if I'm touching something that's been enchanted, I can undo that enchantment. But it's very limited. Only things I touch or see directly. But it's the reason why some like Eirad don't . . . entirely trust me."

"Plus you move with the speed of an elf," Lailu said.

"Probably has elven hearing, too," Hannah suggested.

Ryon looked even more uncomfortable. "Let's not specu-late, okay? I don't make a habit of sharing this kind of infor-mation." He glanced around at the crowded room. "Usually," he amended.

"Enough chitchat," Hannah said. "You need to leave. Now. Before Starling figures out where you've gone."

"Why? Is she going to send someone to collect me?" Ryon smirked. "I'd like to see them try."

Lailu remembered the way Wren's spidery invention had

attacked him, and how he'd been unable to do anything about it. "You should go," she said. "Just in case."

"Is Starling really going to come after me now? She's got her hands full playing the hero, don't you think?"

Outside they could still hear the occasional shriek, but it was getting less frequent.

"This was her whole plan," Hannah said softly. "She found out the elves were going to do something tonight, something big."

"How?" Ryon asked.

Hannah fidgeted. "Gwendyl," she admitted. "I think . . . before she died . . . she talked."

Ryon's expression hardened. "You mean Starling made her talk."

Lailu shivered. What had Starling done to get answers out of an elf? And *this* was the woman Hannah worked for?

"Starling planned to use the chaos tonight as a cover to kidnap you," Hannah finished.

Ryon crossed his arms, clearly not leaving. Why was he being so stubborn about this?

"Ryon, please," Hannah begged.

"No way. If I run now, I'll have to keep running. You really think Starling is going to stop after tonight? If she wants me, she can try to get me."

Bam-bam. Bam-bam. Bam!

Everyone turned and looked at the door. Too late, Lailu realized she hadn't locked it again.

The door flew open.

39

No Escape

Vahn leaped inside, filling the small space and striking a heroic pose, chest out, head up, hair flung dramatically back to flow down his shoulders in a golden river. "Paulie, I'm here to rescue you!" He drew his sword.

"Rescue *me*?" Paulie blinked. "From what? And close the door, would you?"

"The scientists have your shop surrounded. They told me you're being held hostage by an elf. . . ." Vahn trailed off, finally looking around the room. *"Hannah?"* His heroic pose collapsed like a badly made cake. "What are . . . what are you doing here?" He put his free hand to the back of his neck, glancing from Hannah to Paulie and back.

Lailu slipped behind Vahn and kicked the door closed, remembering to lock it this time.

"You know each other?" Paulie asked, voice sugary sweet.

"Er, yes, a bit," Vahn said.

"A *bit*?" Hannah's eyebrows shot up so high they vanished into her hairline. She tilted her head, studying Vahn's reddening face.

"Not to interrupt what promises to be a dramatic and entertaining exchange, but can we get back to the part where the scientists have surrounded us?" Ryon asked quickly. "I'm pretty sure the rest of . . . *this*"—he waved his hands vaguely at Hannah, Paulie, and Vahn—"whatever it is, can wait."

"Yes, exactly right," Vahn said heartily.

"It's not too late, Ryon," Hannah said. "You could sneak out, blend in, escape. I've seen you do it."

Ryon shook his head. "I've made up my mind." He looked around the room. "That doesn't mean the rest of you need to get involved. I don't want anyone else hurt."

"Oh, please," Paulie scoffed. "Most of us can take care of ourselves just fine." She patted her belt, and Lailu suspected she had some sort of magical vials in there. Lailu inched away from her.

Knock-knock-knock.

"Hey? Hello in there?"

Lailu recognized that voice: Neon, inventor of the camera.

"I hate to interrupt, but the king has charged us with the safety of these city streets, and we are certain you are harboring one of those pointy-eared mayhem-creators."

"'Pointy-eared mayhem-creators,'" Ryon mused softly. "I like it."

"Stop it," Lailu hissed. "This is serious." She wasn't afraid of Neon, but all the scientists combined? Her whole body felt like a pot just about to boil. *Focus, Lailu,* she told herself firmly. She'd dealt with a hydra. She could come up with a plan for this. She had to.

"Open your door," Neon said.

"No," Lailu called. "Go away, Neon."

Silence.

"What's the holdup?" someone asked. Lailu didn't recognize his voice.

"They won't open the door," Neon said, sounding hurt.

"Then make them open it, or you'll have to face Starling. You'll have to tell her that you failed. . . ."

"You could help me, Argon," Neon said desperately.

"And get tainted by this brush of failure? No thank you. I like my life. I want to stay in it a bit longer."

"Please, Argon! You know she's just looking for an excuse to get rid of me."

"I don't want her to think I've aligned myself with you and your little mutiny," Argon said. "I saw how that worked out for your buddy, Carbon. Sorry, *friend,* but you are on your own."

Neon went back to pleading at the door, occasionally rattling the handle, and muttering to himself. But Lailu's attention was caught by something much more important.

Click. Click. Whirr . . .

It sounded like it was coming from somewhere behind them. "Paulie, do you have a back door to your shop?" Lailu asked.

"I . . . have a trapdoor in my kitchen," Paulie admitted. "It's not safe to have only one way out of your house. Not when so many people here are mistrustful of us magic users." She glanced sideways at Greg. He flushed and looked down at his feet. "But no one can find it. It's very well hidden."

"By magic?" Lailu suggested.

"Which the scientists are now able to neutralize?" Hannah added.

Paulie's mouth fell open. "Oh."

Crash!

Lailu whirled. An automaton had just burst into the kitchen.

Paulie reacted first, pulling a vial from her belt and hurling it at the automaton. It staggered back as a purple cloud floated around it. The color sizzled and flared . . . and then faded.

Click. Whirr. Click.

The automaton stepped forward, its blue eyes blazing triumphantly.

"That's not good," Paulie whispered. "That was one of my strongest potions."

"They must be coated in some sort of mal-cantation mixture," Lailu said.

Vahn leaped in front of them. He did a fancy forward flip, drew his sword in midair, and slammed the flat of the blade into the metal creation, knocking it to the side. It lurched back up immediately, staggering toward Vahn.

Click.

Knives extended from its fingers, and it swiped them at his face.

Vahn parried, then smacked his blade into the automaton again, sending it reeling. It was down for less than a second before it shot back to its feet.

"The wires!" Lailu said. "You need to cut the wires behind its head."

"I know!" Vahn shouted. "But they've been covered."

Lailu moved closer, and now she saw it too: at the back of the automaton's neck was a freshly installed metal grate keeping all its wires protected. This was an improved model. Even though Starling wasn't responsible for the mutiny at the parade, it was clear that she had learned from it and had taken steps to ensure that no one could stop an automaton under her control.

Lailu didn't have much time to worry about it, though, because already another automaton had stepped through the busted trap-door. And then another. And another.

"Um, guys?" Lailu drew her knife.

Greg moved to stand beside her, his face gray but determined as he drew his own knife. Lailu hated to admit it, but she felt much more confident with Greg at her back. Even an injured Greg was more than a match for a couple of metal beasts.

The first automaton got past Vahn, and Lailu was ready for it. She darted in, slashing with her knife, then ducking as it swiped at her. As they circled each other, she studied that grate on its neck. It had to have other weaknesses.

Dimly she was aware of Ryon fighting two separate automatons, his movements as fast as ever as he tricked them into stabbing each other, their knives embedding in each other's metal plating. Beside him, Paulie threw herbs and cast spells, but nothing seemed to work.

"Lailu, watch out!" Greg knocked her to the side as her automaton sliced the air inches in front of her. It spun, one of its metal hands grabbing Greg around the neck and lifting him off his feet.

"Greg!" Lailu stabbed her knife right through the tiny opening in the automaton between its arm and torso.

Sparks flared out, its hand opened, and Greg tumbled to the ground, gasping.

The automaton stumbled, its arm going up, then down, then up uncontrollably. "Stab them through the joints!" Lailu shouted. "It messes them up."

"*Yah!*" Hannah leaped in brandishing a frying pan and slammed it into the automaton's face. As it fell backward, Lailu stabbed it through the other arm joint, and it hit the ground, fizzled, and lay still.

"Thanks, Hannah," Lailu said.

"Don't mention it." Hannah whirled the frying pan in her hands and spun to find her next target.

Pop!

Lailu turned, but too slowly.

The net caught her, Greg, and Hannah, slamming them together and down to the ground.

Pop! Pop!

Vahn and Paulie went down.

Ryon managed to dodge, the nets no match for his speed.

Neon stepped through the front door with three other scientists flanking him. As Ryon lunged forward, Neon tossed a handful of glittery powder.

It caught Ryon midstride. He coughed, spluttered, and then crashed to the ground next to Lailu.

"Ryon!" She thrashed against the net. Her knife couldn't do anything against the metal fibers. She was trapped. Greg and Hannah struggled next to her, their arms and legs tangling with her own, making it even harder.

"I am truly sorry about this, but it can't be helped." Neon shook his head sadly. "Get him," he ordered, and the automaton next to him stepped forward.

It looked down at Lailu as it passed, its blue eyes glinting beneath the rim of a familiar bowler hat. Then it hoisted an unconscious Ryon over one shoulder, turned, and left the shop, the front door closing softly behind it.

40

WREN DEFIANT

Lailu's fingers were all cut up, blood making her grip slippery, but she was so close. Gritting her teeth, she twisted the metal ends one more time.

"Got it?" Hannah asked. She and Greg had moved as far away as possible, trying to stretch the end of the net so Lailu could work on opening it.

"Almost . . . almost . . ." Lailu slipped the metal coil off to the side, and the net opened. "Got it!"

"Wow, Lailu, you are amazing!" Hannah squealed, jumping to her feet and dancing around.

"I'd be more amazing if I could have stopped this from happening in the first place. Do you know where they're taking Ryon?"

Hannah stopped jumping around. "I've been thinking about it, and it has to be Starling's hidden workshop."

"She has a hidden workshop?" Greg staggered out of the net and leaned against a wall for support.

"She mentioned it to me, but she didn't tell me where it is," Hannah said. "All I know is her most delicate experiments are done there. She said science is too important to be constantly under watch. I think she knew Lord Elister wouldn't approve of everything she was doing."

"Do you have any idea where it might be?" Lailu asked. "Any at all? Maybe Starling dropped some hint?"

Hannah squeezed her eyes shut, obviously thinking hard. "I . . . remember she complained about the stairs. She said it was a real challenge lugging her supplies up three flights of them."

"Three flights of stairs . . ." Lailu frowned, thinking it over. There were plenty of buildings that were three stories tall.

Including . . . the Crow's Nest.

"No," Lailu whispered. But it made a certain poetic sense that Starling would have taken over Mr. Boss's old hangout spot. No one would think to look for her there, and it was pretty well hidden behind the bar and up those creaky wooden steps. It would also explain why that automaton had a picture of the sign in its memory.

"What is it?" Hannah asked.

"I think I know where they are."

"Then what are we waiting for?" Greg asked.

"Um, a little help here first, maybe?" Vahn called out.

Lailu glanced back guiltily—she had almost forgotten about Vahn. He was stuck in the net with Paulie unconscious next to him.

"The net did something to her," Vahn explained. "I think

Paulie doesn't respond well to its magic-canceling effect."

"Oh, and I'm sure you know exactly what she responds well to," Hannah said, sniffing.

"Not the time," Greg whispered.

"Hmph." Hannah tossed her hair to the side and walked to the front door, waiting.

Lailu debated. It had taken her many precious minutes to get her own net open, and she wasn't sure how much time Ryon had. She tried not to picture Wren's den, the way those mystical creatures had been cut into pieces, each limb stretched out and labeled. What were they going to do to Ryon? Were they harvesting him for parts even now?

She made a decision.

"Greg, you stay here and help Vahn and Paulie," she ordered.

"What? Why?"

"Because you can barely stand, let alone run. And I know you'll take good care of them."

Greg opened his mouth to argue.

"Please. Just trust me," Lailu said. "We're running out of time."

Greg frowned, then nodded. "Okay. I trust you."

Lailu turned to her friend. "Hannah—"

"I'm coming with you," Hannah insisted. "I can help with Starling." She slung the frying pan over her shoulder.

"Fine. Let's go," Lailu said.

"Wait!" Greg threw his arms around her.

Lailu froze, completely shocked as Greg pulled her against him in a tight hug.

"Be careful, Crabby Cakes, okay?" he whispered into her hair. Then he let her go.

Lailu stood there a second, not certain how she felt—definitely a little annoyed that he was bringing up her nickname, but also confused. As Greg's cheeks reddened, she settled for unsure; she'd figure it out later. Then she turned, and together she and Hannah ran out the door and down the street toward the one building Lailu had thought she'd never have to see again: the Crow's Nest.

"I have got to . . . get into . . . better running . . . shape," Hannah panted.

"You could always come along on more hunts with me," Lailu suggested as she jogged along next to her. "It's amazing how fast you can run when a hydra's after you."

"I'll pass," Hannah muttered, adjusting her grip on her frying pan as she ran.

These streets were starting to look familiar, and Lailu knew they were close to Mr. Boss's old hangout. It was impossible not to think of her last time here, when Mr. Boss had sent his lackeys to threaten her into spying on Elister and she'd been forced to make the journey out to the Crow's Nest to give her report.

At least this time she had Hannah with her.

"It's just up ahead," Lailu told her friend.

"Can we slow down . . . catch our breath a sec?" Hannah gasped. "I don't want to pass out in front of Starling."

They slowed down to a brisk walk, the night chill seeping in, freezing Lailu's sweaty clothes against her. There weren't as many people on this side of town, and thankfully the few they passed were all human-shaped and too busy with their own celebrations to bother Lailu or Hannah.

"Hey, before we get there," Hannah said suddenly, "I wanted to talk to you."

"Oh yeah?" Lailu's stomach clenched tighter than fusilli noodles. What now?

"I wanted to say . . ." Hannah took a deep breath, wheezing slightly. "I'm sorry."

"You're . . . sorry?"

"Yes," Hannah said. "I haven't been a very good friend lately. I know I've been absent a lot this week, and I never told you that Vahn asked me out, even though I know you liked him—"

"I heard—" Lailu began, but Hannah was on a roll now, her words spilling out faster than griffin stew from a cracked pot.

"I didn't say yes, exactly," Hannah rushed on, "but I also didn't say no, and I never said anything to you about it. I wanted to a hundred times, I really did! But I just, I couldn't. I haven't been honest with you about Ryon, either."

"Wait, what? Ryon?" Lailu slowed down, her heart thumping. "Are you guys *dating*?"

Hannah laughed. "Oh no, I'm just working for him."

"Oh." Lailu relaxed. Then she thought about the line of work Ryon was in, and all her earlier tension came back. "Oh!" She studied her friend. "You're a *spy*?"

Hannah nodded.

"Since when?"

"Since the First Day of Masks. He visited me before Lord Elister's party and told me I had potential, and we struck a deal. Well, two deals, actually, if you count our bet that he couldn't get you to dance."

"That was real?" Lailu's ears burned.

"Sorry, Lailu honey. You're going to have to feed him a full meal. Oh, and I threw in appetizers, too."

"Butter knives," Lailu swore.

"But our other deal was, if I could find an in with Starling, he'd train me to be a spy." Hannah bit her lip. "No comment about Vahn?"

"I tried telling you, I already knew he asked you out," Lailu said as breezily as she could manage. "I'm over it."

They turned the corner, and there was the familiar three-story building just ahead. The full moon made it easy to see the badly inked crow on the swaying sign above it, proclaiming it as the Crow's Nest.

"So . . . the job with Starling?" Lailu prodded.

"Was just a way for me to keep an eye on her." Hannah turned her frying pan over and over. "I should have told you the truth about that, but I know how much you hate all the spying stuff. I was trying to keep you out of it."

Lailu was quiet as they walked up to the front door. She remembered that feeling of loss, that crushing, heavy sadness. "It just made me feel like I was being left behind," she said softly. "By you, and Ryon, and everyone."

Hannah's eyes filled with tears. "I'm sorry. I thought I was protecting you. If we survive this, I promise I'll tell you everything."

Lailu thought of all the secrets and spying. It seemed stressful. "Maybe not everything," she said. "Just . . . some things. You know, big things."

Hannah smiled. "Whatever you want. You're my best friend, and I love you. I would *never* leave you."

Lailu blinked, and blinked again, her vision blurry. "I love you too, Hannah," she sniffled. And then they were hugging, Hannah's frying pan wedged awkwardly between them, and Lailu wasn't sure if she was laughing or crying, but she felt lighter than she had in days.

"I hope we don't die in there now," Hannah sobbed, "but if we do, I didn't want you to die mad at me."

"I wasn't mad at you." Lailu sniffed. "Not really. And we're not going to die in there." She wiped the back of her hand across her eyes. "Probably," she added, since they were being truthful. "We're *probably* not going to die." She sniffed again, pulling away and squaring her shoulders.

Hannah stood shoulder to shoulder with her, both of them gazing up at the door, neither of them making a move to open it.

"We've got this," Hannah said finally, swinging her frying pan around in a complicated loop.

"You've really taken to that, haven't you?" Lailu nodded at the pan.

Hannah grinned. "It's growing on me. I plan to dress it up when we leave here."

If we leave here, Lailu thought grimly. She gripped the familiar splintery doorknob, pushed open the door, and stepped inside.

It was quieter than she remembered, but there was still a sizable crowd of men and women drinking and laughing and talking way too loudly. Lailu was relieved to see that nobody here wore a mask; she'd seen enough masks to last a lifetime.

"How are we going to get past the bartender?" Hannah asked.

"Maybe you and Mr. Smacky there could take him," Lailu suggested.

Hannah's eyes narrowed. "Lailu, I may love you, and I know we just made up and everything, but you are *not* allowed to name my frying pan."

Lailu studied the bartender. Tall and beefy, with a hole where one of his ears should be, he did not look like the kind of man who would kindly let them pass, frying pan or no.

"Maybe he remembers you?" Hannah suggested.

"Doubtful. And even if he did, I don't think he'd care." Lailu bit her lip, thinking hard. For all she knew, this wasn't even Starling's secret den, and all she was doing was wasting time while the scientists drained Ryon of blood. She had to act, and act quickly.

"Lailu? What are you doing here?"

Lailu jumped. "Wren?" she asked. Wren sat at a nearby table looking miserable, a glass of chocolate milk in front of her. "Is your mom here?"

"How did you know? I mean, no. No she's not." Wren sighed. "I just gave it away, didn't I?" She put her face in her hands. "Mama's right, I really don't use my brain enough. It's faulty, just like all my inventions."

Lailu wavered. She was very aware of time running out, but she needed Wren's help. "Wren, is everything okay?"

Wren shook her head, not looking up.

"What happened?"

Wren sniffed. "I invented the neutro-net, and it worked so well, so well." She sniffed again.

"Handkerchief, quickly," Lailu whispered to Hannah. "Here." Lailu shoved the embroidered scrap of cotton at Wren. "Please, *please* use this."

"Thanks, Lailu. You're the only one who cares." Wren blew her nose noisily. "Mama seemed really proud, but then one of my neutro-net launchers jammed, and when Zinc tried smacking it to get it to work again, it . . ."

"It what?" Lailu asked.

"It exploded." Wren hung her head. "Zinc is Mama's current favorite scientist. Mama *had* to rush him out of there and wasn't able to see the fruition of her plan. She hates when that happens. And it was my fault."

Lailu glanced at Hannah. She wasn't sure what to do here.

"Aww, Wren, it's not your fault," Hannah tried.

Wren glared at her. "What would you know? You never mess anything up."

Hannah blinked. "Um, actually, I mess up quite a lot. But I can see I'm going to be no help here." Hannah nudged Lailu.

Lailu wasn't good at this sort of thing. "Wren," she began slowly, carefully, "your mom is wrong. And her plan is wrong. She kidnapped Ryon, and I need to get him back. Will you help me?"

Wren's eyes widened. "You want to rescue Ryon? Why? He's not human."

That was it. Lailu had *had* it with Wren's attitude. "He is so human! *You're* not human," she snapped. "Only someone *inhuman* would allow elves to be chained up or kidnap my friend. I thought you were my friend too, Wren!"

Wren's eyes filled with tears again, but for once they had no effect on Lailu. "I *am* your friend."

"Then prove it," Lailu said. "Help me. That's what friends do."

"Mama would be so mad. So, so mad." Wren's eyes narrowed. "Of course, she's already mad." She stood up. "You know what, I don't care anymore. Let her be mad. So what if I'm a disappointment? So what if she should have just left me in Beolann?" Wren blew her nose on Hannah's handkerchief, then scrunched the cloth in her fist.

"Oh, Wren, she didn't really say that to you, did she?" Hannah asked.

Wren ignored her. "If I help you, Lailu, then you'll still be my friend?"

Lailu nodded.

"Then let's go." Wren whistled, and three of her little spider automatons scuttled out from beneath tables and chairs.

Lailu leaped back.

"Oh, don't worry, they follow my orders," Wren said. "They won't hurt my *friends*." And she led the way to the back of the bar, her spi-trons scurrying along in her wake.

DOING WHAT IS NECESSARY

The bartender glanced at Wren and let all three girls pass without a word. Lailu's mouth was drier than fyrian chicken meat as she followed Wren up the hidden staircase behind the bottles of beer. Would they be too late? What would they find up there?

And what was she going to do? Lailu had no plan and only one knife. Three flights of stairs later, and she still didn't have a plan. She'd just have to wing it.

"Let's do this," she whispered, pushing the door open and jumping inside. She drew her knife, then froze.

The room had been completely transformed. Gone were the rickety tables and tall-backed chairs, the candles and smoke and empty glasses. Instead, Starling sat calmly at a small, polished card table. A series of glowing orbs hung from the ceiling, illuminating the room and glinting off all of Starling's carefully organized tools. Lailu glimpsed a large operating table in back and shelves full of parts, all neatly stacked, with wires hung in tidy coils against the wall.

And Ryon, pinned in the corner by Walton—who held a jagged knife a mere eyelash-blink from Ryon's left eye.

Lailu gasped.

"Hello, Lailu. I can't say I'm surprised to see you. Won't you please have a seat?" Starling indicated one of the empty chairs in front of her, then took a sip of her tea and smiled.

Lailu bit her lip, then started forward.

"Drop the knife first," Starling ordered.

Lailu hesitated.

"Let me rephrase that more accurately. Drop the knife, or your friend loses an eye." Starling pulled a small rectangular item out from her belt and placed it on the table in front of her. "Unfortunately, Walton has been somewhat . . . temperamental with me. It still will not respond to my voice commands, thanks to my daughter's incompetence, but I assure you, *this* it will respond to."

Lailu dropped her knife.

"Thanks," Ryon called.

"Well, the last thing I need is for you to be winking permanently," Lailu said as calmly as she could manage over her galloping heart.

"Your concern touches me," Ryon said.

Lailu took a seat.

"Hannah," Starling called out suddenly, "won't you join us as well? I must admit, I'm very disappointed in you."

"Your hair looks amazing, though," Hannah said brightly as she entered the room. "That style really does suit you."

Starling touched the bronze dragon comb holding her red hair back in an elaborate twist. "It does, doesn't it?" She sighed. "You showed such promise. I was really hoping you would pass my little test. But you know what they say: good help is hard to come by. Now, drop the frying pan."

There was a clatter behind Lailu.

"Sit next to your friend," Starling ordered.

Hannah sat next to Lailu. She looked calm, composed, relaxed even. Lailu wasn't sure how she did it.

"And you." Starling turned her attention to Wren, who had come in behind Hannah. "My own daughter. I have no words." She shook her head. "No words."

Wren flushed and looked down at her feet. "Sorry, Mama."

"Well, it's not any less than I'd expect from you."

Wren sniffed. "I just . . . Lailu is my friend. . . ." Her words died in the face of Starling's scorn.

Starling turned to Lailu, ignoring Wren as if her daughter weren't even there. "Wren always was a little too softhearted for her own good." She took another sip of tea, then set her mug down with a soft clink.

"That's not fair." Lailu's hands curled into useless fists. "Why are you so hard on her?"

"It's okay, Lailu—" Wren started.

"How else is she going to learn?" Starling spoke over her daughter.

"But Wren tries really hard, and she's quite brilliant," Lailu said.

"Her inventions are often rushed. Careless. Faulty."

"She's still a kid."

Starling's eyebrows rose. "That's hardly an excuse. After all, you're still a kid, and look at you, running your own restaurant. And your lovely friend here, well . . ." Starling smiled at Hannah. "She's just a kid, technically, and yet she's been spying on me. I'm beginning to wonder if she's been spying on me this whole time. And for whom? That is the question." Starling tapped her fingers against the remote. Lailu noticed she kept her nails short, practical. They were hands a chef would be proud of. "Who are you working for, Hannah?"

"I don't understand," Hannah said innocently.

"You're very good at playing dumb, but I'm not fooled by the pretty face and wide eyes." Starling leaned forward. "If you want your friend to come out of this with both of *his* eyes, you'll drop the act and tell me what I want to know."

"I'm not working for anyone," Hannah said. "Only myself. *I* wanted to know what you're up to."

"Why?"

"Because I'd hoped I could leverage that information. Or possibly, I could help you. You know my past. You know there's no love lost between me and those elves." Hannah's lips curled. "They deserve whatever you have planned for them."

"I wish I could believe you," Starling said. "Had you come to me openly, maybe we could have worked together."

Click–click–click.

Lailu glanced at the doorway in time to see one of Wren's spitrons scuttling inside.

"As it is," Starling sighed, "trust is impossible at this point." Her gaze slid from Hannah to Lailu. "I know Elister is fond of you, Lailu, but I can hardly take care of your friend and leave you. And I'm afraid I simply cannot tolerate this kind of failure."

"What are you going to do?" Lailu asked, very aware of her knife lying on the ground just a few short feet away.

"I am going to do what I always do," Starling said coldly. "What is necessary."

And she punched the button on the remote.

42

CONFRONTATION

"Walton, no!" Wren shrieked.

The automaton froze.

"Drop the knife," Wren ordered.

"Wren, what are you—" Starling began.

Walton dropped the knife with a clatter and turned to face Wren, its blue eyes glowing beneath its hat. It tilted its head, awaiting further instructions.

Lailu took advantage of Starling's confusion and lunged across the table, grappling for the remote.

Starling was tall and had an adult's strength, but Lailu was used to fighting against kraken and dragons and all sorts of beasties. If she could ride a full-grown griffin, she could handle Starling. She managed to twist the remote from Starling's grasp and toss it to Hannah.

And then the scientist pulled something out of her waistband. A long metal tube with a handle.

Lailu froze. She recognized this thing, remembered seeing Starling fire projectiles at the automatons with it. From this distance, anything that came out of it would go right through her.

"Give me back the remote," Starling snarled, her eyes glittering dangerously as she pulled back on the lever.

"Don't do it, Hannah," Lailu said. "She's only going to kill me anyhow."

Hannah slumped forward. "I'm sorry, Lailu. I can't just sit here and watch."

Click-click-click.

Another spi-tron moved into view just as Hannah tossed the remote at Starling.

Starling caught it awkwardly with one hand, and Lailu ducked, grabbed the spi-tron, and flung it in Starling's face.

Starling moved faster than Lailu thought possible, smacking the spi-tron with the butt of her weapon.

"No!" Wren gasped.

Lailu had already lunged into Hannah, knocking her friend back. She heard Wren yelling orders to Walton, saw the automaton leaping forward just as the spi-tron flared impossibly bright and exploded in a shower of fire and light.

Everything hurt. Lailu's skin felt hot and too tight, like stretched meat. Her chest and arms ached, and her nose burned from the overwhelming scent of peppermint.

Someone was singing. Lailu recognized the voice, beautiful and rich, the lyrics painting a picture of love lost, and a bird in a cinnamon tree. It was one of Lailu's favorite folk songs from her village. "M-Mom?" she croaked, opening her eyes.

The singing stopped, the figure beside her blurring into two figures. Lailu blinked. No, one figure. Her mother, hair unbrushed, eyes shadowed.

"Thank the gods." Lianna put a hand over her heart. "I was afraid . . . but of course you're tough enough to handle a blast like that. Any daughter of mine . . ."

"Blast?" Lailu's memory was hazy. She remembered yelling, threats, Starling's face lit up in bright lights, her green eyes wide, reflecting the glow of . . .

Lailu staggered to her feet, the world twisting beneath her.

"Not so fast." Lianna pushed Lailu back into bed. Only then did she notice she was home, wrapped up in bed like a sushi roll.

"Where's Hannah? Is she okay? And Ryon?" Lailu struggled against her blankets.

"They're both okay, honey. You protected them."

Lailu relaxed, all the fight trickling out of her.

Lianna smoothed Lailu's hair from her forehead. "You took the worst of the blast. Well, aside from the automaton and . . . and . . . Starling Volan." Lianna said this last name softly, sadly.

"Starling, is she . . ." Lailu swallowed.

Lianna shook her head, and Lailu knew then that the scientist was dead.

Emotions warred and mixed in her stomach like an ill-prepared sauce. Starling was dead . . . because of her. What would happen now—to her, to her friends?

What would happen to *Wren*?

"I know what you're thinking, love, but it was *not* your fault. Hannah already told us what happened. You did what you had to do to survive and save your friends."

Lailu thought of Elister, and it was as if the sauce in her stomach had solidified and curdled. What would he do when he found out his star scientist was dead? If he didn't know already. "Sometimes the good of the country must take precedence over justice," Lailu whispered.

"Where did you hear *that* load of garbage?"

"Lord Elister." Lailu closed her eyes. "When I told him I thought the scientists had killed Carbon."

"Well, you were absolutely right about that."

"I was?" Lailu's eyes flew open.

"Oh yes. I told you Elister sent for me because he didn't entirely trust Starling? I've been tailing her and the other scientists all week."

"Really?" Lailu still had a hard time picturing her mother tailing anyone. Her mother . . . the spy.

"I was too slow to help you today, but at least I was able to recover the cylinder from the automaton you faced tonight. Well, some of the cylinder was melted, but I could see enough to prove what happened." Lianna sighed. "Carbon wasn't even the first."

"But why? He was working for her."

"Yes, but he had also started making plans to leave her. Starling wouldn't tolerate that. So she had him killed by his own invention."

"So Walton *did* kill him," Lailu said, remembering the hat and the spot of mud on the rim. Strangely, she felt sorry for the automaton, forced to kill its creator.

"I think Starling wanted to make a powerful demonstration to the other scientists that she could turn their creations against them. And it worked—there was no more talk of leaving. But I wonder what will happen now, without her there to keep them all in line." Lianna pursed her lips. "Such a mess. You know, one of her previous hairdressers turned up dead too? Apparently she was trying to help Carbon and his friends start their own businesses. Hannah discovered that. She said you gave her the tip."

Lailu felt even sicker. "Hannah was always in danger, then. Even before she helped us."

"Oh, don't you worry about Hannah. That girl has a knack for getting herself into and then *out of* danger." Lianna smiled fondly. "You've chosen your friends well."

"Did you know she's a spy now too?" Lailu asked.

"I've suspected as much. Ever since I saw her whispering with Ryon."

"You know him, don't you?"

"I know him by reputation only. If you need answers about Twin Rivers, the word in the spy world is that he's the guy to go to."

"*Your* world," Lailu said, and even she could hear the bitterness in her voice. Her fight with her mother came rushing back, and she closed her eyes.

"Honey, I know you have a lot of questions, and you have a right to feel betrayed, but I've never lied to you," Lianna said softly.

"I've just never . . . mentioned my side job. It was a good fit. I enjoy traveling, meeting new people, and seeing new things, and Elister needed eyes and ears all around the country. It's the reason I was out in Clear Lakes in the first place."

Lailu opened her eyes at the mention of her home village. "Why would Elister want a spy out there?" Clear Lakes was tiny and far from the capital. And then she realized. "The Krigaen border."

Lianna nodded. "I was supposed to check it out. I only planned to stay a few weeks, but your father . . . well. He's very charming."

"Dad?" Lailu asked incredulously. Her father was a very serious, hardworking man. He only spoke when he had something important to say, didn't believe in dancing or loud music, and seemed like the complete opposite of her mother. Honestly, Lailu had never understood what they saw in each other, but mostly, she tried not to think about it. "So you've been working for Elister this whole time?"

"Off and on." Lianna stood. "And don't you worry about him, either. I've already spoken with him. Everything's been taken care of. You'll see." She dropped a newspaper on Lailu's lap. "We'll talk more about this later, okay? Rest up." Then she strode out of the room.

Lailu picked up the paper, the bandages on her hands making everything clumsy.

Elves Banished after Deadly Attack Kills Talented Scientist!

At nightfall on the Final Night of Masks, elves orchestrated a deadly and malicious attack. "Only one fatality," a source close to the palace confirmed, "but hundreds were injured. Thank the gods for the scientists. They saved us all!"

Starling Volan, head of the scientists and the one responsible for protecting Twin Rivers, credited her daughter for this rescue mission just hours before her death. "Wren discovered the necessary ingredient we needed to neutralize the threat magic represents. She has really come into her own as an inventor. I couldn't be more proud." These will unfortunately be the last remembered words of this remarkable scientist, and loving mother.

Even though this attack seemed to be the actions of a small group of elves, Lord Elister had this to say:

"While the elven leader Fahr and I have worked hard on a peace, I cannot ignore this attack and must take steps to protect the people of Twin Rivers. Henceforth all elves are banished from this city's borders. Any elf found within the confines of these walls is subject to immediate arrest."

Although Fahr has vowed to uphold Elister's decision, many insiders have doubts about his ability to do so.

"It seems to me he can't really control his people," said Jonah Gumple, one of the victims of this attack. "How can we trust he will enforce this edict?" Mr. Gumple was particularly distraught since he had attacked his future mother-in-law while enchanted to resemble a skilly-wig.

(story continued on page 5)

Lailu's hands shook as she read the article again. The elves had nothing to do with Starling's death! Sure, they had caused all the mayhem in the city, but to blame them for murder?

Tap. Tap. Tap.

Lailu jumped. A shadow loomed in her window, silhouetted against the setting sun. She dropped the newspaper and drew the knife above her bed before she realized that it was just Ryon.

He pushed on the window, frowned, then tapped again.

Lailu sighed and opened it.

"Got yourself a lock, I see. Clever." He climbed in and sat on the windowsill. "Brr, it's cold out there." He pulled his jacket closer.

Lailu studied him carefully. He looked mildly bruised but otherwise seemed fine, not like someone who'd nearly lost an eye or two.

"You know, you can put the knife away. It's just me," he said.

"That's why I have my knife out."

He grinned. "Fair enough. Although it would be unfortunate if you went through all that trouble to save me just to stab me now."

"Unfortunate," Lailu agreed drily. "Maybe I'll just push you out instead, and then we can see if flying is another one of your 'special talents.'"

Ryon glanced down, then slid off the windowsill and took a slow, deliberate step away from it. "I see someone's still a little upset about my secrets. But, Lailu, you understand why I try not to let anyone know about my abilities, right? It either makes people uncomfortable or it makes me a target."

"You could have told me. I thought we were friends."

"We are. And you're right, I could have. I've just . . . I've gotten used to keeping things to myself. I'm sorry."

Lailu deliberated, then put down the knife.

"Whew! I was getting worried there." Ryon made a show of relaxing. "How are you, by the way?"

"Me?" Lailu asked. "Fine. Never better."

"Awful, huh?"

She nodded.

"Well, you can stop that. Feeling awful, that is," he said. "That woman got what she deserved."

"But . . . I killed my friend's mom! My friend who helped me save *you*."

"First, technically Starling did that to herself. She hit that disturbing metal monstrosity and caused it to explode. The fact that you'd tossed it in her face makes no difference," he continued quickly, stalling Lailu's protests. "And second, while I appreciate your friend stopping the automaton last night, she wasn't exactly an innocent bystander. If it weren't for her, I wouldn't have needed rescuing in the first place."

"But she's just a kid—"

"So you keep saying. But she's not much younger than you, and she's committed some horrible deeds herself—or do you really believe she took no part in the draining of the elves' blood?"

Lailu reluctantly shook her head.

"Well, if that's no comfort, think of it this way: if it hadn't been Starling, it would have been you, it would have been Hannah, and it would have been me. Personally, I think you made the right choice. Don't you?" Ryon crossed his arms.

Lailu sighed. "I do. Of course I do."

"Good. Then quit feeling awful." He inclined his head toward the newspaper. "I see you know about the banishment."

"It's strange, isn't it? That no one was killed last night?" Lailu said.

"The elves made a deal with Elister. They aren't allowed to kill anyone under his protection, and I don't think they've found a loophole in that. Even the people they enchanted weren't able to kill either, only injure."

"Oh." Lailu tried not to think of the screams of pain and terror from everyone who was "only" being injured last night.

"And it turns out, I was wrong about Fahr," Ryon added bitterly. "He was working with Eirad the whole time. This enchantment scheme was done with his approval. What he thought they would accomplish . . . I mean, of course Elister would banish them after this stunt."

"I'm sorry," Lailu said, and she meant it. It had seemed to mean a lot to Ryon that his half brother was not involved.

Ryon ran a hand through his hair. "I thought . . ." He shook his head. "Sometimes you see in a person what you want to see in them, and not what's really there."

Lailu nodded.

"If anyone asks about me, I'll be keeping a low profile. But I'll see you around." He swung his leg over the edge of the windowsill, then glanced back at her. "And thank you, Lailu. It was a lucky day when I started working for Mr. Boss, because it brought me to you."

Before Lailu could think of a reply, he was gone into the night.

She shivered in the sudden draft. "He could have at least closed the window behind him," she muttered. But she was smiling as she leaned out the window and let the chill evening air cool her face.

43

MASTER CHEF LOGANBERRY

*L*ailu kept one hand on the banister as she slowly made her way down the stairs. She pushed open the door, then leaned against it. Getting blown up had taken all the strength right out of her.

". . . shouldn't tell her now," Hannah was saying out in the dining room. "Give her some time."

Sighing, Lailu pulled back the curtain and stepped through. "Tell who what?" she asked.

Hannah and Slipshod immediately fell silent. The fact that they were sitting together in the first place was surprising enough. "You have news for me, don't you?" Lailu realized.

"Oh, Lailu, I'm so glad you're awake!" Hannah rushed over and threw her arms around her.

Lailu stumbled, then managed to catch her balance.

"We've been so worried about you! Sorry, I'll stop hugging you."
Hannah let her go, then lunged in and hugged her again.

"Get off!" Lailu laughed, pushing at her friend. "How long was
I out for?" Had it been days? Lailu had a sudden, terrible thought.
Weeks? Was Mystic Cooking ruined in her absence?

"Hours," Hannah said.

Lailu almost fell over. "That's *all*? Why were you so worried?"

"Well, your mom had to use Paulie's ointments on you as well
as her own. She was worried about your hands."

Lailu looked down at the bandages, dread curdling in her gut like
overcooked cream sauce. Her hands were her life. "Will they be okay?"

"Oh yes—a bit of scarring, but nothing that will hinder your
cooking. Paulie did a wonderful job." Hannah bit her lip.

"Is . . . is everything okay?" Lailu asked. "With you and Paulie?"

"Oh, *Paulie* and I are just fine. We've had a chance to . . . discuss
a few things. I've got no issue with *her*." Hannah's smile was cold
and quite terrifying.

"This is all very well and good," Slipshod said, "but I've got
news I need to tell you, Pigtails."

"I thought we agreed you would wait?" Hannah frowned.

"I did. I waited for you two to finish your reunion. But I'm
afraid this can't wait any longer." He stood up, brushed his hands on
his apron, and cleared his throat. "So. Well. That is."

"Very informative," Lailu said.

"Oh, hush. He's about to tell you he's taking the job with the
king." Hannah sniffed. "I'll be in back. I think someone's knocking." She shot Slipshod a disgusted look, then strode off.

Slipshod looked down at his boots.

"Is that true?" Lailu asked.

"It is," he admitted. "You . . . you could come with me?" he added hopefully. "The king specifically mentioned there would be room for both of us."

"And leave Mystic Cooking?" Lailu shook her head.

"That's what I thought," he sighed. "Which is why I preemptively did this." He pulled a roll of parchment from his back pocket and handed it to Lailu.

Sniffing, she opened it, and read:

Lailu Loganberry has hereby completed her apprenticeship on this, the Final Day of the Week of Masks. Full Master Chef status has been awarded to her. Welcome, Master Chef Lailu Loganberry, and may you serve Savoria well.

It was signed by Slipshod, Elister, her old teacher Master Sanford, and the king. Lailu folded it up again, feeling numb.

"And this is yours too." Slipshod handed her another roll. "You don't have to open it. It's the deed to Mystic Cooking. This restaurant is yours now." He smiled a little sadly. "It's always been yours, truly."

Lailu's fingers curled around the deed. She felt like someone had taken a giant spoon to her insides. But there was one thought that cheered her up. "At least I can say I finished my apprenticeship before Greg."

Master Slipshod cleared his throat. "Well. About that." He picked up his copy of the morning paper, flipped through to a page in the middle, and thrust it at her. "I'm going to leave now before you read that. I'll see you around, Pigtails." He hesitated, then added, "I know I haven't always been the best mentor. . . ." He paused.

Lailu said nothing.

"Okay, that pause was for you to jump in and disagree."

"Oh. Um, you've been the best mentor I ever had," she tried.

"But only by process of elimination, eh?" Slipshod chuckled. "I have nothing more to teach you, Master Chef Loganberry. But I do have one more thing to say." He removed his fluffy white chef's hat and stood up straighter, like he was about to give an important speech. "I have done many things in my life. I have hunted and cooked creatures you've never even heard of, I wrote the most highly regarded book on dragon cuisine, and I served the old king himself. But truly, being your mentor has been my greatest honor."

Lailu's chest tightened, and she wasn't sure what to say. "Thank you," she managed. "For believing in me when no one else did." She would always remember that Slipshod was the one chef willing to take a chance on her and her restaurant idea.

Slipshod scrunched his hat awkwardly in his hands. "No, Lailu. Thank *you*. You've taught me far more than I could ever teach you. Thank you for reminding this old man how to dream." He squeezed her shoulder. "I'm sure you will do amazing things."

Lailu watched until he vanished past the curtain into the kitchen, his footsteps echoing up the stairs. She sniffed and wiped her eyes on her sleeve. That made her think of Wren, and the tears fell even faster, splattering the paper in her hands.

She glanced at it.

A large picture of Greg grinning next to his uncle took up most of the space. Not surprising. He was probably getting credit for something or other. Lailu skimmed the caption, the words *youngest*, *achieved*, and *master chef status* flashing out at her.

Her tears dried up, evaporating in the face of her anger. "No way," she breathed. "That lousy weasel has done it again."

"Lailu, you have a guest," Hannah called from the kitchen.

Lailu dropped the paper and stomped on it. Here she'd finally gotten a step ahead, only to find out that once again, Greg was right there with her.

"Why are you stomping on my face?" Greg asked.

Lailu looked up. Greg stood beside Hannah in her kitchen doorway.

Lailu narrowed her eyes.

"Um, I brought pie?" He held up a pie dish. "If that helps?"

"I was hurt, not dead!" Lailu snapped.

"Well, that's good, since I brought this over to celebrate."

"Celebrate?"

"You know, us finishing our apprenticeships." He grinned. "We're *both* master chefs now, just like we always dreamed."

"My dream was a little more solitary," Lailu complained.

"Oh pishposh," Hannah said. "You can't keep this rivalry going forever."

"Watch me," Lailu threatened, but after a moment she sighed and glanced at the pie in Greg's hands. It *did* look delicious. "Fine, I'll eat your pie," she decided. "But you're still a lousy weasel."

Greg laughed. "I'm willing to accept that. For now."

44

FAIRY STARS

Lailu, Greg, and Hannah settled outside, eating their apple pie in the flickering lamplight on the doorstep of Mystic Cooking. There wasn't a lot of space, but for once Lailu appreciated being sandwiched in the middle. Sitting here with her friends on either side, she felt like she belonged. Like she wasn't alone. Slipshod might be gone, but Hannah was going to stay on and help, at least for a while. And Lailu knew she'd always have her rivalry with Greg. *That* wasn't going anywhere. Even if it was more of a friendly competition now. A competition that she still planned to win.

"You know, we should set up a patio out here," Hannah suggested. "Some permanent seating, a few sun umbrellas. I think it would be really popular."

"I'll have to ask Slip—" Lailu stopped. She took a bite of pie, trying to enjoy its cinnamon-y sweetness. "I'll think about it." It would be her decision now. Everything would be her decision.

Hannah bumped Lailu's shoulder with her own. "We'll be okay." Lailu hoped she was right.

"It's almost time," Greg announced.

"Time for what?" Lailu took another bite of pie. She hated to admit it, but Greg really had a knack for baking a flaky, delicious crust.

"For the fairy stars!"

Lailu frowned. "The what, now?"

"You haven't seen them? They come sweeping through the city every year at this time," Greg explained around a mouthful of pie. He swallowed, then continued, "There are hundreds, maybe even thousands of them, and they fly over the rivers and through the streets until they leave the city through the Velvet Forest. So we should have front row seats here."

"How have I missed this?" Lailu asked.

"Same reason I've missed it the past few years: we were too busy at the Academy. If we weren't hunting, we weren't exactly spending a lot of time outside."

"True." Lailu and Greg shared a smile.

"Oh look, we're not the only ones stopping out here to watch." Hannah pointed at a group of merchants leading horse-drawn carts with all their wares.

Lailu recognized them, with their brightly colored wagon and long, flowing skirts. It was her mom's traveling companions.

Her last bite of pie stuck in her throat. "Actually, they're probably meeting my mom," she said softly. "She travels with them."

"Oh," Hannah said. She and Greg exchanged a look over Lailu's head.

"Surely she'll say goodbye first," Greg began.

"No, probably not." Lailu set her empty plate down. "She usually just leaves."

"Want to go see them?" Hannah asked.

Hannah's shoulder felt comforting against hers, and Lailu knew that she at least had Hannah as her family here in the city. "No," Lailu said. "It's better this way."

The caravan had moved almost out of sight when Greg suddenly grabbed Lailu's arm. "Here they come!" He gestured at the sky with his fork just as a wave of colorful lights came pouring down the streets, their natural glow enhanced by the damp mist. With a start, Lailu realized they weren't just lights. They were pixies. They made everything in this poor part of town more colorful, more beautiful, like frosting on a cake. Lailu could see why they were called the fairy stars.

As the pixies zipped past, she couldn't help but remember Eirad's promise: *Don't worry, little chef. We'll let them all go after the final night of the Week of Masks.*

Lailu tried to enjoy the view, but she knew this was more than just a pretty show of lights. This meant the elves had returned to the Western Travel District to release the remaining pixies. Despite their banishment, they weren't leaving the city.

"Wow," Hannah breathed, eyes wide, and Lailu decided to keep her fears to herself. There would be time for them later.

As the last pixie vanished into the Velvet Forest, Hannah yawned and stood up. "I'll take your plates. See you in the morning, Lailu." She gathered their dishes and headed inside.

Lailu was suddenly very aware that she was alone with Greg, both of them crammed together on the front step. She could feel his shoulder brushing hers through her wool coat, could hear him breathing, could practically feel the beating of his heart.

She reached up to brush a lock of hair from her face just as Greg adjusted the collar of his coat, and as they both lowered their arms, the backs of their hands bumped against each other.

Lailu froze, her knuckles still lightly grazing Greg's. Then slowly, tentatively, he turned his hand, his fingers wrapping around hers. Out of the corner of her eye, she saw him carefully not looking at her.

She swallowed, her face hot, but she didn't pull away. She just sat there, shoulder-to-shoulder, hand in hand, with the boy she thought she hated. And she felt . . . she felt like she did when she was cooking, when all her ingredients were lined up and she was about to create one of her favorite recipes. Like everything was right where it should be.

"So . . . ," Greg said at last.

"Y-yes?"

"Am I still a lousy weasel?"

Lailu laughed, something inside her relaxing. "Greg, you'll always be a lousy weasel." She let go of his hand and stood. "Good night, Master Chef LaSilvian."

His smile was small and sweet. "Good night, Master Chef Loganberry," he returned, and before he could ruin that one nice moment by saying anything else, Lailu slipped back inside Mystic Cooking, closing the door softly behind her.

"Did you enjoy the show?"

Lailu jumped. "Mom? You're still here?"

Lianna sat warming her hands around a cup of tea, the newspaper in front of her. She looked very well settled, not at all like someone about to leave.

"Of course I'm still here, sweetheart."

"I thought . . ." Lailu took a shaky breath, then tried again. "I saw the caravan leaving, and I thought you had left with it."

Lianna set her teacup down. "I was planning on going with them originally," she admitted. "But I thought about what you said the other day. And you're right. Even dragons can choose to stay grounded. And I have decided to stay for a while. That is, if you still want me here."

Lailu's jaw dropped. "Really?"

"Really. I know Sullivan is leaving. He told me his news. And honey, you try to do so much on your own all the time. You need people you can lean on." She stood up. "I want to be one of those people, if you'll let me. I know I haven't always been, but I'm going to try to change." Her hazel eyes filled with tears. "Do you believe me?"

Lailu sniffed. "I believe you." And for the first time in a long time, when her mother hugged her, it didn't feel like it was a lie.

"Hey, Lailu, someone left this by your back door." Hannah waltzed in, a small wooden box tucked under her arm. "There's no note. Maybe a graduation gift?"

Lailu took it. It wasn't much larger than her hand and heavier than it looked. Shrugging, she lifted the lid.

Something metallic sprang from the box.

Yelping, Lailu dropped it and took a step back.

Click. Click. Click.

One of Wren's spi-trons whirled, its blue light flashing as it scuttled in place. "Message for Lailu," it chirped.

"It can talk?" Hannah squealed.

"Must be a new development," Lailu said.

"Message for Lailu," the thing chirped again.

"Um, this is Lailu," Lailu said slowly.

The thing turned, its blue light illuminating Lailu's face. "This is just a test. One . . . two . . . three . . . *die!*"

The light turned red, and the spi-tron exploded.

Lailu moved fast, knocking a table over to use as a shield as Hannah and her mom ducked behind it. When nothing else happened, they peered carefully over the top of the table, coughing at the acrid smell of smoke. A pile of broken, jagged metal parts lay on the ground surrounded by a blackened singe mark.

"Well," Hannah said, breaking the silence. "That can't be good."

"I know. Just look at my cherrywood floor," Lailu fretted.

"Honey, this is much worse than a damaged floor." Lianna's face was pinched with worry.

Lailu sighed. "I know, Mom."

"What does it mean?" Hannah asked.

Lailu had a sudden vivid memory of asking her mom that same

question, just days ago, and she went cold. She knew exactly what it meant.

"It means Wren blames Lailu for her mother's death," Lianna said.

Lailu flinched, but she forced herself to say the rest. "It means war. It means *I'm* at war. With the scientists." She pictured Wren's cold-blooded killing of the cockatrice and hugged herself. Master Slipshod was gone. She would have to deal with this on her own.

Hannah picked up one of the pieces, then dropped it again. "I guess I'd better dust off Mr. Smacky."

"You're keeping the name?" Lailu asked, her heart swelling.

Hannah sighed. "I'm keeping the name," she said reluctantly. "Now let's clean this up. We're open for business tomorrow, after all."

"Yes, *we* are." Lailu grinned, realizing something. Master Slipshod might be leaving, but she wasn't alone. She had Hannah, she had her mother—she even had Greg, who, for all his faults, maybe wasn't so bad after all. And with them on her side, she could handle a rogue scientist and a pack of elves who refused to be banished.

Banished.

Lailu froze, Ryon's words about Fahr echoing through her memory: *This enchantment scheme was done with his approval. What he thought they would accomplish . . . of course Elister would banish them after this stunt.* And then Eirad's words from the First Night of Masks: *Fahr promised Elister that as long as we remained denizens of Twin Rivers, we would not kill anyone under his protection.*

"What is it, honey?" Lianna asked as Lailu's face paled.

"If someone has been banished from Twin Rivers, does that mean they are no longer a denizen of the city?" Lailu asked.

"Right." Then Lianna's eyes widened. "Oh no."

"What?" Hannah asked.

"I think," Lailu said slowly, "that the elves have found their loophole."

ACKNOWLEDGMENTS

We are so thankful to everyone who made their mark on this second installment of Lailu's adventure. First of all, our amazing agent, Jennifer Azantian, who has been Lailu's champion through thick and thin, and Ben Baxter, one of Lailu's very first fans. We couldn't have asked for a better team, and we are grateful to be part of the ALA family.

Another huge thank-you to Sarah McCabe and Fiona Simpson, our rock-star editors. You consistently amaze us with your thoughtful notes and edits, and we feel so privileged to be working with you both.

Also thanks to Angela Li for a truly fantastic cover illustration—we got chills the first time we saw those glowing red eyes—and Nina Simoneaux and Karin Paprocki for the cover design. And thank you to everyone else at Aladdin who helped in the making of this book: our publisher, Mara Anastas, and deputy publisher, Mary Marotta; Carolyn Swerdloff and Catherine Hayden in marketing; Christina Pecorale and the rest of the Simon & Schuster sales team; our production editor, Katherine Devendorf; and our publicist, Audrey Gibbons.

Writing a sequel was very challenging, and we couldn't have

done it without a lot of help and feedback from several incredible writers. First, Alan Wehrman, who not only noticed a gaping plot hole but helped brainstorm ways to fix it. We can't thank you enough. Teresa Yea, for always keeping an eye on our pacing and helping us slash those unnecessary words. Suzi Guina, who was willing to read this series out of order to help us. And Moana Whipple, whose fast reading skills are seriously a superpower.

To the rest of our critique group: Miles Zarathustra, Colleen Smith, Meg M., and Joan McMillan—all those pages and pages of critiques are what helped shape our writing today. Thank you, always. Also a shout-out to Stephanie Garber—we think of you every time we write "slightly." And to Sarah Glenn Marsh—any time we've needed a friendly, supportive word, you have been there. And to Liz Briggs—we'll be #TeamBriggs forever.

To our family: Lyn and Bruce Lang, thank you for supporting this "writer in residence" and for your constant enthusiasm; our cousins Christy and Paul Buncic, who introduced us to anime when we were young and thus set us down this treacherous path; Rosi Reed, who has patiently tolerated our fictional depictions of villainous redheaded scientists; Ed Reed, official tiger buddy and enthusiastic support-giver; and our parents, Rose and Rich Bartkowski, who taught us to dream big and never doubted we'd make it.

And finally, to Nick Chen and Sean Lang, our partners in all of our undertakings, including this one. And to Ember—we hope you grow up to love Lailu as much as we do.

And to you, our readers and the reason we're here. Thank you for joining Lailu on this next adventure.

Turn the page for a sneak peek
at Lailu's thrilling new adventure!

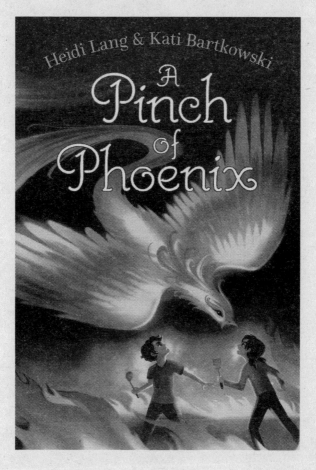

1

Surprise Visitor

Lailu scrubbed a thick coating of her own homemade finish into the mark burned onto her cherrywood floor. The scent of beeswax and wine filled the air, drowning out the sweet aroma of her cockatrice cooking in the kitchen. But no matter how nice it smelled, or how hard she scrubbed, the burn remained. Taunting her. Reminding her of Wren's threat and her exploding spi-trons.

"*One . . . two . . . three . . .* die!" Lailu shuddered, remembering the way that creepy metal spider had chanted at her before exploding, leaving behind metal parts and the black streak now scarring her floor. Wren's little present, which apparently was here to stay.

"It's no use," Lailu sighed, sitting back on her heels. "It's not going away."

"Well, I think it looks much better," Hannah said. Hannah had been living with Lailu and helping out at Mystic Cooking for several months, but she had been Lailu's best friend for far longer. They had grown up together in the same snowy little village in the mountains before chasing their separate dreams to Twin Rivers, Lailu to attend Chef Academy and Hannah to enroll in Twin Rivers's Finest, a school for hair and fashion.

Unfortunately, school hadn't worked out too well for Hannah, who couldn't resist the temptation of all those glittery hair combs and had gotten caught "re-homing" one. Luckily, their sneakiest friend, Ryon, had noticed her light-fingered talents and had recently taken her on as an apprentice spy. Lailu still wasn't sure what that entailed, and she preferred to keep it that way. Spying was trouble, but she was very glad Hannah had stayed.

"I doubt any of your hungry customers will notice a little scar on the floor," Hannah continued. She took a sip of tea, then set her mug down on her table. "Not when they're enjoying your tasty cooking."

"Master Slipshod will notice." Lailu's former mentor had left Mystic Cooking to return to his old job: cooking for the king. However, he'd promised to drop in from time to time, and she didn't want him to see how she'd already let the place get damaged, not after he'd just turned it over to her.

Hannah shrugged. "It's not really his business anymore, is it?"

"I guess not." Lailu tossed her scrub brush into a wooden bucket, then subtly stretched her hands, her fingers stiff and achy beneath their thick bandaging.

"Still bothering you?" Hannah's forehead creased.

"It's not so bad," Lailu lied. She'd thrown one of Wren's

spi-trons at Starling in self-defense. When it exploded, the blast had killed Starling and burned Lailu's hands. The constant pain felt like a reminder, both of the battle she'd fought and the war to come. Lailu knew Wren's attack last night was only the beginning, and she hoped her poor restaurant could handle whatever came next.

Lailu stood and stretched her back just as the bell over the front door rang.

A tall, well-dressed man entered the room. A man with the cold green eyes of a killer.

Lord Elister the Bloody.

Lailu's chest tightened. "L-Lord Elister," she greeted him. "Welcome to Mystic Cooking—"

"No need for pleasantries," he said. "I'm not here to eat."

Lailu gulped. She knew she was *not* his favorite person right now. Not after her hand in the death of Starling Volan, the talented scientist who had been working for him. True, Starling had been trying to kill Lailu and her friends at the time, but did that fact matter to someone like the king's executioner?

Elister looked the restaurant up and down, his gaze lingering on the burn mark.

"Search it," he said. Four guards swarmed inside, one of them stationing himself at the door while the other three made straight for the curtain that separated Lailu's dining room from the rest of the restaurant.

"Hey, stay out of my . . ." Lailu stopped. This all felt eerily familiar. On her opening day, her restaurant had been invaded by both the elves and a shady loan shark. She hadn't been able to stop them, either. She let her outstretched arm fall limply to her side and took a deep breath as the sounds of crashing and things falling came from her kitchen. Those guards weren't just searching her restaurant; it sounded like they were tearing it apart brick by brick.

She glanced at Elister. His face was as expressionless as one of Starling's automatons.

Until Lailu's mother came storming through the door, her fury swirling around her like one of her brightly colored skirts. "Eli!" she snapped. "What is the meaning of this?"

Lord Elister took a step back, then caught himself. He straightened. "Lianna," he said, almost pleasantly. "Since we appear to be dispensing with titles and formalities, I'll get straight to the point. Mystic Cooking is a business with ties to the elves. As you well know, due to the pandemonium they caused on the final day of Masks and their 'involvement' in Starling's murder, the elves have been banished from my city." He glanced at Lailu when he said "involvement," and she shuddered.

It was true that the elves had created fear and mayhem during the final day of the Week of Masks. Their magic had turned many of the citizens of Twin Rivers into the monsters they were masked as, but they had nothing to do with Starling's death. Elister knew that, Lianna knew that, and Hannah . . . Hannah had also been there when Starling died. The only ones who didn't know the real cause of Starling Volan's death were the guards. So . . . who exactly was this show for?

"Therefore . . . ," Elister drawled.

"Therefore what?" Lianna narrowed her eyes. "You're *not* shutting us down. We don't belong to the elves, we just owe them money."

Lailu noticed how her mother said "we," and her heart filled with warmth. Even if that warmth was surrounded by cold terror. Elister wouldn't really shut her restaurant down, would he? *Could* he?

Of course he could. He basically ran this city. Technically he was acting as joint regent with the queen until the king came of age, but everyone knew he was the real power behind the throne.

"I'm not shutting you down. I'm just ensuring that no elves are being harbored here."

"Why would we harbor any elves?" Hannah asked.

"Or anyone of elven descent," Elister added pointedly.

Hannah looked away, her cheeks reddening. Ryon was half elf. It was supposed to be a secret, but Starling had found out, so clearly Elister knew as well.

"There's no one here but us," Lianna said, her face giving nothing away. "As I'm sure you know. This really isn't necessary."

"Perhaps it would be less necessary if there were someone I truly trusted nearby. Someone who still worked for me, for instance . . ."

"Oh, stop with the weighty pauses," Lianna snapped. "You might intimidate everyone else, but you forget, I've known you a long time. And my work is here now."

Elister studied her, taking in the apron tied over her skirts, the flour smudged on the side of her neck. "I see that. I suppose that is . . . understandable," he said in a tone that suggested it was anything but. "Just as I'm sure *you'll* understand that part of *my* work is to search every business that has a connection to the elves, just in case." His lips curled back in a cold, hard smile. "For your own safety, of course."

"Of course," Lianna said blandly.

"And we'll continue to enforce our ban by any means necessary," Elister continued.

"Hey, there's a trapdoor in here!" one of the guards in the kitchen called, followed by the sound of more crashing and then, a moment later, the tinkle of glass shattering from below.

Hannah gasped. "Your wine cellar!"

Lailu clenched her sore hands into fists.

"If you use this display of force with all the businesses, you won't be making any friends on this side of town," Lianna warned. Pretty much every business near Mystic Cooking had some connection to the elves, who lived in the Velvet Forest just outside of this part of the city and regularly loaned money to the citizens in the poorer districts.

"My job is to make the city *safe*, not to make friends."

"Then maybe you should be more worried about this." Lianna pulled a newspaper out from one of her skirt's voluminous pockets and shoved it under Elister's nose.

All Lailu could see was the back advertisement about LaSilvian's special roast.

Elister snatched the paper from her hands. "I told them not to put that on the front page."

"My lord." One of the guards poked her head out from behind the curtain. "You'd better come see this. We've found . . . well. Something."

Elister rolled up the paper and tucked it under his arm. He looked at Lailu over Lianna's auburn head. "Is there anything you want to tell me?"

Lailu felt the color drain from her face like water from a

colander. *Was* there something to tell him? Ryon did have a tendency to lurk around here. For all she knew, he was close by now. She really, really hoped he wasn't, but if he was . . .

Lailu shook her head.

"Very well. Come."

Lianna started forward.

"Not you," Elister snapped at her. "Or you." He pointed at Hannah. "Just Lailu."

As Lailu followed Elister, she caught Hannah's dark, worried eyes and wondered if it would be the last she saw of her.

THE GENERATOR AND THE SPY

ailu's hand trembled as she brushed past her curtain into the kitchen. Her huge steam-powered stove, designed by the murderous—and now dead—Starling Volan, took up about a third of the floor space, and cupboards, pots, pans, and other cooking essentials took up another third, making the space in the kitchen pretty cramped. Normally Lailu found it cozy, but with Elister's imposing presence and the guard hovering over her wine cellar's trapdoor, it had become as claustrophobic as a hydra den. And as messy.

She had to step over several pots and pans, all heaped on the floor next to shattered dishes, and someone had left the stove door open. Lailu snuck a quick peek at her cooking cockatrice, glad that at least no one had destroyed that.

She turned her back on everyone and blinked away her tears.

All of the damage in here was fixable. Even though she knew she'd never get it all back in place before the dinner rush began, she could deal with it when Elister and his minions left. Still. It felt like a betrayal.

Elister had saved her life in this very restaurant. He'd helped her when she was dealing with the backstabbing loan shark, Mr. Boss, *and* he'd complimented her cooking. She thought he at least respected her as a chef. But this treatment of her restaurant? It was unforgivable. It was as bad as Mr. Boss, and she'd never thought Elister would stoop that low.

"What is it, Seala?" Elister asked the guard.

"I don't know. But it's large, glowing vaguely bluish, and humming."

Lailu turned away from her broken dishes. "The power generator," she realized. *Wren's* power generator.

Wren, Starling Volan's daughter, had convinced Lailu to let her "modernize" Mystic Cooking with hot and cold running water and lights that would turn on and off with the flick of a switch, all thanks to the generator installed in Lailu's cellar. Now that Wren wanted to kill her, coupled with the fact that Wren's inventions had a tendency to be a little . . . unstable, that generator suddenly seemed like a terrible idea. Lailu could practically feel its malice throbbing all the way through the floor, and she wrapped her arms around herself.

She had to get rid of it.

"Shall we?" Elister said, jerking his chin at the open trapdoor.

The guard fingered the cuffs of her dark-red uniform, which seemed a little large for her. Maybe she'd grow into it; with her wide brown eyes and wispy hair escaping the tight professional braids, she looked barely older than Hannah. She eyed that dark square leading below and then turned to Lailu. "Chef!" She pointed. "You first."

Lailu scowled. "That's *Master Chef* Loganberry."

"Exactly so," Elister said. "Go first yourself, Seala. Unless you're afraid to?" He glanced at Lailu. "Seala here is rather young and inexperienced, you see."

The guard's face tightened. She shot Lailu a murderous glare, as if Lailu had somehow set her up, before disappearing below, followed by Elister. Lailu sighed and reluctantly went down after them. The stairway was narrow and dark, but enough bluish light from the generator filled the room for them to see where they were going.

When Wren had first installed the generator a week ago, it hadn't given off more than a gentle glow. But over the past two days that glow had gotten brighter and brighter. It reminded her eerily of Wren's spi-trons and how their lights brightened right before they exploded. Just like the one that had killed Starling.

Lailu shook her head, pushing away the memory of two surprised green eyes caught in a glow of fire. Then she noticed her wine cellar. "What did you *do*?" She was shaking she was so angry. "You smashed half my bottles!"

The other two guards stood among the shards. "Don't worry. We spared the LaSilvian," one of them said. "Only a few of the Debonaire broke."

"You carry LaSilvian now?" Elister said, raising his eyebrows. "Interesting."

Interesting? All those smears of wine soaking into her cellar's packed-dirt floor like blood and *that* was his comment? "Is *this* protecting your city?" she demanded. "Or do you not consider *this* to be part of *your* city?"

"Don't worry, Master Loganberry. We will see that all damages are paid for." Elister turned his back on her, studying the generator. "Did Wren make this?"

The generator took up all of the wall space next to Lailu's icebox. Pipes stuck out of the top, sending out occasional bursts of steam, the whole machine humming continuously. When Wren had offered to install it, Lailu had pictured Mystic Cooking becoming the very image of a modern and revolutionary restaurant. Now, staring at it, the thing filled her with dread. Dread, and sadness.

Wren had been her friend back then.

"Yes, Wren made it," Lailu said stiffly.

Elister nodded. "I recognize the design. One of her mother's original creations. Such a pity."

"Sir?" Seala called. "There's something underneath it. It's . . . moving." She dropped her hand to the hilt of her sword, crouching to see better.

Click, click, click.

Cold terror shivered up Lailu's spine. That noise sounded exactly like the clicking of one of Wren's explosive spi-trons. But there was no way . . .

Lailu moved closer, scanning the shadows beneath the hulking generator. Was that a glowing blue light? It moved, darting to the left, and Seala gasped.

One of the other guards moved in closer. "It's under the icebox," he said.

It moved again, farther back. *Click, click, click.* And then it vanished.

"Maybe it—ahh!" Seala fell back as something black and metallic shot out from beneath the generator, its long spindly legs extended toward her.

Lailu grabbed one of her intact wine bottles and smashed it on top of the metal creation, slamming it into the ground in a shower of wine.

Click! Click! Its legs trembled and jerked as the gears in its back crunched around the shards of glass, its single eye glowing the same eerie blue as the power generator. Aside from the clockwork gears and the many-jointed legs, it looked almost like a giant beetle, about the size of a frying pan.

"An elven spy." Seala pushed herself to her feet. "Should we arrest the chef?"

"Hey, I just saved you," Lailu said.

"From a trap *you* set." Seala's eyes narrowed to ugly slits.

"What?" Lailu looked down at the broken wine bottle in her hand. "I sacrificed one of my best wines for—"

"Stop," Elister commanded. "Both of you. Obviously this is science, not magic." He sighed. "Much less predictable. Unfortunately."

"But, sir," Seala began.

"We're leaving. Grab the beetle."

"Wait!" Lailu flung her arm out to stop them. "Last time Wren sent one of those . . . it exploded."

"Intriguing." Elister glanced at the guard, who had backed away from the spi-tron. Scowling, he grabbed the clockwork creature himself.

Lailu threw up her arms.

Nothing happened.

Elister wrapped his new pet in the folded newspaper he'd taken from Lianna and headed up the stairs, trailed by his guards. Seala paused at the bottom of the steps, blocking Lailu. "Just so you know, I didn't need your help."

"Are you sure about that?" Lailu asked.

"*I* didn't need to go to a fancy academy to learn a thing or two. Don't think I don't know exactly what you were doing."

Fancy academy? Lailu scratched her head. "Um, what was I doing?"

"Don't play innocent. You were trying to make me look bad in front of Lord Elister." Seala's scowl grew uglier, darker. "It won't work." She stomped up the stairs and slammed the trapdoor closed, leaving Lailu in the semi-darkness.

Lailu sighed. She had enough enemies already.

She spared one last glance for the generator, pulsing behind her. It did *not* seem safe, and the fact that a spi-tron had managed to hide beneath it made her feel about as secure as a lopsided cake. She'd prefer it openly attack her like last time, rather than scuttling around in the dark, doing the gods only knew what.

Lailu shivered and made her way up the stairs. One way or another, she'd have to get rid of that generator, or she was afraid she'd end up going the same way as Starling.

Molly Bigelow is NOT your average girl. She's one of an elite crew assigned the task of policing and protecting the zombie population of New York. *The Hunger Games* author Suzanne Collins says *Dead City* "breathes new life into the zombie genre."

From Aladdin • simonandschuster.com/kids

EBOOK EDITIONS
ALSO AVAILABLE

CHARLIE HERNÁNDEZ

must navigate a world where *calacas* wander the streets, *brujas* cast spells, and things he couldn't possibly imagine go bump in the night. That is, if he has any hope of saving his missing parents . . . and maybe the world.

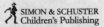